ADVANCE PRAISE FOR

Let Not Your Sorrow Die

"*Let Not Your Sorrow Die*, otherwise known as The Brutality of Bracken, is the omitted sixty-seventh book from the Bible, a wrathful assortment of tales better told with your fists than words, given that MacLeod bloodied his knuckles while writing them. These stories punch you straight in the face with every flip of the page."

—CLAY MCLEOD CHAPMAN, author of *Wake Up and Open Your Eyes*

"Are you ready? Take a deep breath. Sign the waiver. Enter the dark. The fearless and wildly talented Bracken Macleod is going to spike your adrenaline and hurt your heart. *Let Not Your Sorrow Die* is a haunting, beautiful collection that tours you the best and worst of the human condition and leaves a shadow in you like a bruise."

—BENJAMIN PERCY, author of *The Ninth Metal, Red Moon, Thrill Me,* and *The End Times*

ALSO BY
Bracken MacLeod

<u>NOVELS</u>
Closing Costs
Mountain Home
Come to Dust
Stranded

<u>COLLECTIONS</u>
13 Views of the Suicide Woods
White Knight and Other Pawns

Let Not Your Sorrow Die

A Collection of Stories

Bracken Macleod

Let Not Your Sorrow Die
Copyright © 2025 by Bracken MacLeod

Page 319 constitutes an extension of this copyright page.

A list of content warnings is provided on pages 321-322.

Print ISBN: 979-8-9924837-5-8

Cover Art & Design by Sarah Sumeray
Interior Design & Formatting by Todd Keisling | Dullington Design Co.

First Trade Edition

No part of this work may be reproduced or transmitted in any form or by any means without permission, except for inclusion of brief quotations with attribution in a review or report. Requests for reproduction or related information should be addressed to the Contact page at www.badhandbooks.com.

Without in any way limiting the authors' and publisher's exclusive rights under copyright, any use of this publication to "train" generative artificial intelligence (AI) technologies to generate text is expressly prohibited. The author reserves all rights to license uses of their work for generative AI training and development of machine learning language models.

This is a work of fiction. All characters, products, corporations, institutions, and/or entities in this book are either products of the author's imagination or, if real, used fictitiously without intent to describe actual characteristics.

Bad Hand Books
www.badhandbooks.com

for
Andrew Vachss
and
Jim Moore

my friends

AARON:

Oft have I digg'd up dead men from their graves,
And set them upright at their dear friends' doors,
Even when their sorrows almost were forgot;
And on their skins, as on the bark of trees,
Have with my knife carved in Roman letters,
'Let not your sorrow die, though I am dead.'
Tut, I have done a thousand dreadful things
As willingly as one would kill a fly,
And nothing grieves me heartily indeed
But that I cannot do ten thousand more.

—William Shakespeare, *Titus Andronicus*
Act 5, Scene 1

TABLE OF CONTENTS

Epilogue (For A Story Yet Unwritten) 11
Pigs Don't Squeal In Tigertown 17
Weightless Before She Falls 43
Lost Boy 59
The Loneliness Of Not Being Haunted 77
Not Eradicated In You 97
A Short Madness 115
Memories Of ~~You~~ Me 147
The Girl In The Pool 159
Extinction Therapy 171
No One Who Runs Is Innocent 193
Dreamers 209
Pareidolia 229
Back Seat 253
Everything We Lost In The Fire 271
Lying In The Sun On A Fairy Tale Day 305
Acknowledgments 315
About The Author 317
Publication History 319
Content Warnings 321

EPILOGUE
(FOR A STORY YET UNWRITTEN)

Sofia rubbed the key the locksmith had given her with her thumb like one of those worry stones people used for self-soothing. She hadn't anticipated how much it would mean to her that the man who'd installed the reinforced strike plate and multi-bolt lock hadn't stared at her like everyone else did. He smiled and told her it'd take a tank to breach this door as casually as if he was explaining the features on a TV remote. She tipped him an extra hundred dollars, despite his assertion that it wasn't necessary. It wasn't, but she still felt it was well-earned. No one was more aware than her how difficult it was not to stare. She couldn't look in the mirror without having to force herself to focus on some unmarred detail of her appearance. The soft line of her jaw (above the scar on her throat), the arc of her hairline at her temple (next to her now-pointed ear, missing the piece they couldn't reattach), the blue of her (remaining) eye. Yeah, he'd earned that hundred dollars.

She twisted the key onto a spiral ring connected to the little toy Vespa scooter Jesse had bought her. She pulled the little bike off the ring and took it to the trash bin under the kitchen sink and tossed it in. She shut the cabinet door before she could change her mind and fish it back out.

What would Jesse think?

Nothing. Not anymore.

Not ever.

Tears loosened the tape holding down the pad covering her right eye socket.

"What am I doing?" she said, wondering aloud if it was it too soon to be back in her own place. Alone. Her mom had wanted her to come live with her after the rehab hospital, but Sofia couldn't face moving back home.

I am home. This *is home, goddamn it.*

She'd been grateful for her mother's presence in the hospital most days, but the woman who'd always abhorred silence now seemed absolutely *terrified* of it. She talked incessantly about the price of knitting yarn, traffic on the Mass Pike, and her dogs, keeping at bay the demons who crept in through quiet gaps in thought. It was understandable; she'd almost lost her only child to a monster. Her therapist's admonition intruded on the thought. "But he was *not* a monster, Sofia. Only a man." She'd *killed* that fucking *man*, and if she wanted to live in silence for a while she'd earned the privilege. After the saw and the screams and that constant drone in the walls like being aboard a plane that never landed, if stillness was an invitation to demons, she'd gladly open the door to Hell for a minute of it.

I'm doing the Lord's work. You'll see, Sophia. I'll show you His divine grace.

She banged the heel of her hand against her head trying to knock his voice out of her mind, but unlike Jesse and Melisa and João, it lived on. She let out a long, shuddering breath and returned to the

EPILOGUE (FOR A STORY YET UNWRITTEN)

kitchen for the bottle of gin she'd ordered the night before from the place up the street that delivered. It was already half empty. She promised herself she'd order another tomorrow and add the pros and cons of self-medicating to the list of things to discuss with her new therapist.

Sitting on the sofa she poured some of the liquor into last night's glass, still on the coffee table, and sipped at it, mindfully drinking her way into another blackout. It was better than dreaming. The Oxy wasn't blanking her mind.

I miss morphine.

The silenced phone vibrated against her hip. She fumbled it out of her pocket and looked at the screen. Another DM from a stranger about appearing on their podcast. She clicked on the sender's profile knowing there was no way she was going to reply, but still curious. The cartoony kitchen knife stabbing into the wincing moon from that silent film where there should have been a rocket made her feel ill. This one, like so many, was hosted by two guys who looked like together they made a whole lumberjack, and a woman in a Wednesday Addams dress holding a cat and a martini glass with equal care. She blocked all their profiles and the show page before marking the message request as spam.

This is my home.

They can't get me here.

Not if I don't let them in.

The traditional news media had given up on talking to her almost right away. They were more interested in *him* anyway. They wrote articles titled, *What we know about the Berkshires Butcher* and *Killer's manifesto reveals long-planned murder spree*. The podcasters were different. They had a sole survivor to fixate on like a fetish object. She hadn't been particularly interested in true crime shows before and had negative interest in them now. The nurses at the hospital had loved them, though. They listened avidly, and seemed to often forget her room was right next to their workstation. Put there on purpose, so no one could sneak in to try to get pictures of her all bandaged up for the tabloids, though somehow (again, probably a nurse), they still managed.

"She's a pretty mess," she overheard one of them say, talking about one caster's opinion of her looks "post-incident." As if she should've come through it like some horror movie survivor, covered in everyone else's blood, some scrapes and maybe a wound in her thigh or calf that would make her escape dramatically slow, but not ruining her sequel appeal. One of those bitches even called her a "final girl." That got Mom so worked up she went out and screamed at them until security came. After that, they whispered their episode recaps and avoided making eye-contact when they came to attend to her iv and dressings and bedpan and all the things that made her feel infantilized and powerless.

I am not powerless.
I fucking killed him.
Final girl.

She took a drink to help forget the girlfriend who wanted to buy her a Vespa for her birthday but could only afford a toy. Another to banish the memory of the best friend who'd rented the cutest place out in the Berkshires to get away from it all for a while, just us girls, who at the last minute invited her boyfriend along. One more for the good friends who checked in on her after to make sure she was all right, and then ghosted. She took a drink, toasting the podcasters and newsreaders and everyone else who thought this was the end of the story. Her survival, merely an epilogue. Fuck all of them. *This* was the *beginning* of the emotionally crippled, mentally ruined, physically disfigured new life inside these four walls where no one could get to her.

She survived but what's left of her?

And for good measure, the last sip for her.

This can't mix well with Oxy.

Stories don't end just because you want them to.

PIGS DON'T SQUEAL IN TIGERTOWN

FRIDAY

The muzzle flash lit up Raymond's mouth and nose like that jack-o'-lantern trick kids play with a lit match behind their teeth. Light spilled out from his lips and nostrils and it all seemed like a joke in the half second between him pulling the trigger and the top of his head spreading against the dusky wallpaper like a red fireworks fountain bought from a plywood shed on the roadside. Except, instead of sparks, his head showered blood and brains and bone around the room. Just like the Fourth of July, the air smelled of smoke and sulphur and the scents of bodies too long in the sun waiting for dusk to come.

The second before Raymond stuck the pistol in his mouth, he said, "Nature don't give a shit about fairness." Immediately before that he'd said, "Fuck you and fuck the Dead Soldiers too." Before Orrin had thought to warn Raymond about watching what he said, his heart skipped a beat and he'd told the man that if he didn't want to have it shoved up his ass, he needed to put that gun away. And prior to that, he told Raymond that if he thought the motorcycle club was being unfair about his debt, he could take it up with the club president, Bunker. All those seconds in time, from Orrin banging on the door, to the creaking of his Chippewa boots on the steps, and the rumble of his 2,294cc engine at the end of the driveway to Tigertown were gone in silence, as though they never existed—just like the back of Raymond's head and his memories and all of his dreams. And all that remained was the thrum of Orrin's heart and the ring of his concussed eardrums.

Before he'd driven his Triumph under the WELCOME TO TIGERTOWN sign hanging from a gallows arm over the access road entrance, he'd read the hand-painted markers along the side of the state highway spaced out like old Burma Shave ads.

OTHER ZOO'S

YOU MIGHT OF PAST

BUT TIGERTOWN

IS WORTH IT!

THE MEMORIES WILL LAST!

½ MILE ON YOUR LEFT

Even though he'd seen them on his other visits to Raymond and his old lady, there was something about the visual rhythm of them passing by as he sped up the road, throbbing in his eyes like a dull strobe. They commanded his attention and he read each one of them every single time, as if the visit before and the one before that and the third and second and first didn't matter. He needed reminding. Yes, this way to Tigertown. The memories will last.

Before he took the turn for Route 30, Orrin glanced at the

plywood board affixed with rusted baling wire to the EXIT 42 marker that read:

TIGERTOWN NEXT EXIT—2 MI. EAST

Before that were the entrance ramp and the city streets in Bannock Falls and the driveway of the Dead Soldiers MC clubhouse. Setting all these future memories in motion was President Bunker sitting on a barstool smoking an American Spirit unfiltered and saying, "You tell him, if he couldn't afford the interest, he never shoulda taken out the loan."

The movement of time seemed to still while Orrin existed in a ghost world of memories. If he hadn't bought his first bike, if he hadn't met "Demon" Langan in The Rising Phoenix bar, if he hadn't become a Prospect and earned his rocker patches, if he hadn't been loyal and dependable and stood for the vote to be Sergeant at Arms, if he hadn't had the day off of work and gone into the clubhouse for a whiskey and a few laughs, everything might've turned out differently.

If.

But none of that had gone differently. These were the choices he'd made. The collection of decisions that brought him to the present moment where he sat in a straight-backed chair in a rundown ex-farmhouse turned roadside attraction halfway to Vulcan Hot Springs trying not to puke at the sight of brains and the smell of blood and gun smoke.

The distant clack of the hand cannon dropping onto the glass tabletop, and the sharp crack of it giving way and spilling hot steel and shards into the floor below set time moving forward again. Reality surged into motion and flowed around Orrin as his legs spasmed straight, trying to propel him away from the blast that was already long gone. His chair tipped and he went over, falling backwards, sprawling gracelessly on his back as the ancient boxy television on the entertainment center behind him wobbled and threatened to mash his own brains into the deep-pile carpet.

Orrin scrambled to his feet, his head swimming and lungs struggling for fresh air while all he breathed was the stench of the piss and shit filling Raymond's Wranglers intermingling with the other odors of squalor. He bent down and put his hands on his knees, panting, trying to slow the beat of his heart. He was fluent in the language of violence—it had been taught to him early—but ever since his fourteenth year when he grew taller than his old man, it had always been uttered in *his* voice. He guided the hand that determined when and where and how that language was recorded and what message was sent. He'd done terrible things to living men before, but he'd never seen anyone blow his *own* head off. That troubled him in a deep place he didn't know existed until now. A place of uncertainty and loss of control. Writ on the wall in front of him was an accusation in someone else's script, an indictment he couldn't answer, but one he might be held to account for anyway. His command over the situation had been wrenched away, and he couldn't see what was coming next any better than Raymond could see anything anymore.

It was time to go.

He tugged his riding gloves up tighter, assuring himself he was still wearing them and didn't have to wipe any fingerprints off of the chair or the doorknobs. His hearing slowly came back to life and he heard the ambient sounds of a house return. The refrigerator was running. A fan in the window struggled to move the summer heat around. He was repeating, "Aw fuck, aw fuck, aw fuck," and hadn't noticed that he'd been speaking until that moment. He backed up and pawed blindly at the door handle, unwilling to turn his back on the corpse, knowing it couldn't get up to follow him, but still too unnerved to look away. The latch clicked and released and he pulled the door open and pushed against the screen with his ass. The hinges shrieked, and behind him he heard a low huff and growl.

He turned and saw the thing a hundred yards away, sniffing at the seat of his bike. He owned the largest, loudest motorcycle in the club. His brothers joked about it, asking if Triple A would send a crane to help him pick it up if it got knocked over in the parking lot. But the thing standing next to it, the tiger, was bigger than the bike.

The screen door slammed shut behind him with a loud bang. The animal raised its massive head and looked at him, its eyes full of intelligence and intention. It opened its mouth and growled. Since the club had discovered Tigertown, seeing big cats was as common for Orrin as spying cows in fields along the highway. But, unlike a cow, he'd never seen a tiger with nothing in between him and it but distance. And that's all that separated them now: a frighteningly short distance. No cage, no moat. Just open space.

He grasped at the door, desperate to rejoin a dead man and get back inside. Behind him, he heard the footfalls of a perfect predator making short work of maybe twenty-five yards. Fifteen. Five. The screen swung open, and Orrin leaped into the house, flinging the solid front door shut behind him. It slammed as he heard the beast land on the porch, yowling its frustration. He threw his back against the wood and twisted the deadbolt, squinting his eyes shut, waiting for the feeling of the door and six hundred pounds of hungry beast falling on top of him. Instead, he heard the creature pacing back and forth on the boards outside. It roared. The sound scared Orrin worse than the report of Raymond's forty-five, worse than anything he'd ever heard.

He jerked his pistol out of its holster, aiming it at the door with a quivering hand. For the first time in his life, it felt perfectly impotent in his grip. He hadn't had a chance to draw it when Raymond had pulled his piece from between the sofa cushions.

Worthless then.

And the tiger between him and his bike was waiting on the other side of a door without a window. He couldn't see it to even *try* to get a shot off.

Worthless now.

He stepped away from the door, crouched low, and crept to the window to get a look out onto the deck. Though he couldn't see the tiger, he could hear it walking away from him on the creaky boards. He imagined it was searching for another way in. It roared again, and Orrin's pulse thrummed in his ears both faster and louder.

He had no idea if his piece even packed the kind of punch to kill a tiger. The thought of such a thing had never even occurred to him; his handgun was made for killing men. To him, tigers were the sort of animal that seemed untouchable. Like some kind of creature from myth that existed in the liminal spaces between light and dark and only stepped out to take what *they* wanted. He knew they weren't mythical creatures, though. He'd seen them often enough right here in Tigertown.

Orrin had toured the "zoo" with the rest of the Dead Soldiers a couple of times. The cages were made of chicken wire stretched around scrap wood from pallets and who knew what else. He assumed, like everyone else, that the cages, however ramshackle they appeared, were sturdy and secure. He'd thought, *Raymond and Val wouldn't live here if they weren't. Right?* But then, he knew people who did stupid, self-destructive shit all the time. They rode in the rain, they shot smack, they borrowed money from the Dead Soldiers, and they visited places like Tigertown off of Route 30, halfway to Vulcan Hot Springs. *Of course* one of the cats had broken free; it was an inevitability. And it was his bad luck that he happened to be here when it happened. Not luck. *Bunker.* Bunker had sent him instead of coming himself because he wanted to send Raymond a message. I don't come when you call, like a dog.

The sound of the big cat's steps on the porch grew louder, and for a brief moment, out of the corner of his eye, he caught a glimpse of an orange-and-black blur in the window. He aimed, and it was gone. He thought maybe if he went *upstairs*, he could lean out and try to get it from above, taking his shots from a safe position. He reckoned, whether or not his piece was capable of killing one, a mag full of nine mil rounds would discourage it at least—but only *if* he could hit it. His hand was shaking so badly he was uncertain he could even hit the door right in front of him. His gaze returned to Raymond's gun resting in the mess of glass on the carpet. It held fewer rounds, but packed a bigger punch. If he could kill the thing with five bullets, then he could put the piece back where he found it, and maybe it'd look like Raymond had greased himself in despair over having to off one of his precious cats. He slipped his own pistol back into its holster and reached through the chrome table frame to pick up the Taurus revolver. It felt better, heavier, in his hand. He tightened his grip and walked out of the front room.

But before that.

※

TUESDAY

The Fort Basin County Sheriff parked her truck in the driveway a few yards from the front door and killed the engine. She sat for a moment, listening, waiting for the proprietor to come out like he always did when someone first arrived at Tigertown, waving like an idiot and welcoming them to "The best safari this far from Darkest Africa!" Pat had brought her kids here once and instantly regretted it when she saw the condition of the cages holding the animals. They were cramped and ramshackle and, worst of all, filthy. She led her boys through the tour, pretending everything was all right, but feeling fearful and increasingly angry at the people who kept the animals in these conditions. Before that, the kids had been so excited to see tigers they'd practically jumped out of the car and run up ahead as she eased up the driveway, afraid of hitting another visitor or wrecking the already struggling suspension on the deep frost heaves and ruts in the road. Kyle and Patrick had seen big cats before at the Salt Lake City Zoo, but they'd heard stories from their friends about *this* place. About how close you could get. About how many tigers there were. They were as excited as she'd ever seen them, and couldn't turn around without losing the little credibility she worked to establish with young boys embarrassed to have a cop for a mom. They were good kids, though, and were as disappointed and disgusted at the state of the place as she was.

Now, she held the papers in her hand and felt a tinge of satisfaction at the idea that she was starting something that might lead to better lives for the animals behind the house. She pushed open the truck door. It creaked loudly on rusting hinges and she winced. While the city PD an hour up the highway was getting all sorts of secondhand military equipment from the Feds, the County still had her rolling around in an old Bronco with a hundred and fifty thousand miles and a rebuilt engine. She left the door hanging open and crunched through the gravel on the way to the front porch. Before she got to the steps, Raymond burst out the front door, tucking in his denim shirt and looking like he had just woken up. Pat checked her watch. A quarter to eleven.

Raymond nodded at her with his chin and spat on the porch. "What're ya' after, Officer?"

"That's Sheriff Trudell, Mr. Pawlaczuk. I'm here on official business."

"Mr, *Pawlaczuk?*" Raymond said his own name with contempt, as if being called anything other than Raymond was an insult to his age. Pat herself did the same thing anytime someone called her Mrs. Trudell. She'd reply with a folksy, *Aw hell. My grandmother is Mrs. Trudell. I'm Patricia. Pat for short.* Her grandmother was now twenty years in the ground, and Pat was in her late forties. There was no arguing she wasn't the elder Trudell woman in Fort Basin County. On top of it, her husband had died more than five years ago in Afghanistan. She wasn't Mrs. Anyone. All her affectations of youth were falling away with the passing days. Still, Raymond had at least twenty years on her. Maybe more.

She held the twin envelopes out. He refused to reach for them or even come down the steps. She took a step up onto the first riser. "That's just far enough, Sheriff. Whatcha got there?"

"An order to cease and desist all operations on this … *animal preserve*, and a notice of foreclosure from the county. This zoo is operating illegally without permits or any of the licensure a man'd need to keep exotic animals. The conditions are a violation of county and state health requirements for both humans and livestock. And the county had condemned this house as well." She failed at suppressing a smile. "You're out, Raymond. We're closing you down."

FRIDAY

The stench grew stronger as he made his way deeper into the house. Competing smells of unwashed dishes and old garbage hovered on top of the scent of wild animal seeping in from outside. Just standing in this place made Orrin feel filthy.

Turning the corner on his way to the stairs, he passed the kitchen and half expected to see an orange-and-black monster sitting at the dinner table, licking its lips, wearing a barbecue bib, with a knife and fork clutched in its paws. Instead, all he saw was last night's dishes and a pile of junk mail on the table. Beyond that, the back door. He crossed the room and checked the lock. He knew a tiger couldn't turn a knob, but still, it made him feel slightly better to know the deadbolt was thrown.

The oppressive heat muddied his already jangled thoughts. He stared out the window in the kitchen door, and tried to remember the layout of the property, wondering if there was a way to flank the animal the long way around and get to his bike. While he'd toured the "zoo" a few times, it had been with his brothers along, distracting him. They'd laughed and talked shit and paid no attention to anything around them because they were the Dead Soldiers and the world stepped aside when they rode or strode through. They didn't bother with exit strategies or future plans. A man, especially a Dead Soldier, walked out the same door he walked in. Except, Orrin was *merely* a man. And—one percenter or not—he couldn't outfight a fucking tiger. His bike was parked in front, and that was his only way out. He had to outsmart the animal.

He went back out of the kitchen and found the stairs to the second floor. He took them three at a time. Somehow, it smelled worse upstairs than down. He approached the door on the south-facing side of the hallway. It was closed. His hand hovered by the knob as he imagined Raymond's old lady, Val, waiting inside with a shotgun in her lap ready to cut him in half, leaving him to die like his father, bleeding out on the floor of a strange woman's bedroom. He assured himself that Val wasn't on the other side. If she was, she would've come running when Raymond checked out. He reached for the knob, and as soon as he cracked the door, he knew she was right where he feared he'd find her. Except, instead of sitting on the edge of the bed, waiting for him with a twelve-gauge, she was laid out, arms folded across her chest, face pale, a dark red stain under her hands. The high-pitched drone of flies buzzing in the room was maddening. He steadied himself against the doorjamb and tried to breathe, but the smell of her invaded his nostrils, made him feel like smothering, like he was being drowned in filth. He breathed her in and gagged. How long had she been lying there dead, waiting to be found? How long had Raymond been planning this?

Orrin recalled Bunker telling him to go to Tigertown. "That fucker Raymond's been calling for two goddamn days," he'd said. "You go find out what the fuck he wants and give him a reminder that he doesn't get to demand a meet with me. I'll talk to him when *I* want, not when *he* fuckin' feels like it."

Two days. She's been in here two days.

Summer in Tigertown stank. The heat baked the dry dirt outside like a kiln and the smell of sun-cooked tiger piss hovered, pungent, in the air. And under that, there was rot. Raymond and Val tossed sides of beef, whole chickens, pigs and whatever else they could get their hands on into the cages to keep a dozen big cats alive. But they didn't pick up after them, and whatever the cats didn't eat sat in the sun, swarmed by flies and growing ever rank with decay. Compared to the bedroom, though, the cages smelled like the Yankee Candle shop in the mall.

Orrin put a hand over his mouth. The effect was minimal, merely adding a hint of leather to the fetor of the room. He pressed harder with the back of his glove, held his gorge, and staggered toward the window next to the bed.

The window fought him as he tried to yank it open with his left hand. The frame was old and neglected and it got stuck at an odd angle halfway open. He wanted to smash it. The sound of recalcitrant things breaking was often how Orrin measured compliance. Wood, glass ... bones. But shattering the window wasn't going to help him get away without leaving a trace. When the police finally showed up, he didn't want them to find any sign the Dead Soldiers had been here. He put the pistol on the sill, held his breath, and slid the window down before lifting it open again more gently with both hands. This time it rose without sticking. He pushed the screen out, letting it clatter to the ground, leaned through and took a deep breath of merely distasteful air.

He looked down and muttered, "Fuuuck me." The eaves below the window blocked his view of the porch and the tiger. He couldn't hear it anymore either. Had it just stopped moving or had it moved on? He'd half expected to see it react to the falling screen, but it wasn't a housecat. He didn't figure he was about to distract it with a ball of yarn or a laser pointer.

In the distance, his motorcycle gleamed in the sunlight like an oasis. Shimmering in the hot air distortion as if it would vanish if he got too close. While the path from the house to his Triumph looked clear from up where he stood, he knew that was the real illusion.

Then he saw it.

The animal was stalking away from the house into the tall weeds on the other side of his bike. He watched it turn and crouch down. A shiver passed through Orrin as he realized the thing was lying in wait for him. Hunting. But the cat's pelt was brighter than the dry brush in which it hid. He had it dead to rights.

He knelt down in front of the open window and took aim. His hand trembled with adrenaline and the unfamiliar weight of Raymond's hand-cannon. The thing wasn't right below him anymore. At this distance, he'd be better off trying to get the shot with a deer rifle. Raymond almost definitely had a thirty-aught somewhere in the house. He knew the old bastard had to be poaching deer to feed the cats. There was no way he could afford to buy enough meat from the butcher for his zoo. Not the way he kept coming to the Dead Soldiers for money. But Orrin had the tiger in his sights *right now* and didn't want to risk losing that advantage while he went looking for a better weapon. He aimed, let out a slow breath, and squeezed the trigger.

The report of the gun deadened his ears. The fucking thing was loud. His own pistol made demure little *pop pop pops* compared to this one.

A small cloud of dust kicked up from the ground where the slug hit yards away from his target. He blinked in the bright daylight and tried to re-aim, but couldn't see where the tiger had gone. It moved so fast. And now, instead of knowing where it was, he was blind to it again. *I should've waited. Fucking stupid.* If he'd had any illusion about what his role in predator and prey was, it was dispelled.

He stared at his bike. He reckoned the distance between the front door and his ride wasn't one he could cross before the tiger cut him off. Even though the animal was probably half-starved from its keepers' neglect, it could see, hear, run and kill better than he could on his very best day. The damn thing had almost got him when all he was sprinting for was the door at his ass. He had to find the rifle. He needed more power, and a scope. Hunt it like they did in Africa or India or whereeverthefuck a tiger like that was from. He ducked inside and immediately wanted back out again.

Orrin breathed through his mouth, trying not to smell the rot breaking down Val's body. She smelled worse than the carcasses they threw in the animals' cages. Of course she did. She was whole, guts and all. She was human.

That was his way out.

But before that.

TUESDAY

"So, you're the lawyer for the county now, too?" Raymond asked.

"Nosir. I'm just doing my job. You asked and I told you. And since you're here looking me face to face, it doesn't matter if I put these in your hand or toss 'em at your feet. You been duly served as I see it." She held the papers out and waited another couple of seconds. Raymond reached over and snatched them out of her hand with a sound like "Fuck you" beneath the rattle of the envelopes, but definitely not a clear "Fuck you," or else Pat would have been inclined to take another step or two up onto the porch after him.

"Unconstitutional!" he shouted. "It's my goddamned property, and I can do what I want with it."

"Tell it to the judge. Afternoon, Raymond." Pat didn't need to stick around to watch him open the envelope. She'd done her duty. Though she wanted the extra pleasure of seeing the results of her effort play out on his face, it would only aggravate him more to linger. Her job was to deescalate conflict. So, she tipped her hat and turned to leave. Pat stepped down and started back toward her truck. She heard the sound of paper being balled up, but didn't care. If Raymond ignored the summons and they issued a bench warrant for his arrest, all the better. She'd be happy to come out again and gaffle him up personally. She'd even do it on her day off. Hell's sake, she'd do it on Christmas if it meant shuttering Tigertown for good. It wasn't until she heard something hard sliding against leather that she realized she shouldn't have turned her back on the man. She spun around, flipping the leather tab off the hammer of her revolver and tried to draw. The bullet from Raymond's gun caught her in the thigh and sent her sprawling. She lost hold of her gun and it bounced out of her hand and slid away in the dirt. Heavy footsteps raced toward her as she tried to scramble for it. But the broken bone and screaming hole in the back of her leg kept her from reaching it in time. A shadow fell on her and she turned over, holding up her hands.

Raymond loomed over her, his expression dark and angry. He hadn't had time to regret what he'd done yet, but it would come. His face would change when he realized what a terrible mistake this was.

"It's a fucking injustice and I won't stand for it. This is *my* property and this is still America."

"S-stop. Stop this. The D-deputy Sheriff knows I'm here. Everyone … knows. Th-this is … is official business. It's not personal," she lied. She hadn't told anyone she was coming out to Tigertown. She'd seen the envelopes awaiting service and, instead of handing them on to her deputy, had taken them herself. She wanted to see his expression when she served him. Because it *was* personal.

Raymond's face fell. Fury changed to fear and the realization that he'd just lost everything. His house, his farm, the cats, and now his freedom. Maybe, eventually, his life at the end of a needle. No matter what, he was going away. Pat felt a hint of satisfaction at the idea of it. But while the day was hot, she was starting to feel cold and tired and satisfaction soon became fear and realization. *Oh, shit. I'm bleeding out.*

She tried to reach for the radio transmitter on her epaulet. Raymond stepped on her arm and bore down. It hurt less than her leg, but still, it hurt goddamn bad. She couldn't help it and cried out in a way she never had done on the job. The only female sheriff in all the state's forty-six counties, she didn't have the luxury of a high-pitched cry. In her own ears, she sounded like one of her sons. The seven-year-old had a way of keening high at his hurts. Pat thought she sounded like him just then.

She thought of her sons.

Raymond reached down and yanked the transmitter cable out of her radio. He took the whole thing and threw it back up toward the porch. It squawked once and was silent. "Pigs don't squeal in Tigertown, Sheriff. It gets the cats too excited."

☆

FRIDAY

Orrin found the gun locker in a room downstairs. It might have been a dining room once, some place for the family that built this house to gather at the end of a long day of honest work and eat together. Orrin knew hard work, though he wasn't sure he could call much of it honest. And if his family had ever taken a meal together, it was before he was old enough to hold on to such a memory. In the corner stood an oak gun cabinet like the one his grandfather had owned. The glass door and tiny lock wouldn't keep anyone from getting their hands on anything inside—it wasn't a safe, it was a china hutch for rifles. And Raymond had a collection. Any other time, Orrin would be considering taking the lot of them home with him. There was a pump shotgun, a pair of .22 caliber rifles, and exactly what he was looking for: a Remington bolt-action .30-

06 with a scope. He tried the door and wasn't surprised to find it unlocked. He grabbed the thirty-aught and considered taking the shotgun as well. He could only fire one rifle at a time, though, and if his plan worked, he wouldn't need the shotgun at all. Still, while he'd have to leave the deer rifle behind to make it look like Raymond had put down the cat before taking himself out, the Mossberg was going to be Orrin's reward for having to endure this mess of shit.

He pulled out the drawer underneath the cabinet. Boxes of ammunition were stacked neatly inside. It seemed to him the only space in the house that had any order. He dug through until he found the right caliber and took the box. He loaded four long rounds into the rifle, stuffed the remainder, still in the box, into his jacket pocket and returned upstairs.

His stomach did a hard flip in the doorway to the bedroom and he gagged again. Time in the house wasn't doing anything to help him get used to the smell. He set the rifle by the door and shrugged out of his leather jacket, letting it drop to the floor. The buckle on the kidney belt made a loud clank as it hit the hardwood and he flinched a little. He pulled off his T-shirt and wrapped it around his face the way he'd seen kids playing in his neighborhood do, pretending to be ninjas. He tied the short sleeves behind his head. The shirt was sweaty and smelled like his body odor and engine grease. Though the house was stifling and breathing through the cloth only made him feel hotter, the smell of it was soothing in its familiarity. Those were the aromas of sitting in his garage working on his bike, smoking a little weed and drinking a beer. They were the smells of normality and peace. Still, there was much more than a hint of Val's stench getting through. He'd heard stories of how the smell of a dead body never came out of things. That you could smell it in a house for years afterward. He could burn his clothes and buy himself brand new ones, all except for the denim cut-off jacket he wore over his leathers—his kutte. He couldn't replace that or the club patches sewn on it. He'd slice off the tattoo over his heart and throw that in the fire first. His kutte was therefore destined to always stink. If he survived this, he'd happily smell like a corpse. But first he needed to get out with both it and his skin intact.

Orrin took a deep breath through his mouth and approached the bed. Val's skin was grey and mottled with long purple streaks, like her veins were swollen with dark ink. Her lips were the same purple and starting to blacken on the inside. Touching her felt like a very bad idea, even with his gloves on. As if death itself might rub off onto him. Bacteria was eating her up from the inside. He knew it couldn't hurt him. He could wash up and everything would be fine. Still, he felt a powerful repulsion at the idea of getting too close to her, like the prehistoric fear of death he'd inherited from his most distant ancestor, calling out to him from across millennia: *this is unclean. This is a bad thing.* But he couldn't listen to that voice. Moving Val was the only plan he'd come up with, and nothing else was springing to mind.

He grabbed her wrist and yanked. He'd expected her to be stiff with rigor mortis, but she wasn't. Her body was loose, and he pulled harder than he meant to, jerking her to the edge of the mattress. Moving her made the smell worse and a wave of stench hit him like a fist even through the shirt covering his face. He looked at the mattress where she had been, and though there was an indentation, there was no bloodstain. The bullet that killed her hadn't exited out her back. He was thankful for small miracles. He bent over, slid an arm behind her shoulders, the other under her knees, and lifted her off the mattress. She was skinny and light, though her limp body was uncooperative. He had to hold her tightly and close. She was dressed for summer in a crop top and a pair of shorts. The feel of her cool skin against his naked belly made him feel ill. He hadn't thought to put his coat back on and zip it up, and now it was too late. They were skin to skin, and he didn't want to prolong it. He kept breathing through his mouth and walked out of the room holding the dead woman.

He carried her down the stairs and into the front room where her old man still sat cooling on the sofa. Orrin felt angry and wanted to kick the shit out of the fucker. Even if he was dead and couldn't feel it, at least *he'd* know Raymond was getting the beating he deserved. He left the dead man alone and looked outside. There was no sign of the tiger that he could see. Just the porch and the drive and his bike.

At the door, he dipped down like he was curtsying to twist the deadbolt latch. Val's head lolled around and he reflexively squeezed tighter to keep from dropping her. Like it would matter if he did. The feeling of her body giving in his arms broke him a little. She was soft and felt like a person. There was something wet on his arm. He tried not to think about it. Pulling the door open, he waited for a second, ready to kick it closed if he saw the blur of a big cat racing toward him. When nothing came running out of the weeds, he let out a breath he didn't know he was holding and pushed at the screen door with Val's hip. It opened with a pop and a loud creak. He stepped outside.

The stairs groaned beneath his weight as he descended. The sound made his back tense and his heart beat a little quicker. At the bottom, he stopped and listened. He couldn't hear much above the breeze and his own breathing in the makeshift mask. He hazarded a glance back at the porch. Though there hadn't been anything there a moment ago, he wanted—*needed*—to be certain he could get back inside. It was one thing to run a few feet into the house, but if it cut him off and he had to run the other direction, it was all over. It was a comfort to see nothing in between him and the front door. He took a few more steps out into the open and knelt down to lay her body in the dirt. He looked over his shoulder at the window to the second-story bedroom. Crouched where he was, the window was clear of the eaves. Good enough.

Sunlight glinted off the rear-view mirror of his motorcycle, and with no sign of the animal around, the urge to sprint toward it pulled at him like a hook in his flesh. *But my fuckin' kutte's in the house.* Orrin chided himself for leaving it behind. Stress and fear were going to kill him as sure as an escaped tiger. He needed to get his shit together if he wanted to ride away from this place.

He stood and began walking quietly, but quickly, back to the house. Behind him he heard the rustle of the tall weeds. It might have been the breeze. Or it might have been a beast. Either way, his bladder almost let go and he sprinted for the front door.

He leaped up the stairs, stumbling as he cleared the bottom four, but not the last two. He scrambled across the deck and ripped open the screen. It banged against the side of the house, and Orrin was inside and slamming the front door before the screen swung back into place.

"FUCK! YOU!" he screamed, ashamed at his naked terror. He shook and slammed a fist into the door. Pain reached up from his knuckles into his wrist, but he didn't care, and he punched it again, shouting out his frustration. Taking a deep breath, he looked at his hand while he flexed it. It wasn't broken. Sprained maybe, but as long as he could hold a throttle it'd be fine. More importantly, he felt sure he could still pull a trigger.

A soft sliding sound and a muted thump made Orrin jump again. He spun around, arms up in front of his face.

Raymond's corpse had slumped over on the sofa. Whether it had been the reverberations of Orrin's violence or simply gravity, the result was the same: Orrin's chest felt tight and he was breathless. His vision blurred as he tried to keep from hyperventilating. "I hope you're sweating in Hell, motherfucker!" he hissed from between clenched teeth. He went to the window and looked outside. If the tiger had been behind him, it wasn't there now. He was beginning to feel like the animal was a dream. Like Raymond had drugged him somehow and he was hallucinating everything. Except, he could see Val out there dead in the road, and Raymond was spilling what was left of his brains onto the couch behind him. And this was still Tigertown. He wasn't hallucinating. Somewhere out there, death was waiting, tooth and claw.

He stumbled into the kitchen and searched the cupboards until he finally found what he wanted in the one above the refrigerator. A big plastic jug of tequila stood next to a smaller bottle of cheap margarita mix with a woman wearing fruit on her head on the label. He grabbed the tequila, twisted off the cap, and took a healthy couple of gulps to settle his nerves. He forced himself to stop, replaced the cap and then the bottle. Just enough to give him the Dutch courage he needed.

He stomped upstairs, snatching his jacket off the floor and slinging it on without untying the T-shirt from around his face. He grabbed the rifle and went to wait at the window.

Earlier.

⛥

WEDNESDAY

Val stood in the doorway watching Raymond pull his stained shirt up over his head. He dropped it on the floor. She picked it up to throw in the fire pit along with the Sheriff's uniform. "Did you get through? Did you try calling again?"

He shook his head. "Nope. They ain't answerin'. I can't imagine what the Soldiers can do to help, anyways. With what we already owe 'em too? There's nothin' in it for them."

"Horseshit. They won't get *any* of their money if we go to jail. Cats're already takin' care of the bitch. We throw this in the burn pit with her uniform," she said, holding up his shirt, "and all we got left to do is get rid of the truck in the barn. Choppin' a truck is the least bad thing those sons a bitches get up to. It don't cost them a thing."

Raymond stepped out of his pants. His tight, off-white underwear sagged from a skinny ass that was twenty-five years past firmness. He looked at his wife with tired eyes and said, "We're fucked up way past fixin'. You ought to pack a bag and go. I reckon they'll be out tomorrow at the latest lookin' for her. I'll say you went to see your sister up in Mercy Lake and you weren't here when she came by to give me the papers. Takes a whole day to get there, so nobody'll be able to say for sure just when you hit the road. Evelyn'll vouch for you."

"And what are you going to do?" Her eyes went wide and her mouth dropped open. "You're not gonna … "

"Go grab your bag." He stepped into a pair of jeans he pulled off the top of the overflowing hamper. "Pack up what you need and get on the road. No sense in both of us getting caught up in this."

Val didn't say anything as he walked out of the room. She didn't ask him to come back or offer a better plan. She just let him go.

When he returned, she had the bag on the bed and was stuffing clothes into it. She looked up from what she was doing. Her brow knitted as she saw the gun in his hand. "Are they here already?"

He raised the pistol and fired.

FRIDAY

Sweat moistened the shirt on his head, but the cloth kept it from dripping in his eyes while he watched the road. He'd scanned the weeds and the far edges of the property with the rifle scope, but he wasn't catching sight of the tiger. He'd thought for certain Val's body and the promise of an easy meal would lure it out, but it had been forty minutes and it hadn't taken the bait. He wondered whether it had wandered off, looking for other prey. There was no shortage of horses and cattle in the countryside around the county. Sheep and a few alpacas too. He decided he'd give it another twenty minutes, and then he was going to try sneaking out to get away. And then he saw it.

It was stalking around the opposite side of the house by the barn, instead of where he'd seen it when he tried to take the shot with the pistol. His heart thumped harder at the sight of it. The thing was big and moved like liquid. It was beautiful and terrifying. A perfect thing. He almost regretted having to kill it.

The tiger slowed its pace and lowered its head as it came closer to Val's body, sniffing at her. Orrin centered the crosshairs on the top of its skull and waited.

What are you waiting for? Dig in.

The animal looked around as if it was trying to figure out where Val had come from. It reached out with a paw and grabbed at her. Val's body jerked like it was a child's doll and the tiger bit down on her neck and quickly started to drag her back the way it had come. At the edge of the road near the weeds, it plopped down and tore off a long strip of her flesh.

Bile burbled up Orrin's throat, stinging and threatening to choke him.

He swallowed, re-aimed, and squeezed the trigger.

The sound in the bedroom was deafening and he thought he might have let out a yelp of pain, though he didn't hear it if he did. His ears were dead and ringing; his head hurt a little. He pushed past all of that to pull back on the bolt handle and eject the spent casing. He shoved the bolt back into place and chambered a new round. Through the scope he saw the tiger lying next to Val. A pool of dark blood was spreading from its skull and muddying up the dirt. He contemplated putting another round in it, but deaf or not, the rifle was loud, and he didn't want to risk attracting any more attention than that shot might've already. Even this far out in the boonies people didn't like hearing rifle reports near where their kids got off the bus, or where they were grazing their livestock.

He stood up and shook out his legs. His knees and his fist ached. The ride home was going to be long. But it didn't matter. It was going to be the best ride of his life. He'd just killed a fucking tiger. None of his brothers were ever going to be able to top that no matter how many points the next buck had. He just had to trade rifles and he could get on his way.

Earlier in the day.

⛤

FRIDAY

Raymond ran out the back as soon as he heard the motorcycle pulling up the drive. He'd just about given up hope that Bunker was coming. He pulled the keys out of his pocket and looked at his zoo. He thought that he'd miss his cats. But then, probably not.

"Time to raise hell."

⛤

FRIDAY

Orrin stepped out onto the porch, pulling the door shut behind him and took a deep breath of fresh air. He walked down the steps, not looking over at where he'd shot the tiger. He'd made sure it was dead before he came down from his roost. He'd put the rifle back in the gun cabinet and took the Mossberg along with the ammo. It wouldn't do for the cops to find shells for a shotgun that wasn't in the house. He wrapped the box of shells in his T-shirt and stuffed that into his saddlebag. The shotgun he tied to the side of the bike with bungee cords. It wasn't perfect, but it'd get him home.

He swung a leg over the bike and turned the key. The engine roared to life and he twisted the throttle. His hearing was coming back slowly, but it was still muffled. Between that and his pipes, he never heard the animal behind him.

When it pulled him off the seat into the tall grass, he had no idea what was happening until he was already on his back. Everything was a blur. He felt claws puncturing his jacket and his flesh underneath. He felt its hot breath, and then the thing's teeth biting down on his neck. Orrin wanted to reach for his pistol, but it was under him in the holster at the small of his back. He beat uselessly against the animal with his fists. He struggled and kicked but the tiger knelt down on its elbows and held him there. He tried to gasp for breath, but the jaws holding him were tight and he couldn't breathe.

He felt a hard tug at his leg and a searing pain as his leathers ripped open and a long muscle tore away from his bone. Another tug. The tiger that had taken him down tightened its hold on his neck. The sound of his spine breaking echoed inside his own skull like when he'd bite down on a piece of gristle. It was a vibration from *inside* his body, not a sound outside.

The bright day grew dim, even though the sun wouldn't be

going down for hours. And he slipped away while the other hungry tigers ate him, leaving nothing left in his life to come.

Before that, he had been a man who would have liked to have taken a last ride.

Long before that, he had been a boy who loved his bicycle, and the feeling like flying when he rode it down the tall hill behind his house and took his hands off the handlebars.

And earlier still, he was a child and occasionally his mother held him and whispered to him, her breath tickling his ear like a warm bourbon breeze.

And before that, he wasn't yet born and was exactly like he was now.

Gone in silence, as though he never existed.

WEIGHTLESS BEFORE SHE FALLS

for Jennifer McMahon

"If a train is coming at you, closing your eyes won't save you ... but if you look right at it, you at least have a chance to jump."
—Andrew Vachss, *The Weight*

The distant hills along the horizon were autumn painted, red and yellow and orange; bright color spreading into the valley in a carpet of brilliance that reminded her of Fiver's apocalyptic vision of Sandleford Field. New England in October was a sanguineous landscape. The scene crawled along, gliding slowly under billowing white clouds that barely moved against the blue sky behind. A river wound along, lacerating the scene, sparkling in the early day's sunlight, glinting striking white like broken glass. A house nestled in the trees: white siding, green roof. Dark windows. No movement, other than to glide past with everything else resolute in its place as the train sliced through the countryside.

The rhythmic sound of steel wheels on rail like a mother's

heartbeat against an infant's ear—*tchuk-shuk tchuk-shuk tchuk-shuk*—settled her nerves, lulling her to a near calm she hadn't felt in so long, the sensation was as much a stranger to her as feeling whole. She left her headphones hugging her neck, enjoying the ambiance of the train. In the city, she rarely took the clamshells off. Why would she want to hear car horns, drivers shouting criticisms out windows at each other that would be reflected back at them by the next light? The thunder of busses and garbage trucks, motorcycles driven by men much too old for their performative toughness—half of them lawyers, anyway. No. Who wanted to hear any of that shit? Not her. But the sound of the *train*. That was just all right. She could listen to it all day. Except, she knew undisturbed peace wasn't in her future.

Enjoy it while you can.

She dared close her eyes and wait. It wasn't long before—

⛧

"Excuse me, do you mind if I sit here?" The man in the aisle gestured at the seat facing hers. He wore a sport coat and jeans, but not a casual tweed sport coat with the elbow patches like her dad. No, this was a suit jacket, dark blue and almost shiny. Its formality contrasted with his faded dungarees. He wore it naturally, though it didn't look good, not to her. She shrugged, knowing he wasn't about to accept a refusal. The act of asking was obligatory, yet meaningless, like saying, "How are you doing?" when greeting someone. No one ever listened for an answer; it was enough to have ritually uttered the words. He was already bending to take the seat as she shrugged her assent. He smiled. Their car was empty. So many unoccupied seats. Though she wanted to return to gazing out at the landscape, he continued looking at her, forcing her attention.

"You know, I know you," he said.

"Yeah?"

"I've ... seen you in the waiting room at Counselors' Cooperative." He laughed, trying to feign nervousness. "No one in the lobby ever says anything to each other. We're there, hanging out before our appointments, and trying not to make eye contact. It seems, weird, you know? Not to even say 'hi.'"

She knew. She recognized him—had seen him there more than a few times. He wasn't as shy as he claimed. Others would come in and try to find a seat in the waiting room far from anyone else. Protected in a bubble of short distance. They'd stare at their phones or thumb through an old copy of *Psychology Today* or *People* from the rack on the wall, until they were called. Even when it was a couple in for counseling, they wouldn't talk to each other. The unspoken decorum of the therapists' waiting room was to save conversation for the clock. For behind a closed door. Odd little cream-colored noise machines sat on the floor outside of each of the offices, droning on in a pink noise monotone, obscuring the tears and confessions, raised voices and recriminations on the other sides of doors, while people in the lobby waited their turn to peel back the bandage, show their wound some sunlight. Silently waiting helped further the illusion of not being seen in this place of vulnerability. Not being exposed as one of the broken. Except this man. He'd come in and sit, not looking at a device or a magazine, but staring ahead into the room, looking around like it was a dentist's office, and he was waiting to compare smiles with other patients. She'd started staggering the days of her sessions with her therapist to try to avoid seeing him. He showed up on Thursdays, she'd try a Friday. He came on Friday, she moved to Wednesday. Despite her efforts to add an element of randomness into her schedule—and the difficulty it caused her at work—she still saw him there.

And now here.

"Okay," she said.

"I'm Allan, with two L's two A's, like Edgar Allan." He smiled. A smug look like he was trying to show how much he knew about her from her black clothes, her dark mien. "It's nice to meet you."

It doesn't matter, she reminded herself. "Alice," she said, not shaking his proffered hand.

"Alice. *Very* nice to meet you. It's funny," he said without waiting for any sign she was interested in more than introductions. The sound of her name on his voice felt bad, like touching her tongue to rust. Bitter and metallic, not quite like blood, but close enough. "To run into you here, I mean. I see you around town too. Your look is … pretty distinctive; you're a hard person to miss, you know." She was aware. Though he stood out less than she did, she always knew when he was near. "You like to walk," he said. It was an accurate observation. That time alone felt good, especially after spending a shift with customers who treated her like one of the weird things they stocked in the store instead of a person.

"I don't have a car," she replied.

"I figured. Ripton isn't that big, but still. You've got to clock the miles on your tracker." He glanced at his expensive smart watch, ignoring the fact she wore strings of black beads around her wrists, but no devices. "I know I'd like to spend more time out of the car than I do, but you know how it is. I've got client meetings all over the place, and if I walked between them, I'd be out of a job."

He paused, and she knew he was expecting her to ask what it was he did. She didn't care. Whatever it was, it gave him the freedom to be out of the office, driving around all day in his BMW. Those didn't have a name like Legacy or Intrepid or anything. It was a something series—X9 or whatever. Cars didn't interest her, though she knew his by sight. It was some color between brown and red that the dealer probably had a fancy name for instead of maroon, and had thin tires around big black wheels you could see the brakes through. They looked like sci-fi wagon wheels to her. The thing was always shiny clean, even when there was salt on the roads or it had rained. At a distance, it looked to her like a blood clot with headlights.

The slight side to side motion of the train increased a little and she felt slightly queasy. Though he was the one facing backwards, he seemed unperturbed by the motion. She took a deep breath and let it out slowly. His cologne didn't help settle her tummy.

"Anyway, I've seen you around town, but never got the chance to say 'hi' until now. You always seem to vanish every time I think we're going to the same coffee shop or something." He laughed again. Forced.

"Right?" she said. "I guess I've seen you around too." Alice didn't mention that when she did, she usually darted off into someone's yard or through an alley he couldn't follow her down. Nearly every time she spied the clot coming toward her, her guts seized and she tried to vanish, but in a way that wouldn't make it *look* like she was deliberately avoiding him. That timeline had so far been avoidable. But eventually, it would play out to its inevitable end. Unless …

He smiled broadly at the admission that he hadn't escaped her notice. "What luck we're on the same train, then. Where are *you* headed?"

"Vermont."

"Well, yeah. Me too. Stowe, specifically. I have a ski cabin up there. I take a few days every fall to go up and unwind before winter gets its hooks in."

"You have a nice car. Why don't you drive?"

His smile faded a little. "It's part of getting away. I work in my car, so when I travel for relaxation, I like to take the train. I'll call a MyRyde whenever I need to go into town, but most of the time I just hang out at the cabin. You know, cook, listen to records, get a taste of the good life, if I was set enough to retire and be a homebody slash ski-bum." Big smile.

"It's too early for skiing."

"You have to open up the house ahead of the season. Get it ready. That's what I do. Get everything set up so I can escape whenever I want and hit the slopes when the powder does come."

It was bullshit. They both knew it. He was on the train because she'd dropped her phone in the waiting room when she got up to go into her session the week before. He'd had an uninterrupted hour with it. Looking through her photo gallery, texts, Instagram. Her e-mails. He'd seen her e-receipt for the ticket she'd bought on the Nor'Easter Line to West Hall, Vermont. She'd have bought a ticket all the way to Ashford, but West Hall was far enough, so she tried to save a little money. Neither of those towns were anywhere near Stowe. But here he was. On *her* train.

After her session, she'd come out to find her phone sitting on the children's table in the waiting room instead of on the floor under her seat. The app that took a selfie every time the device was woken up had stored a picture of him staring right into the camera. His eyes wide and lips pursed in a look of delighted surprise she assumed came from finding no security code enabled on the wakeup screen. That face made her shudder. The battery icon was at sixty percent. It had been at seventy-two when she went in. Though it probably would've been a good idea to save it, she deleted the picture, disabled the selfie app and reactivated her unlock code.

She sat there gently rocking in her seat as the train seemed to pick up speed.

tchuk-shuk tchuk-shuk tchuk-shuk

her stomach in knots wondering what to do next. She wanted to glance at the clock on her phone. But, knowing what time it was wouldn't help. She had to do this by feel.

Here he sat with her in the empty train car, his salesman's smile so broad she could see the dark hole where the molar behind his right canine should've been. "What are the chances, right?" he said. "I know you're thinking, 'why sit right here when this whole car is empty, except for the two of us?' It's just, when I saw you, I felt like I had to stop. I see you in the Co-op and all around town and I think, *there's* somebody who looks interesting. Somebody who knows what it's like."

"I don't."

"Or … at least gets it. We both go there to get help with our problems. We talk to people we barely know to try to gain some insight into why we are the way we are. They know all about us, but they don't *know*. Not the way you and I do." He tilted his head a little to accentuate his feigned uncertainty with his prepared monologue. "My bet is, you probably feel a hell of a lot more in tune with my feelings than Bob or Holly. You see Holly, right?"

She nodded.

"Is she good?"

Alice shrugged. "I guess so. She gets me, I guess."

"But not a hundred percent, am I right?" He pointed to her shirt. It read, *LOVE ME LIKE MY DEMONS DO!* She didn't answer and he didn't pause. "Bob is okay. He hears what I'm saying when I tell him how … "

"You don't have to—"

"It's okay. I can talk about it now," he said, ignoring her subtle plea to not overshare. Then again, she knew what he was about to say was almost certainly a lie, like everything that'd come before. Sure, she saw him in the waiting room often enough. But she never saw him go in, or come out of Bob's office. For all she knew, maybe Bob was a just a friend, and Allan with two L's and two A's dropped in from time to time for lunch or something else.

He continued. "Since my dad passed, I ... the old man was a son of a bitch—always hard on me—but I guess, he was still my dad, right? I sure you get it."

He'd taken a stab. A pretty safe one, she thought. Daddy issues seemed likely for her. Either abusive or absent. Too harsh and out of touch with the way she looked, the things she liked. But her dad was all right. It wasn't him that'd sent her to therapy.

Allan sat there waiting for her to answer, letting the silence lengthen to an uncomfortable duration, one he was counting on her to fill. So, she did. "Holly gets me okay. She helps. But, you know. It's hard. My problem is ... " she let the sentence dangle. Like she felt: hanging at the end of a hook.

"You can tell me." He leaned forward, as if to say, it's safe for you to whisper it. No one in this empty train car will hear but me.

"Complicated," she finished.

He sat back, a trace of disappointment in his voice. "I'm sure it is." His face darkened. He looked so subtly frightening no matter his expression, but now there was nothing understated about him. Her heartbeat quickened in time with the train.

tchuk-shuk tchuk-shuk tchuk-shuk

"No one believes me," she said. "Not even Holly. But you will. Right?"

"Of course, I will."

She looked at her hands in her lap. Her bag under them. Inside was her notebook, allergy meds, makeup, wallet, and phone. That last was in the front pocket, just under her hands. Useless. There wasn't a soul on Earth she could call to fix the situation she'd gotten herself in. She knew that would be the case beforehand, being in motion, on the train, but she'd done it anyway, because of all the times she'd ducked him on the street as he passed her in the clot, she knew she wouldn't elude him forever, and the one time she didn't would be the end of her problems. Of everything. Forever.

His eyes shifted to the bag. She could see him thinking things through. Whether to take it from her. He stayed still, knowing he could reach it before she could pull a Taser or pepper-spray out of the zippered main compartment. She had neither. Just an inhaler. That wouldn't do shit. He wasn't a cosmic spider-clown hiding in the sewers. He was a *real* monster. She went on.

"Holly gets it. I mean, she understands how I *feel*, but I know she doesn't *believe* me, no matter how much I prove it to her."

He leaned forward again, trying to force closeness. To disarm. "You shouldn't have to prove a thing." He put his hand on her knee. Her stomach lurched, and the back of her throat burned. This gentle resting of a hand on her, the first of many touches. None of which she'd consent to. None of which he cared to seek permission for. She wanted to jump up and run right then.

Not yet. It's not time yet.

She said, "Yeah, well, I get why she can't. It's … a thing that's … hard to swallow."

His eye twitched. She pretended she didn't see it. "What is it?"

She took a deep breath. "I kind of … can see the future."

He sat back in his seat, smile broadening, even though it was a slip in his caring persona. He was laughing at her on the inside and couldn't hide it. "It can feel like that, but self-fulfilling prophecies—"

"See? You don't believe me either."

His brow furrowed but the unkind smile lingered like the last vision of the Cheshire cat. "I do! I mean, I want to understand, it's just—"

"Weird, right? I know. I have real *visions* of the future. I see things before they happen. It's not like, *knowing* what's definitely going to happen. But I know when something is, like, so possible it might as well've happened already."

"That's ... different."

"How?"

"It's ... " he seemed to be searching for words, genuinely intrigued by her delusion. Delayed, but not derailed, from his true intent. "A lot of people are good at putting together pieces of predictive information. Hell, that's how traders on Wall Street make a living. They study what's happening in the market and make predictions about where to put their clients' money. Lots of people do it. Horse racing betters and people like that." It was the first thing he'd said to her that wasn't rehearsed.

"It's not the same. Like, I knew you'd be on this train."

"Yeah?" His face dropped into that darker expression again as she reminded him why he was there. "How'd you know that?"

She shrugged again. "Just knew it. Same way I knew when you were following me in your car. I saw it, and then it happened."

His face reddened, fists balling up. "So, I've been *following* you, have I?"

"But I can change things. I know what, and kind of when, depending on how close. I know that when you're driving up on me, I better get lost."

"Or what?"

"And I know when you're in the office before I go in, or if you're coming in while I'm waiting. I mean, I don't know a lot of things, but big strokes. Like, I know this train is going to crash."

His eyes widened with amusement. "It is, is it?"

She nodded, clutching her bag tighter to her abdomen. "Uh huh. Right now, the driver or conductor or whatever, is passed out. I don't know why. He's drunk or epileptic—I guess if he was epileptic, they wouldn't let him drive trains—anyway, he's lying on the floor in the engine compartment and we're going to be going too fast for a curve coming up."

The man looked out the window at the increasingly blurry landscape, his brow furrowed. It was obvious he didn't believe her, but the expression on his face belied the creeping uncertainty settling into his mind. She knew the evolution of that look—disbelief turning to fear. Like seeing someone in a dark mask through the window of your back door. Though it was locked, a person in that situation would know the intruder was coming in. Normal people's houses weren't impregnable; not like castles, no matter how much anyone liked to think of them like that. A broken window next to a doorknob, and he was in. Faster than you could get to a phone and dial for help. Much quicker than you could reach the gun with the trigger lock on in your nightstand all the way at the other end of the house. He'd be in. And then reality would change. The thought was like that. The speeding landscape, the feeling of increased velocity in his body was a man outside the window, looking in. She knew the sensation exactly.

"I feel like I'm already dead and I'm just waiting for time to catch up to me," she'd said to Holly, thinking of the man driving the clot. The one who was going to kill her. He was going to do it on a Tuesday afternoon. Snatch her in his car and take her home. She ducked into a hardware store and hid. He was going to do it on a Friday evening on her way home from work. Same idea, except this time, he wanted to take her to the park. She lit in between that pizza place and the Haitian church. And again, on a Saturday. And again. Until she didn't see a way out. His masked face at her window.

And then, she dreamt the train. And the driver. And the river.

"You're full of shit." He stood up, rocking on his feet as the train swayed from side to side. He reached over and grabbed her arm, pulling her up out of her seat. She resisted him, but he was bigger. The bones in his hand popped, he squeezed her wrist so hard. Loud enough she heard it over the sound of the tracks.

tchuk-shuk tchuk-shuk tchuk-shuk

The car swayed again and he took an awkward step into the aisle, holding on to her as if she could keep him from falling.

"Not yet," she said.

"Fuck you! I've been waiting for this for a long time. You have nowhere to disappear to this time." He yanked the bag from her hands and dragged her away from her seat into the aisle, toward the bathroom at the end of the car. He jammed the door open revealing a space not much bigger than an airplane toilet, but big enough for two people. Big enough for him to close his hands around her neck and watch her face turn red as autumn and then purple over his white knuckles, see his own face in the mirror over her shoulder. His ecstasy reflected behind her while her tongue stuck out, her eyes bugged, her voice a whisper as she asked him to … please … stop. And he wouldn't. He'd squeeze until he felt that pop under his thumbs, until it felt right, until he felt her weight in his hands pulling down and the tightness in his pants lessen. All those things she knew he'd feel because they were all the same things in her visions whenever she saw him. The ecstasy of her death.

He shoved her into the bathroom, she fell and hit her back against the sink. He smiled at her wince, and took a step into the room toward her. Maybe she wanted to die sometimes, but not like this.

She reared up with a knee and kicked at him with her boot. "It's not time yet!" He staggered back into the wall opposite the bathroom door, slipping on the corrugated metal floor in his nice smooth-soled shoes. Before he could get his feet under him, she slammed the door and latched it.

His cries on the other side were deranged, but muffled. So soft confined in her box swathed in the sound of steel wheels on rails like a pulse in her ears.

tchuk-shuk tchuk-shuk tchuk-shuk

He banged on the door. Kicked it. He had to know she couldn't outwait him; he could just sit down and bide his time until she had to emerge. But he believed her that time was fleeting.

And then it happened. To Alice, it felt like being at the apex of an imminent drop. So slow, but pulling at your stomach with the promise of descent. A pause before the fall. Like being in the front car of a rollercoaster going over the first rise.

She braced herself, sitting on the toilet, pressing her hands to opposite walls and her feet against the sink. It wouldn't help, but it was better than standing in the aisle near the door between cars, where there was only open space and metal and window to break against.

The car tilted and the soothing rhythmic churn of the wheels stopped.

*tchuk-*_____

She felt a kind of sick weightlessness. Her body lifting from the seat despite her best effort to stay braced. She dared close her eyes and listen.

⛧

A groan of metal, long and elegiac. And somewhere in another car, the screams of other people headed north for vacations, romantic getaways, and just the thrill of a train ride during leaf peeping season. A population she'd increased by two, knowing what would happen. Hoping it would happen, because she didn't know any other way to stop the *other* outcome. The other vision where, instead of gazing through a window at hills and rivers and lonely houses, she was trapped in the dark of a car trunk. The luxurious cargo space of a BMW X9 or whatever. Until that sudden bright white of the lid opening and nothing more after that.

Weightlessness became sudden embodiment. The feeling of a hard surface against her, breaking, bruising. She, bleeding. The ring and the pain and the sensation of a sudden stop and a slower renewed descent. And that new sound. Water.

She fumbled with the latch on the door. The bolt slid, but the door stayed shut. Bent in its frame. Stuck in place. She braced herself and shoved at the hinged middle. It hurt so much. Her shoulder. A rib too, she thought. It was hard to get a deep breath. She soldiered on and pushed until it gave. And then gave again a little more. Until she could shimmy out.

The ever-tilting car gave her aid, and she fell from the bathroom into the aisle landing heavily in the angle between floor and wall.

It was dark. She couldn't see the man. Maybe she'd heard him hit the floor. Maybe she heard something else, but it satisfied her either way. Because she knew what she knew. What the vision had given her. Blood rolling over bright New England hills, and a train slipping off its tracks into the rushing river below. And he, no longer in her dream. Unable to dream of killing her.

Water rushed in through the gaps in the door. She reached for the emergency handle on the passenger window above her. Freeing it to a cascade of bracing water that battered her with frigid violence, shoving her away from the opening.

Just like the vision.

She held on to a seatback and waited for the car to fill enough she could swim out. Finally, when it seemed like her last chance, she took as deep a breath as she could and ducked down under the rising water to pull herself out of the car, into the river, swimming for the bright sparkles of sunlight on the surface, thinking only of the dream.

And the headline in it:

FEW SURVIVORS OF TRAIN DERAILMENT IN VERMONT

LOST BOY

Out on the wastes of the Never Never—
That's where the dead men lie!
There where the heat-waves dance for ever—
That's where the dead men lie!
That's where the Earth's loved sons are keeping
Endless tryst: not the west wind sweeping
Feverish pinions can wake their sleeping—
Out where the dead men lie!
　　—Barcroft Boake, *Where The Dead Men Lie*

Sam tried to pay attention to his date, but the child at the other end of the restaurant wouldn't stop staring at him. He looked at his plate, at his hands, at the tables to his left and right—anywhere but at the woman sitting across from him, because the gaze of boy over her shoulder was relentless and unnerving.

She furrowed her brow and said, "You haven't heard a word I've said."

He held up his hands in protest. "I have. Really. You were telling me about your co-worker who strapped their 'Fatbit' to a ceiling fan to win a step challenge. It's funny." He *was* listening. Joye was interesting. She was smart and witty, told good stories, liked jazz and thrillers, and looked absolutely nothing like his wife.

"What then? What is it?"

He looked up from his hands, leaning slightly to the right to angle her head in between him and the inerrant gaze of the child. "It's ... nothing. I'm just ... It's ... " He shook his head. "It's me. I'm sorry. This is my first date in a really long time—like a decade. I'm rusty, I guess."

He could almost see the red flag snake up the pole in her mind and flutter in the breeze of her building judgments. Her eyes darted to his left hand resting on the tabletop. He resisted the urge to pull it back and set it in his lap. He didn't have a tan line, but when he looked, there was still a slight indentation where he used to wear his ring.

"Your profile doesn't say you're divorced."

"I'm not."

"But you're not married, right? *Right?*" She smiled, but it was unconvincing. Behind her eyes, he could see she was thinking of ways to end things early. She took a big drink of her wine, and set the glass on the table a little too forcefully. The stem didn't break, but a little of her pinot gris splashed up over the side of her glass and slipped down the side. In a few seconds, she'd polish the rest of it off, and that would be the end of their date.

"Not anymore," he said.

She wiped at her mouth and folded her napkin, getting ready to push back her seat. "My profile very clearly says, no divorcées. I'm not interested in someone with—"

"I'm not. Divorced. My wife ... she died a year ago." He looked around at the tables nearest them. No one was looking at them, but it felt like the words he spoke had resonated through the restaurant, echoing off the walls and wine glasses. Saying those words always seemed louder than anything else he ever uttered, even when he whispered them. He felt like he was sitting at the epicenter of a sonic boom and everyone was staring. But no one was. No one but the kid in the back. Still staring.

He wanted to hold up a hand to encourage her not to leave, but instead kept them flat on the table so she wouldn't see them shaking. He explained, "There wasn't a box to check for 'widower'. It seems like it should be a thing, you know, but I guess there aren't too many of us on *30 and Flirty dot com*. I'm sorry."

He raised his arm to signal for the check. She reached out and pushed it back down to the tabletop, leaving her hand on the back of his. Her skin was dry and cool. She had thin fingers that didn't get enough circulation, no matter what she did. He didn't know that for sure about Joye. That was his wife, Liv's explanation. But, making the association felt good. Joye looked nothing like Liv, but deep down, he kind of wished she did. When he'd filled out the online questionnaire, he'd put in preferences that were opposite of the ones belonging to the person he'd married so long ago. As it turned out, a complete opposite was as much a reminder of her as someone with a resemblance.

He enjoyed the familiar sensation of her touch. It had been a while since anyone touched him and let it linger. Still, as welcome as her touch was, it made him feel that ever familiar tinge of loss that had been in him since Liv's last days.

Maybe he wasn't ready yet.

"I'm sorry," she said. Her face softened. He still didn't know what to say. *It's okay?* It wasn't okay; it was killing him. He had opted for "Thank you" for the longest time, though that still felt wrong somehow.

"Thank you."

Joye stared in his eyes with a look that was part sympathy and part fear. Though she was visibly relieved he wasn't a philanderer, she didn't seem to be fully committed to riding the night through either.

He slipped out from under her fingers and patted the back of her wrist softly before placing his hands in his lap. He smiled, but knew it looked strange. He was still getting reacquainted with the expression. In that moment, it felt false. Like he was wearing a mask that didn't fit quite right. A clown face drawn over a frown. He tried again, letting his mouth relax and the smile shrink a little. He tried to think of something that made him feel good. Surprisingly, the night with Joye up to this point was it. He got the expression right the second time.

"I am not a project. I promise." He held up his hands in defense. "And I know everyone who says, 'I promise' is lying, but I swear I'm not. I am *not* a project, and I'm not looking for someone to fix me. Soooo, you know. That."

She grinned, raising an eyebrow. "Well, that's good for you, because I am shit at projects. I have a whole apartment full of half-built Ikea furniture."

"I can't read their instructions. You have to have a degree in Egyptology to assemble their bookshelves."

Her smile grew. "I don't take the fake families out of the frames I buy. I just prop my pictures up in front of them."

"I never even print out the pictures I take of my friends. That way no one can complain about how they look in them." They laughed. He put his hand back on top of hers. She didn't pull it away. There was a pause while they both searched for another witticism to share about their mutual inability to complete simple tasks. They laughed at the same time as if the growing silence itself was evidence of their lack of follow through.

"See?" she said.

It felt good to share a real joke. Not one that was forced through the filter of grief, but honest playfulness. He wanted more of it. Searching for a way to get the conversation going again, he fished for something to say and alit upon the worst possible idea. "Seriously, though. I'm not looking for anyone to fix me."

"Say it again, and maybe you'll believe it." She winked, but he was wounded nonetheless. Her expression changed as he felt his own darken. The ghost of his wife felt like someone sitting in the next chair at their table. Joye placed her other hand over top his before he could pull it away. "It's okay. I'm not interested in fixing you. But I am interested in *you* right now. Is that good enough?"

"That's perfect."

Their server approached the table and asked how they were. Joye looked at her plate. Her jambalaya was almost all gone. Sam's salmon, by contrast, had barely been touched. He said, "Everything's fine. Can we get—" He meant to ask for another couple of glasses of wine. Instead, Joye broke in.

"The check, please. And a to-go box for Mr. Follow-Through's fish."

"It never reheats well," he said.

"Like you'd even try."

The waiter frowned with confusion, while they laughed at the private joke. He pulled the bill folder from his apron pocket and set it on the table, saying, "Whenever you're ready," walking off before Sam could get his credit card out of his wallet.

Joye said, "I know a place around the corner that serves the best cocktails. Before we go, I need to use the powder room. I'll be right back."

"Take your time. I'm sure our waiter will." He stuck his card in the folder and set it on the edge of the table.

She smiled and walked off, looking over her shoulder once before disappearing into the ladies' room.

He turned back in his seat, to face the child still staring at him. Without Joye sitting across from him, Sam had no one to hide behind. Sam pulled his phone out of his pocket, turned sideways in his seat and opened Facebook, even though he didn't care what anyone on the app had to say. He scrolled past all the people who hadn't called him in months looking for something to distract him while he waited.

Still, he felt the kid's gaze burning through him.

When Joye came back from the bathroom, the waiter still hadn't been by to take the folder. Sam pulled cash out of his wallet and substituted it for his card. The tip was less than he intended to leave, and it left him with nothing to take to their next stop, but that was the price of wanting to leave in a hurry.

"Let's grab that cocktail!"

"What about your fish?"

"You're right. I'll never reheat it." He probably would have eaten it eventually, but he just wanted to get out of the restaurant. And away from the kid.

⁂

There was a line to get into the bar, but the night air was nice and Sam didn't mind a little wait under the stars—all three of them that could be seen from the city. The temperature had dropped a little since the start of the evening, but Sam felt a hot flush rise in his cheeks as Joye slipped her hand into his. Despite the evening chill, he felt the urge to take off his sport coat before she could see him sweating through it. But that would mean letting go of her hand to slip it off. What if she didn't reach for him again? What if he tried to take her hand and she pulled away? He told himself he was being ridiculous—she'd reached out for him, after all. Self-doubt got the better of him and he decided he'd rather sweat than break the contact.

She asked about his job while they waited. He told her as much about being a copyeditor for a textbook publisher as he could without utterly boring her. That conversation lasted less than five minutes and didn't get them any closer to the door. "I am writing a novel, though."

"Ooh," she said, with apparent sincerity. "About what?"

He shrugged and waived his free hand dismissively. "It's nothing serious."

"Oh, you don't get to tease me. Spill it."

"It's about a person who finds a thumb-drive in a bathroom with a video of what looks like a murder on it. The police tell him it's just a prank when he takes it to them. He spends the rest of the book trying to get away from the killer who's tracked him using a Trojan on the same memory stick. I told you, it's just a genre novel."

"I love thrillers. Have you read Neil Hunter's *Missing Autumn*? It sounds kind of like that."

His eyes went wide. He'd never met anyone else who'd read Neil Hunter.

The line moved forward and they inched closer to the door talking about their favorite books and Sam felt less and less like he needed that drink after all to help him relax into the conversation.

Eventually, the bouncer waved them in when space opened up. They descended into the basement establishment and found a pair of empty stools on the far side of the square bar. The bartender wiped his hands on a towel, leaned over, and asked what they'd like. With his vest sleeve garters and handlebar mustache, he looked like a time traveler, or a ghost. Joye told him she wanted something "tart, with whiskey." The bartender nodded, said, "Gotcha covered," and went to work. A minute later, the man set a drink in front of her and waited. She took a sip and said, "Perfect." He nodded, turned to Sam, and asked what he wanted.

Sam opened his mouth to ask for a Manhattan, when a flash of movement in the window behind the bartender caught his eye. He glanced up in time to see a child's legs walking past the window. Sam waited a moment for a pair of adult feet to come chasing after them. But none did. A knot in his throat choked him as the bartender asked him again what he'd like.

"Um, a … Manhattan, I guess."

The man furrowed his brow, and said, "You can get that anywhere. Let me make you something worth coming in for." Sam nodded and the man went to work. This time, however, Sam wasn't interested in watching him pour intuitive volumes of ingredients into a shaker and chip ice off of a block with a pick. He kept staring out the window.

"Are you all right?" Joye asked.

He nodded, though he felt certain his face was as white as the bartender's shirt. "I'm okay. I think I just need to duck into the bathroom real quick. It must be the fish I didn't eat." He winked at Joye, but she still looked worried.

Sam blushed again. He wanted so badly to sit back down and grab ahold of her hand. Instead, he leaned over to give her a small peck on the cheek. She turned into it and he ended up kissing the side of her mouth. Her lips tasted like rye and lemon and he wanted to kiss her again. Taste more. Instead, he straightened up, shrugged off his sport coat, and draped it over his stool. "Save my seat," he said, patting his jacket. "I'll be back in two shakes."

"Any more and you're playing with it," the bartender said as he mixed the ingredients for Sam's drink in a Boston Shaker.

"You should leave that to me," Joye purred. The bartender let out a wolf whistle and started stabbing at the block of ice in front of him with a long metal pick.

A lump grew in Sam's throat and he tried to think of something witty to say in reply. Nothing came out but a hoarse whisper that was lost in the din of the bar. He turned and headed for the door.

The bouncer sitting at the door said, "No reentry," as Sam stepped past him.

Sam stopped and looked at the man perched on the tall stool. "I just want to get some air," he said. "It's, uh, stuffy in here." The air conditioning was cranked, but needing some air sounded more reasonable than that he thought he'd just seen a child walking all alone up a city sidewalk at ten at night and if he didn't make sure he was all right, he was going to have a panic attack.

The doorman seemed unsympathetic. "Whatever, bro. Your call. In or out. You can't be both."

An anxious woman standing on the other side of the glass door opened up her palms as if to say, come on—just leave already. Sam held up a hand and mouthed, "Sorry," to her. She rolled her eyes and began talking to her friend in line. Her raised voice filtered softly through the door. "Will you look at this asshole?"

Sam turned and nodded at the doorman who didn't nod back and went to the bathroom instead.

At the sink, he splashed some water on his face and stared at himself in the mirror for a moment trying to push his anxiety down. The man who stared back wasn't a stranger; he had the same haunted look Sam was very familiar with. He'd been wearing that look for over a year now.

In the reflection behind him, he saw a pair of feet dangling under the first stall door. Small feet in bright colored sneakers that couldn't quite reach the ground. Sam's breath caught. He squinted his eyes shut and held his breath while he counted to ten. He opened his eyes when a man shoved his way into the bathroom took a place at a urinal, sighing loudly. Sam turned and looked at the stall. The door was open. No feet. No child.

He turned off the water and plucked a handful of paper towels off the counter beside the faucet handle, refusing to look at his reflection—or what might be behind it—again.

When he returned to his seat he found his drink waiting for him. Joye's glass was still full as well. Either she hadn't drunk any of it during his absence, or she'd ordered a second already. He apologized for being gone so long. Joye said, "I was starting to worry." He smiled and told her that everything was just fine. He took a sip of his drink and murmured his approval. Joye reached out and put her hand on his. "You sure everything is all right?"

"Right as rain," he lied. He tapped his glass to hers and smiled before taking another sip. Joye lifted hers and took a big swallow. She pulled her nearly empty glass away from her mouth and smiled. Her lips glistened with whiskey and his stomach knotted at the memory of kissing her a moment earlier. He wanted to shoot his cocktail and order them both another. He wanted to look like he had his shit together more and kept sipping instead. Joye finished and slung the strap of her purse over her shoulder.

"I'm sorry, did I say something?" he asked.

Joye leaned forward and kissed him squarely on the mouth. "You better finish that. Unlike the fish, I hate to see good whiskey go to waste."

"I ... are you ... "

"She left a twenty and a ten on the bar and stood. "Are you coming?"

He slammed the rest of his drink, not regretting for a moment not taking the time to savor it.

⁕

Sam opened his eyes in the dark and felt a moment of panic overwhelm him. He was disoriented with sleep and the dark room felt cavernous, less like a deep hole than a void. He lay there for a long moment, breathing deeply and letting the darker shadows in the room deepen into the silhouettes of his familiar things and ground him. His dresser, the bookshelf, the open door to the hallway came into focus as his eyes adjusted and revealed to him the things returned from nothingness. He turned his head toward the unfamiliar shape in bed next to him.

Another person. It had been so long since there was another person in his bed. He recalled Joye's enthusiasm as he unlocked the door to his condo and let it swing open. Without waiting to be shown in, she'd stepped through first and reached back to pull him in after her. Liv hadn't been assertive like that. She'd liked the dance they did when she dropped a subtle hint here or there, and Sam would wrap his arms around her and place a soft kiss on her neck, waiting a moment for silent permission to kiss her again. She'd lean her head back into his shoulder and he'd kiss her and nudge her toward the bedroom, and she'd say something like, "Oh you think so, do you?" reminding him who was in control.

Once again, Joye was her opposite and wasn't.

He watched the shadow outline of her shoulder against the deeper black of the room beyond her body. He watched until he saw the subtle rise and fall of her shoulder with her breath. Then he let his out.

He touched her hip with a timorous hand. Her bare skin was warm and soft and felt like electricity under his fingers. He let his hand slid down the arc of her hip, to thigh, to bent knee. She didn't stir, but let out a contended sounding sigh. In the dark, he had only hints of the features of her face. A small chin, a long thin nose, and hair that seemed like a burst of darkness. A dark stain that made his stomach tighten and his heart beat a little faster.

Everything's fine, he told himself. He pulled back the sheets gently and slipped out of bed. He found his boxer briefs on the floor and stepped into them, though he thought he might slip them off again when he came back to bed. Even though he lived alone, it felt strange walking around the house without anything on. As if he might have to run out into the hallway in a hurry and beg a neighbor to use the phone because *oh god she isn't breathing and my battery is dead and please just call 9-1-1 and tell them to send someone right away because she's not breathing and cold and I don't know what to do because I can't find her phone and mine is dead and please help me,* and he didn't want to ever feel as vulnerable as that again, and wearing clothes felt a little like being in control. He was in control of his body, if nothing else.

He stepped into the bathroom and lifted the lid, careful not to let it bang against the tank behind. He tried to pee into the bowl at the edge of the water so the splash of his urine wouldn't wake Joye. He felt a little splash against his shin and re-aimed, frustrated that he'd missed. But he was still groggy from wine and whiskey and sleep and hadn't turned on any lights.

So not to wake Joye.

Because when she woke up it would all be over. She would get dressed, maybe kiss him a little, and then she would collect her things and go home, because even though she'd slept with him, this was still a first date and she wouldn't want to stay the whole weekend. It was too early for a weekend together. Slowly. One day at a time.

Just like surviving.

He finished, closed the lid quietly and debated whether to flush. He decided the noise was a better risk than leaving that for Joye to find if she woke up before he did. He waited until the loudest part of the process was finished before opening the door and returning to the bedroom.

He padded down the hall and stopped in the doorway. It took him a minute to make sense of what he saw. She was sitting up in bed.

"I'm sorry. I didn't mean to wake you," he whispered. She said nothing. "Joye?" He turned on the hallway light, thinking that she might have to use the bathroom too, but didn't know where to go in the unfamiliar dark. Light will cast out the darkness.

The child sitting on Joye's chest looked at him with black eyes that reflected the hallway light. It stared at him the same way it had in the restaurant.

He wanted to scream at it to get away from her, but he lost his breath. His throat felt constricted like strong little fingers had wrapped around it. The child leaned forward, closer to Joye's face, but didn't turn its gaze away from him.

"Stop," Sam choked out. He took a rasping breath and tried to say it again. "Stop, please. Don't."

The child's eyebrows knitted, and it titled its head a little to the side. "Why?" it asked.

Same didn't know what to say. Why? *Why?*

"Because, I like her. Please, stop. I need this. I need her."

The child's face shifted, upturned eyebrows knitting together, making its expression as dark as any moonless night or bad intention. "I needed you."

"I ... "

Gooseflesh rose on Sam's body and his breath billowed out of his mouth in a humid cloud that fell apart as fast as his courage. He felt a sheen of filth in him that couldn't ever wash away. No matter what he put in the past, walked away from, it was there coating his mind, his heart, his entire essence. It was as black as the boy's eyes and shiny like them too. And nothing he could ever think of to say would wash him clean. Not after what he did.

"I'm sorry."

He knew saying I'm sorry never stopped a hand already swinging. It never took away the sting of a struck cheek or the feeling in a child's stomach after the threats were made. Sorry did nothing. The child looked away from him toward Joye, still sleeping, a look on her face that mirrored the child's own frown. It leaned forward and put its hands on her throat.

"Please. No. PLEASE! STOP!"

"Make me," it said.

A child's dare. *Make me.* Said in the full realization that he absolutely could not make it do anything. Not without touching it. And he knew that touching it was something he absolutely could not do. Not ever.

Not even to save Joye?

Make me.

He took a single step forward. A hollow threat. The child knew it, and its fingers tightened. The image of Joye and the boy astride her blurred as tears flooded his eyes. His knees felt weak, but he stayed upright and attempted another step.

Make me.

He reached out. His hand not held up to push or slap, or even to signal for the boy to stop. He reached out to merely lay his hand on the child's back. To let it know he was sorry. For not being the person he needed to be, for not being strong enough to stay, for everything he had been too weak his entire life to face.

He was sorry for burying the boy without ever saying a word of regret for what that loss meant.

But sorry was not enough to heal a single scar.

It couldn't bring back a lost boy.

It was worthless.

Forever.

He touched the child. A chill spread through his body, raising gooseflesh on his skin. His breath billowed out again in a cloud of condensation like his spirit escaping. The boy shimmered and Sam's hand passed through him and settled on Joye's chest. Her eyes fluttered open, and her frown became a smile. "Hey, you. You're freezing."

"Hey," he said, trying not to sob out loud and failing.

"Are you okay?"

Sam shook his head. She took his hand from her chest and held it up to her mouth. She kissed the palm with which he'd tried to comfort a lost boy and felt only hurt and hate. When he moaned, his breath hitching at the pain of her kiss, she pulled him down to her and held him against her warm, bare skin, and smoothed his hair, whispering "Shhh," and "It's okay. You're okay."

Eventually, he fell asleep on her chest, listening to her breathing—to her heartbeat.

In the morning, Sam awoke alone. He felt the emptiness of his bed gnaw at him and he placed his hand flat on the mattress, trying to feel the heat of a woman who wasn't there. Another woman, who wasn't there. But it was cold. He'd told her he wasn't a project, but of course he was. He was a terrible, ruined project that had been started and abandoned and restarted and broken a little worse until he was a collection of pieces barely held together by a bond that was wearing away. He didn't blame her for leaving. She'd said she was shit at projects. And he was an unfixable one.

He heard the clink of the coffee pot and sat up straight. He jumped out of bed, still in his underwear, and ran into the kitchen where Joye stood pouring herself a cup of coffee, wearing one of his t-shirts and a pair of his boxer briefs. Her hair was a mess and she'd scrubbed her face clean and was radiant. She smiled at him and he let out a long sigh.

"Good morning," she said.

"I'm so sorry about last—"

Joye held up a finger to silence him. It worked. She took a sip of her coffee before asking if he wanted a cup. He nodded, still unsure whether he was allowed to speak. She grabbed down a mug that read, "Shhh," at the top, "Almost," in the middle, and "Now talk," at the bottom. Liv's favorite. She filled it to Shhh and handed it to him.

Leading him by his elbow over to the breakfast table, she pulled out his chair and waited for him to sit before pulling a chair over next to him. She sat and leaned against him while he drank, and didn't say anything for a long time. She just touched him and was there.

Eventually, she broke the silence and said, "I was looking at your pictures." She nodded toward the collection of framed photos hanging on the wall. Liv had said she always wanted them to be together for meals, even if they were apart, so she'd gone on the hunt for photos in shoeboxes and albums and thumb drives. She framed them and hung them in a cluttered collage on the wall beside the table. They clashed with the rest of their décor, but somehow she made it work. "Is that her?" Joye asked, pointing to a shot off to the side of the array of a woman smiling devilishly behind an ice cream cone.

"That's her. She had a thing for ice cream." He directed her gaze to another picture of a child holding a cone. Same smile. Same pose. "That's her when she was a kid."

"And who's that?" Joye pointed to one next to it. The boy from the restaurant, from the street, and the stall … and the night stared at them from the frame. The boy's face was solemn and drawn. He'd been told to stand there and smile, but he hadn't wanted to have his picture taken. He didn't want to smile. A woman's hands gripped his shoulders, holding him in place. They could make him do that much.

"That's me when I was a kid."

"He's cute."

He swallowed hard. "I don't like it. I asked Liv not to hang that one up."

Sam hated being that boy, and as soon as he could manage, had made himself into someone else. Someone who couldn't be told what to do, or how to feel. Who couldn't be forced to endure things he didn't agree to. He'd hated that boy for being weak. Hated him so much that he killed the thought of him and buried it deep in the desert of memory, certain there was no way back.

Joye snuggled up closer, leaning her head on his shoulder. "Aw. *I* like it," she said. "He looks sweet. I want to know who he grew up to be."

Sam snorted a short laugh. "He's been lost for a long time."

"I found him, didn't I?"

He nodded. But he'd found his own way back. The ghost of a boy back from the Never Never.

THE LONELINESS OF NOT BEING HAUNTED

1.

The antiques dealer had assured June that the object was an authentic railroad watch—named so because it was accurate enough for railroad time service. But that's not why she'd wanted it. Mr. Jackson also insisted that the timepiece had been in the possession of the previous owner when he died. Not just owned by him, but beloved and held close *at the moment* he passed away. "It was his great grandfather's watch," Jackson told her as he pushed the box across the counter, closer to her. The object had been a dying man's connection to a personal history. Then, his children took it from his hands and sold it. Its personal worth as dead as its third generation of owner. She bought the watch and hurried home. She unwrapped it at the dinner table and began to admire its detail, turning it over, focusing on the scrollwork around the engraved backplate instead of the liver spots and wrinkles on the backs of her hands. The pocket watch was older than she was, but it existed in a slower state of entropy. The timepiece was already over a hundred years old, and, if cared for, would persist for a hundred more, where she would be "lucky" to see a century pass. It wouldn't be long after that failed milestone that there would be nothing left of her but bones. And after another hundred years, maybe nothing at all—not even a memory.

Young people think it's fortunate to live a long life, but June knew differently. Time is not kind to transient beings. It takes breath and weakens bone. And if you're "lucky," you'll live for years with the memory of all your lost loves. Everyone you have ever loved will eventually die. And if you live a long time, their absence will never leave you, like the ghost on a wall where a painting used to hang.

She turned the watch over again and looked at the face. Black lacquer hands stood still in a chevron over a bright white face, ringed by bold numbers. In a smaller circle where the numeral 6 should have been, the second hand stood still, pointing at a hash mark between 40 and 45. She considered winding the device to see it come alive, but decided she didn't want to observe the hands moving or even hear it tick. Its stillness was better. For it, time remained quietened at a quarter to noon. Or midnight.

And now it was hers. She clasped her hands together over it. It felt nice in her palms. Heavy and cool and solid all the way through—a corporeal thing. A thing with weight. But that was it—only weight, nothing else. At her prime, in her forties, when she felt most alive, most rapacious, and ready to kick down doors, she'd had weight. Height too. But, that was half a lifetime ago and the years had made her light and frail. Worst of all, though, they'd left her alone.

Throughout her life, she'd had lovers and friends, but age, disease, and misfortune had taken every one. Taken her lover and their daughter on the very same night that had broken her and left her bedridden for months. That had been the start of her decline. She who was once strong withered in the wake of that loss. She who had loved was left alone. And eventually her friends, one by one, faded away as well. Some moved, some died, others just disappeared. She'd heard on the radio that the kids call it "ghosting," when people just gave up on you and vanished.

She had gone on a ghost tour once with a friend. Kat—short for Katherine—stood beside her in the thick, humid afternoon while the guide told them about the spirits haunting the trees at the edge of the plantation property. As he told the story, her friend gasped and stepped back, holding a hand over her mouth. The guide had smiled and said, "Sometimes, she appears to people from behind the trees." Kat pulled her hand away from her face, mouth agape and asked, "Was she blond?" The man nodded and smiled. The crowd gathered around oohed and aahed. Some looked at her like she was a plant—someone there to sell the story, not actually a tourist. But Kat was a tourist. June felt a stab at her center. Kat didn't even believe in ghosts. *She* was the one who wanted to believe; *she* was the one who needed them. She didn't see anything but trees, a plantation house, and a group of people all wishing they'd seen what Kat said she had.

Later, over drinks at the rotating bar in the Hotel Monteleone, Kat rationalized her experience as a suggestibility inspired by the heat and morning cocktails, but June knew her friend was still moved. The ghost of a long dead woman stepped up beside her, smiled and then faded away as if she'd never been there at all. That was how Kat described it, anyway. June hadn't seen anything but Kat jump back and act shocked. Her friend wasn't the type to fake it. She was sincere to a fault and didn't believe in ghosts. Not until that trip, anyway.

Kat was killed in 2001.

June still had Kat's glasses. The same pair through which she saw the spirit in the trees sat on the table in front of her. But at that moment, she was focused on the watch.

Though her hands always felt cold, the watch gradually warmed between her palms until only its weight assured her it was still there. She wanted to reach into it and find the spirit of the man who'd died with it in his hands. She wanted the connection to it that he'd had and, through it, the connection to him. She wanted his hands to close around hers and hold it with her.

June sighed and spread her palms. It was just an object. Though it would move and tick if she wound it, there was nothing in it that lived. Nothing special. It was just another thing in a lonely place full of silent things.

The distant sound of someone laughing outside drifted up through her from four flights below, and the neighbor's footsteps above creaked and thumped as he paced from one end of his apartment to the other and back. A car horn honked and a man yelled and tires screeched abruptly as the driver jammed the gas and a bus stopped, its hydraulics hissing as it "knelt" to release riders and accept more and the city kept on all around her.

She set the watch on the small ritual table, between Kat's glasses and a rubber duckie that had been in the bathtub with a toddler when she drowned. June lit a tall candle and placed it in the center of the star engraved in the top of the table, next to a wedding ring and a pair of dog tags, and waited. Nothing changed. Her room was a muted mélange of city noise boxing in the stillness of her apartment. After a while, she got up and set about the task of making herself dinner. The aroma of her meal soon overtook the scents of matchstick sulfur and candle wax.

She sat at the dinner table by the window and ate, looking out into the street at the people rushing to get from one place to another.

Not one of them looked up at her. They only saw each other, and even then, most of them pretended not to. It was the way you survived in a city. By creating a personal illusion of isolation in a press of forced intimacy.

After dinner, she washed her dish and set it on the drying towel next to the sink. There was no point in wiping it dry and putting it away in the cupboard. She'd have breakfast on the same plate in the morning. And lunch. And then dinner again. One plate. One seat. No waiting.

She turned off the lights and headed for bed. Along the way, she blew out the candle. Nothing had been attracted to it or the watch. Not tonight. She'd try again tomorrow.

2.

The man on the other end of the line stammered as he told June that something had come into the shop she might be … interested in. She asked why he was calling instead of Mr. Jackson. "He usually lets me know himself when he has something new." She glanced at her table. At the things there. The new addition was nice enough, she guessed. Though, the watch would look better in a dome on the mantle than in the middle of the star.

"This item isn't really his style. But I think it might be yours."

June wasn't feeling up for a trip out of the apartment, but the man wouldn't agree to tell her over the telephone what it was he found. He kept insisting it'd be better if she came in to the shop to see it in person. And it had to be today. Mr. Jackson wasn't ever coy or insistent like that. When he called, he told her what he'd set aside, according to her standing request, and asked when she would be able to drop by. June tried not to leave anything waiting too long, but there was never any urgency in their transactions. Whenever she could find time to get to his shop was soon enough.

The man on the phone assured her it would be worth her time, saying this wasn't a thing she was likely to ever find again. Not like the watch or the fountain pen or any of the other things that had made their way onto the table before being replaced by another once-loved object. This was unique, and available today only. She said she'd try to make it in before lunch. He seemed satisfied and said he looked forward to seeing her, though there was something in his voice that seemed off when he said it. Like it was a lie. Mr. Jackson was always very kind to her. Every time she visited his shop, he asked how she was doing and made pleasant small talk. More importantly, he seemed to take her odd interest seriously. Not everyone did. She imagined some people talked behind her back. Called her morbid. She didn't think Mr. Jackson did. If he did, he hid it well.

June collected her things, put on a sunhat, and blew out the candle before stepping into the hall. She could hear her neighbors behind their apartment doors—televisions and children and yapping dogs. But no one peeked out when she pulled her door shut. It clicked too quietly for any of them to hear over their own lives, and when she turned her key, the deadbolt slid into place with a soft scraping like a faraway librarian with a finger to her lips. "Shh," it said to her.

Outside, the morning was hot and humid and June could tell it was only going to get worse. The air had that thick feel like slight smothering. She immediately wanted to go back inside, ride the elevator up home and spend the rest of the day next to her window air conditioner, listening to records and reading. She'd light a candle. But she wanted to see what it was the man who worked for Mr. Jackson had found.

She took a step away from her building. And then another, until she was at the entrance to the subway and she'd gone far enough that she might as well keep going.

⛧

The bell above the door tinkled as June pushed through. Mr. Jackson's employee—she recognized his face, but couldn't remember his name—looked up from the counter and, instead of smiling like his boss usually did when she walked in, waved her toward the far end of the counter. He lifted the barrier and stepped out from behind it gesturing with a pale hand toward the back of the store. There, he opened the storeroom door and held it, waiting for June to go ahead of him. She hesitated for a moment before stepping through. She'd never been invited into the back and she didn't know this man. Sure, she'd *seen* him before, but had never actually spoken to him. And he'd never even nodded at her, let alone spoke. Suddenly, they were doing business. In the back room. *There's nothing to worry about*, she assured herself and walked through the doorway.

The storeroom was small and packed tight. There were antique radios and swords and books and even a stuffed owl up on a high shelf looking down at her as if she were a mouse. She marveled at the noisy clutter of objects, ordinary and otherwise, that Mr. Jackson deemed unfit for the front of his shop. She wondered why he'd buy something he didn't intend to put out. Maybe he had a second shop somewhere else. Maybe he had his own interests, and this was *his* collection.

The man closed the door, propping it slightly ajar with a cast iron Boston terrier doorstop and walked around to the other side of a round table in the center of the room. "It's … well, it's not an antique," he said. "It's not … But then I remembered your particular … interest, and I, well, let me show you."

He turned around and slid a grey, rectangular box out from behind a group of objects concealing it. It was about the size of a toy bed for a baby doll—longer than it was wide or tall. He shoved aside a pile of papers and bric-à-brac cluttered on the table and set the box down. She felt more than a tinge of disappointment at the sight of it; it was plastic and cheap looking. And *this* was why she dealt directly with Mr. Jackson. She'd suffered the sidewalk heat and the stifling subway humidity for something that came in a beige plastic box. The trip back to her apartment would be doubly exhausting, for the frustration of going home empty-handed. She decided then that she would call back later to have a discussion with Mr. Jackson. She didn't appreciate being taken advantage of. There were other places to get what she wanted.

"I don't understand the need for all this cloak and dagger. That doesn't look like anything I'd be interested in. I'm sorry, but you've wasted my time."

"Trust me." He opened the lid and removed another, smaller container from inside, the size of the doll that would sleep in that bed. He set the second box in front of the first. This one was wooden with a pair of brass inlay laurels arcing out from the center of the hinged lid. On the front were two tiny matching handles, though there was no drawer or front hinge on the box that she could see. Her breath seemed harder to draw for a second. She wasn't certain why. The object he removed wasn't that striking. Still, it took her breath away for a second. A feeling about it. Like something had come with it that she couldn't see.

The man pushed it toward her with a finger, immediately pulling his hand back after an inch or so. He stepped away from the table rubbing his hands on his pants and nodded, inviting her to step forward and inspect it.

"What is it?" she asked.

"The seller called it a 'burial cradle.'"

"A *what?*"

"A burial cradle. It's a casket ... for a miscarriage," he whispered. In her day, no one ever said "miscarriage" with volume. It was always whispered along with the words, "affair" and "barren." He wasn't from her day, though. This man was young. A third her age at most. Still, he whispered it. *Miscarriage.* Too terrible to say aloud.

Her forehead wrinkled and she frowned. She opened her mouth, and hesitated a moment, wanting to address him by name. "As morbid as my request might seem to you, I'm not interested in objects that haven't been—"

He grimaced. "Before you make up your mind, open it."

That breathless feeling returned. She took a tentative step forward and reached for the box to inspect it more closely. When she lifted it, she felt the contents shift away from her. She gripped it tighter, afraid of dropping it, though the impulse to throw it was almost as strong as the urge to hold it close. "What's inside?" she asked, fearful of the answer. He didn't say. He nodded. She opened the box.

Inside, was a satiny pink pouch tied with a black ribbon. She reached in with a finger and touched it. Whatever was in the pouch was smooth and hard and curved. Like a cylinder. A bottle, she realized. It was in a bottle. She went to untie the bow, but the man coughed loudly and shook his head.

"Are you telling me there's a—"

He held up a finger before she could say "baby." He said, "We're not supposed to have this, you understand. It's ... illegal for us to sell something like this."

She closed the lid, but kept hold of the box. "Then why are you?"

He looked around the room as if an answer was hiding in the

shadows behind a steam trunk or under a mid-century end table. Or as if someone might hear. "Because, I think it's what you're looking for. Do you want it?"

She hesitated. It was awful. This wasn't a thing borne through a lifetime that someone held onto for comfort as their final moments passed. This was … different. It wasn't a thing *near* loss. It *was* loss.

She wanted it.

"How much?" she asked. The bell at the front of the store cut off the man's reply before he could quote her a price. His head whipped around to look through the gap in the door and his face went paler. He turned to June and glanced urgently at the emergency exit in the far back of the storeroom. He was urging her to flee.

She stood her ground. "How much?"

"Geoffrey? Are you back there?" Mr. Jackson called out.

"You've got to go," the man whispered as he lurched toward the door. He stood in the crack and poked his head through. "Hey Miles! What are you doing here?"

"I came to catch up on a little paperwork. No rest for the wicked." He laughed. "You feeling all right? Need me to watch the front for a minute?"

The man—Geoffrey—waved his arm at June to go. She shut the box and set it in the larger, plastic container. Putting the thing away felt bad. It tugged at her. She hadn't paid, but she wasn't leaving without it either. She told herself she could return some other time and pretend that she'd picked something else up while Mr. Jackson was out. That was it. Go now and come back later to settle up.

Geoffrey waved again at her from behind the door to go. He said, "No, I'm good. Just got out of the bathroom. But you know, now that the tank is empty, I'd love a cup of coffee. My treat, if you run out to get it."

"No, that's okay. I'll cover you. Take a break and go get yourself something. I want to get started on the inventory. I feel like I need to purge to storeroom. I can't stop thinking about that ghoul who came in last night. Can you imagine trying to sell such a thing?" He groaned. "The thought of it makes my skin crawl."

Geoffrey faked a laugh and agreed.

June felt a pull from within her arms. She turned and started for the door. The space in the back of the store was tight with clutter. She had to suck in her stomach to brush between a secretary desk and a bicycle. Behind her she felt some small thing catch on her clothes. It shifted with her and she stopped, hoping it would also stop along with her. It didn't. She wasn't quick enough to catch it and it clattered to the floor, shattering with a bright sound.

"What was that?" Mr. Jackson's footsteps were hurried and heavy. June was frozen. She clutched the box to her chest. Geoffrey started to say, "It's noth—" but Mr. Jackson had the door open before he could finish.

"Ms. *Porter*?" Mr. Jackson said. "What are you doing back here?" He seemed surprised, almost pleasantly so. His reflexive smile started to appear, but died as his eyes tracked down to the box cradled in her arms. His face flushed red. "Ms. Porter!" He turned. "Geoffrey! What is going on here?"

June spoke up. "Geoffrey was trying to—"

Mr. Jackson silenced her with a stare. "I know what Geoffrey was doing; I'm not an idiot. Though, I am surprised at you, Ms. Porter. I thought better of you than this. But then, it's your standing order that brought *that* to my store in the first place."

"I don't ... "

"I have other eccentric customers, to be sure. But this is beyond the pale. I can only imagine someone thought that was a thing he could sell to me because word has gotten around about your … tastes. Well, if you want to collect … medical oddities, this is not the place for you. My reputation is worth more than you spend here." He turned toward his employee, who seemed to be trying to slowly slide through the door Jackson was blocking. "And you, Geoffrey, are fired. Get your things and get out."

"But Miles!"

Jackson raised a finger and Geoffrey flinched. "You heard me. I'll send your last paycheck tomorrow. Don't bother coming in to get it."

Geoffrey looked at June as though he wanted to complete their transaction. Like he was signaling her to meet him outside. Or even just offer him cash right then. She felt sure he'd paid out of his own pocket for the box, but she didn't imagine that Mr. Jackson was about to let them conclude their transaction. Still, whether or not she was able to reimburse the man for what he'd spent, she wasn't leaving without the box.

She began to walk toward the door. Jackson held up a hand. "You're taking *that*?" he said. She didn't say anything, just held it closer. "Fine. Get it out of my shop. I'm happy to be rid of it. But leave though the back. I don't want anyone seeing you come out of here holding that."

June didn't wait for him to change his mind. She turned and, stepping over the shards of whatever it was she'd broken, pushed through the steel door into the alley.

The smell of a dumpster broiling the waste from the Chinese restaurant next door hit her solidly. Sweet rot. Her stomach turned, but she held her sick down and rushed as fast as she could past it and out of the alleyway.

She stepped from of the shade into the open street and the sunlight on her skin felt shameful, as though she was lit with judgment. It shone on her brightly, reflecting off the blank tan box in her arms like she carried a piece of its starlight with her. A beacon that blinked a message to everyone who saw her.

Ghoul.

Feeling too uncomfortable to take the subway home, she hailed a taxi instead. She did her best to hide the box as she climbed into the back seat. The driver didn't ask. He drove her home in silence, looking at her the whole way in the rearview mirror. At the end of the trip, she threw cash through the window in the divider and jumped out of the car as soon as he unlocked the doors. He squealed his tires pulling away from the curb.

The feeling of breathlessness subsided. She was home with the box. It was hers. She covered it with an arm to conceal it and climbed the steps to her building.

3.

The box sat alone on her dinner table, and she felt a sting of shame at having brought it home. Mr. Jackson had been a friend, though a distant one. Though he hadn't said it, she was sure she wasn't welcome in his shop any more than Geoffrey was. But in the moment, she'd felt compelled. That Geoffrey had lost money didn't matter. That Jackson has lost respect for her didn't matter. The box mattered. But not the box. What was *in* the box. Not even that, really. What the box invited was what mattered. Though, that feeling of urgency had worn off now that she was home with it. And it wasn't pushing or pulling at her.

She opened it and pulled the smaller container—the cradle—out. She set the plastic case on the floor under the table and stared at the brass inlays and what she realized now were faux pallbearer handles on the front. As if the miniature casket would be borne to the grave by other tiny hands.

With trembling fingers, she opened the lid and peeked in at the satin bag. June had a good idea what she'd see if she untied the ribbon holding it closed: a tiny body, barely formed—arms and legs no bigger than twigs and eyes that had never opened. Was it pink or brown? Was it some other color? Gray? Or purple, like rot. She both wanted to know and didn't. It didn't matter. It was here and hers and whatever it looked like didn't matter.

June traced one of the laurels with a finger. The fear that she might outlive her child had always been there in the back of her mind, urging her to say things like, "be careful," "don't talk to strangers," and "look both ways." And while she'd thought maybe, some distant day, she might survive her spouse, she'd never imagined losing her entire family at once. And then, there was no one to say any of it to anymore. A car crash crushed her child's body before she could say, "look out." There was no sleeping lover to whisper "goodnight" to when she came late to bed, because of that one deafening, wordless moment. And then forty years passed like some kind of dream and she woke up and realized that all her life was spent looking back until there was almost no more ahead.

She stood and moved over to the ritual table with her collection of other people's treasured things. One by one she removed them from the table and placed them in the plastic outer box under the dinner table until she could think of a better home for them all. Perhaps, in her storage unit in the building basement.

Unlike the small things, the cradle didn't seem to fit anywhere except at the center of the star. June moved the candle out of the way and set the cradle down. She lit the wick and whispered her invitation.

"Please come. Please stay."

Nothing.

She hadn't had time to ask about the box. Who first owned it, who sold it, and why? Was the woman who'd filled it still alive? Even if she had asked, Geoffrey probably hadn't gotten any sort of provenance for it or its contents. Mr. Jackson's reaction suggested this transaction was performed in the same alley to which he'd banished her. She imagined that was how things like this were always sold. In secret places, hushed voices in the dark bickering over price and no more. No questions asked.

June closed her eyes and sat in front of the table waiting for something to change. But nothing did. The neighbor upstairs continued to pace, while cars honked on the street below, and people shouted to each other in both pleasure and frustration. The air conditioner hummed and only cooled the dinner table.

That feeling of embarrassed regret returned. Reality and self-consciousness returned and said what she was doing was absurd and stupid and she was a fool for wanting to believe in ghosts as badly as she did. If it weren't for Kat and the girl in the trees, maybe she never would have done any of this. Maybe she would have gone on dates and maybe had another child. Once, she'd still had time to have a whole other life.

The thought that she should get rid of it came to mind. She hadn't spent anything on the casket. She could dispose of it respectfully, make a couple of calls and ask if she could pay to have it cremated or buried. She could bury all of it. All the things that should be in coffins in cold earth with their owners.

She could let go of it all.

And then she could go apologize to Mr. Jackson.

She stood and pulled the plastic box out from under the dinner table. Filled with the things she'd piled in it, there was no room for the little coffin. Not if she wanted to replace the lid. She upturned the box and dumped its contents out onto the ritual table with a clatter and a heavy *thunk*. The pocket watch tumbled out last and fell into the open casket. It clanked against the jar. She gritted her teeth waiting for the sound of cracking glass and the smell of formaldehyde and ...

She didn't want to think about it.

Nothing broke. No horrible smells revealed what an awful thing she had brought home. She reached down to pluck it out, but hesitated. The air near the cradle felt thicker. Colder. She pulled her hand back and the cold reached up for her. The chill radiated out of the cradle and brushed up against her belly. It wasn't an unwelcome touch; it felt like a caress.

There was a hint of something like a whisper in her ear. She thought it sounded like, "I'm here." Or, perhaps, "Come here." She leaned closer. The cold caress moved from her belly up over her breast, to her cheek, where it stopped like a loving hand holding her face still before a kiss. She closed her eyes and waited for the pressure against her lips. But the touch faded.

"No. Don't go," she said, her eyes springing open. "Please stay." Her breath billowed out in front of her. It faded in the hot apartment and was replaced by her next and the one after that. She was panting with excitement, her heartbeat thundering in her ears like the thrum of the ocean.

She picked up a class ring and the dog tags and the glasses and dropped them all in the casket along with the watch and jar until it was overflowing. The chill enveloped her and she felt movement around her sides and behind her. Small breezes that ruffled her clothes and made her hair dance. She thought, a hand on her hip would be so welcome—that little push that moved her around the floor in tandem with a partner.

The speakers behind her began to peal with Chet Baker's trumpet and she spun around to see who'd started the record player. Something shifted like a movement out of the corner of her eye, though it wasn't in the corner, but dead ahead. She tried to track it, but the distortion faded before she could get a bead on it. She took a step toward the stereo. The pull of something that didn't want to be far from her stopped her. A clinging presence begged her to stay, holding her skirt. Like her daughter had always done.

"Janice?" she said, whispering her girl's name. "Is that you?" The tug came again, harder. She faced the casket on the low table and felt cold.

The lights dimmed and there was pressure on her shoulders. A brush against her neck that flipped her hair away. She laughed, tears falling down her cheeks wetting thin lines that felt the cold more than the rest of her face. More hands. There was pressure at the small of her back and encircling her legs. She felt unsteady, like she might fall. Another touch righted her and stuck close.

They'd come.

They were all around her.

She tried to take a breath. She couldn't get a deep one and wheezed, trying harder. The cloud of exhalation that hovered in front of her mouth was smaller than before and took longer to dispel. The air was thick and felt impossible to draw in.

She staggered a step away from the table. The presence clutching at her skirt pulled and the one at her back held on and the others all around her slowed her movement. It felt like pushing through water. Clutching hands with insistent fingers pulled and pinched and held her.

"Not … all … at once," she gasped. It was too close, too intimate. There were too many. How many of their things were in the apartment with her? How many had she collected? Dolls and rings and necklaces and favorite books and crosses and a knife and the watch. And the glasses. She reached for Kat's glasses.

Don't be afraid, the familiar voice said in that same voice that had once told her. *It was the heat and the Ramos gin fizz. There's no such thing as ghosts.*

Her wedding ring tingled and felt heavy on her finger.

We're here for you.

A tug at her skirt again.

Here for you.

Her chest hurt.

Always together.

Like fingers squeezing her heart.

She opened her mouth, gasping. Everything was cold and quiet. Though it turned, her record was silent. The neighbor upstairs had stopped walking. The cars stopped honking. All she heard was the faint murmur of voices inside her apartment.

Stay with you.

Always.

Together.

June picked up the cradle with trembling hands and carried it around to the sofa, holding it close so nothing spilled out. She sat heavily, falling more than lowering herself carefully. The glasses rattled next to the bottle. She steadied everything inside with a hand, and balancing the cradle in her lap, looked at her treasures. There was just enough room for one more thing. She slipped off her wedding ring and dropped it in along with everything she'd collected from the dead. It made a small noise as it settled into its own space among everything else that she'd been able to fit inside. She closed her eyes and listened to her ghosts as the air got colder and thicker and harder to breathe. The pain in her chest spread up her neck and down her arm and she felt afraid.

What if she dropped the box and it spilled?

What if her ring fell out?

And she was left out.

What if none of this was really happening, because there's no such thing as ghosts?

She let out a shuddering breath and waited while the dark got darker and all the voices hushed until she couldn't hear anything at all anymore.

Some people just faded away and you never heard from them again. The kids called it ghosting.

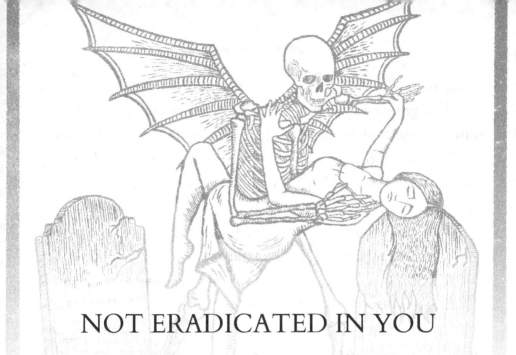

NOT ERADICATED IN YOU

Look how desperately you wanted to bond with "parents" who would not love you. That is not a defect; indeed, it can be a strength. It proves that the ability to love has not been eradicated in you.
　—Andrew Vachss

HARLOW

Harlow had handed him the money already—the most she'd ever saved, the most she'd ever spent at once on anything—but he held on to the paper bag, looking down at her with narrowed eyes. "You sure you know what you're getting into? I mean, anybody ever showed you what to do with something like this?"

She shook her head. "Huh uh. But I'm good at figuring shit out."

"Yeah, I bet." The guy smirked.

"Is there a problem?" The problem was the same as it was for everyone she dealt with: no one took her seriously because she was a kid. A *small* one at that—when other girls her age shot up past the boys, growing tall, filling out, she stayed short and slender. Her torn, oversized black sweater made her look even smaller. Some people thought that because she was petite, she was meek. Being underestimated allowed her to get away with things other girls couldn't.

She held out her hand. She wanted what the guy had promised to sell to her. What he'd told her he could get, "no problem." Finding a dealer had been easier than getting the money. Mostly she collected a little at a time, scrounging change here and there, sponging from friends. "Hey, can I borrow a dollar for the Coke machine?" Her friends knew she wasn't "borrowing," but it was easier to ask that way than to outright request a handout. She'd take their dollars and later, produce a can of soda she'd hidden in her backpack from the fridge at home so it looked like she'd done what she said she would with the money instead of pocketing it.

She kept everything she saved in a jar hidden in her bedroom closet behind a box of old stuffed animals where her mom never looked.

It felt like it took forever to set aside enough, but she was patient and resisted the urge to spend even a little of her stash on other things… no matter how hungry she got. Eventually, she had the price to be paid, and now she stood in front of this man, having given it *all* away, waiting for him to hand over what was hers. Waiting to see if he'd treat her like every other adult she knew, or if he'd respect her.

"I don't know. You fuck this up and there's no taking it back. There ain't no training wheels on this shit."

She didn't say anything, just held out her hand. He reluctantly passed the paper bag to her. It was smaller and lighter than she'd imagined. Harlow badly wanted to peek inside and reassure herself she hadn't just spent a personal fortune on this man's lunch. It seemed rude though. As if she didn't trust him. She didn't, of course, but she wanted to appear worldly, like she'd done this before—a hundred times, more often than she could count—and knew how something like this felt in her hand. Though they both knew this was her first time. Maybe it was a first for him too. Selling to someone as young as she. Probably not, though.

"Thank you," she said.

His jaw flexed as he gritted his teeth. They were done. It was time for them both to leave. He sighed and held up a finger, silently asking her to wait a moment. He went to his car and leaned in through the window. A moment later, he turned around with an envelope in hand. "I shouldn't do this," he said as he walked back, holding it out. "I shouldn't be selling *any* of this to you, but..." he trailed off. He told her that he wouldn't be doing this deal except for the name she'd dropped. Dierdre—her best friend's old after-school babysitter who sometimes bought them pints of Ruble vodka—said this guy owed her and gave Harlow his number. At first, he'd accused her of making a prank call. But then she said Dierdre's name and he listened. Whatever he owed the babysitter, it had to be something.

She reached out for the envelope and he yanked it back. "Look. I'm not fuckin' around about how serious this shit is. You gotta do it right, okay? I mean, for real. People get hurt."

"I get it." Her voice was as thin as she was.

He let her take it. "Everything you need to know is in that or the bag. *Pay attention.* You can practice without the works, okay? But once you start *using* what's in there," he pointed to the bag, "it's for real. No... backsies."

Frustration burbled up in the back of her throat. As much as she hated being spoken to like a child, she appreciated the warning. No matter how things turned out, she figured screwing it up still had to be better than not ever trying it. "Thanks," she said.

"Yeah," the man sighed as he walked away. He waved a hand as if her gratitude was something he knew he ought to deflect. He climbed into his car and started it up. The thing rumbled like a storm, and Harlow felt the engine's vibration throb in her chest. They were meeting under the Route 2 overpass because it was private, but then he showed up in a car so loud no one could miss it. She didn't get adults.

He stuck an elbow out the window and looked at her a last time before peeling out, kicking up gravel and dirt. The sound of his car lingered in the neighborhood for a long time as he sped off to wherever it was that guys like him went when they were done selling their stuff to kids. Harlow turned and stalked back to the bushes where she'd stashed her skateboard and backpack. She slung the pack over her shoulder, and dropped the board on the asphalt. She kicked off and rolled home.

Harlow pulled the house key out of her shirt collar and bent forward to unlock the door. The aluminum beaded chain she wore the key on was too short to reach the keyhole without taking it off, or leaning close. Stooping over was more difficult and embarrassing, but she was too nervous about dropping it to take the necklace off. She'd had a different key on a nicer chain that had once been her grandmother's; she'd removed it to unlock the door one afternoon and dropped it. The key fell perfectly, slipping between the boards of the front porch as though they weren't even there, and before she could drop and snatch at it, the chain slithered through the gap, into the dark. It was after dark before she got inside, got something to eat. And then her mother had been furious about having to get another one made. Still, the next day, her mother gave her a replacement. She recognized the potentially damaging appearance to the neighbors of her still tender-aged child sitting outside on the steps waiting to be let in. Harlow stole a new chain off of a rotating display on the counter at the record store downtown. She threw away the dog tag with the stupid peace sign on it and replaced it with her key. The chain wasn't as nice as her grandmother's necklace had been, but it felt sturdier and was longer. Long enough, she could bend down to unlock the door instead of having to take it off and risk losing it in the hungry porch flooring.

Once inside, she shut and locked the door behind her. If she didn't remember to unlock it later and her mother had to use *her* key to get in, she'd undoubtedly say, "What? Are you afraid someone's going to *steal* you?" Then, she'd laugh that bitter laugh at the too-familiar-by-repetition jape and lock the door after her as if it weren't the exact same gesture of self-assurance her daughter had made. It wasn't that Harlow was afraid of someone coming in to kidnap her, but she felt better behind the locked door. It was something in her life she could control. However small that was.

The house was dark. Though it was still early and bright outside Harlow didn't bother to open the heavy curtains. She took her skateboard to her bedroom and propped it next to the door inside, using her backpack as a brace to keep it from sliding down and clattering on the hardwood floor. Her stomach rumbled loudly and she thought about going to the kitchen to find something worth eating. She thought there might be some leftover Chinese in the fridge, though it was from last week and she wasn't sure if it was still good.

The thought of the paper bag still concealed in her backpack tugged at her like a hook in her skin. Though she was excited to see, she hadn't opened it. Not outside. She didn't want to be caught out with what it contained. What she *hoped* was there. Her "works" the man had called it. It might still be a rip-off—she could imagine the guy now, getting high with Dierdre and laughing about the stupid girl who gave him all her money for nothing. It made Harlow want to cry. The babysitter had been so convincing—she'd seemed so sympathetic, like she wanted to help. Told her to tell the guy Dierdre said she was cool. But, Harlow had no idea what something like that really meant. So here she was with an expensive lunch sack filled with probable nonsense and a deepening despair over her proven naïveté.

Sniffling and pushing down her disappointment, Harlow forced herself to confront her gullibility. She unfolded the top and peered in. Her heart quickened and she pulled out a small cardboard package of skinny black birthday candles. She dropped to her knees and spilled the rest of the contents on the floor in front of her. A stubby compressed charcoal stick fell out, the tip chipping on the floor shedding little pieces of black like brittle shadow. Two plastic film canisters tumbled after and rolled away, labeled with light brown masking tape—one read GYD and the other BLD. An incense cone and a small, rolled piece of paper followed last. She opened the paper and read it.

She hadn't been cheated. This was exactly what she'd asked for.

It didn't seem like much, and most of it had likely cost the guy less than five dollars to get, but then, you couldn't just go to the Rexall Drug and ask the pharmacist for *everything* he'd given her. The candles and incense and charcoal were easy to find, sure. But that last part. The little slip of paper. That wasn't something just anyone could just get. *That* was special. You had to *know*. That was worth the price.

Excited, she dug in her pocket for the envelope the man had given her. He'd seemed to go back for it as an afterthought, but opening it and unfolding the page within, she saw he'd prepared it for her carefully. She didn't know why he'd held it back, or exactly what she'd done to convince him to give it to her, but reading over it, she felt a shiver of anticipation streak up her back. Everything she needed to know was written out for her in clear detail. Step-by-step instructions. And the incantation.

She jumped to her feet and ran into the kitchen, snatching a bowl for the blood and earth in the black plastic film canisters and a long, sharp knife from the drawer. On her way back, she darted into the living room and grabbed her mom's lighter out of the drawer in the coffee table. She consulted the list again and found the last thing she needed in the hallway closet. A pair of scissors.

In her bedroom, she sat on the floor and began reading the page carefully. The dealer's voice in her head like an echo trapped in the walls of her room slowly escaping.

Pay attention. You fuck this up and there's no taking it back.

She read the words in a whisper, "Asmodel king of the East, Azazel king of the South, Paimon king of the West, and Mahazuel king of the North, send and bind your servant to me..."

Slow down. People get hurt.

She started over, careful to say each name as it was written on the page with the man's hints at pronunciation. *Az-mo-del. Ma-ha-zoo-ell.* She studied the symbol drawn at the bottom of the page and traced it on a piece of paper before attempting it on the floor. Using the round, removable lid to her laundry hamper, she traced a circle on the floor with the charcoal. Surely it was big enough. She began drawing the sigil on the page inside of it, careful to get all the lines and angles right, and placing the six black candles at the points.

"By your mistress, Lilith, I call you. I know your name."

She pried the lid off the first canister and poured the desecrated graveyard dirt into her bowl. Dark menstrual blood followed from the second—she couldn't use her own, she was a virgin—beading on top of the dry earth and turning muddy black. Fertile soil; infertile blood. She lit the cone of incense and set it in the lid of one of the canisters. "By the bowl and blade and blood and soil, answer me. I know your name."

Finally, she took a small lock of her hair in her fingers, and cut. She dropped it in the bowl and whispered, "Come to me and stand in my circle. I know your name; you are bound to it and to me."

Harlow picked up the kitchen knife with a trembling hand and held the tip over her wrist. It was going to hurt. But *everything* hurt. Why shouldn't her pain get her something that *she* wanted for a change.

She pressed the tip into her skin and watched the swell of blood rise up out of her and slip over the side of her arm into the bowl.

"I know your name. Come stand in my circle. I know your name, Ertzibat."

CAROL

Carol felt a tinge of exasperation at having to pause to fish her keys back out of her purse. The kid was home and there was no reason for her to lock the goddamn door. The porch light wasn't on and it was dark and the keys had somehow slipped down to the bottom of her bag, though she'd just dropped them in a second ago.

One annoyance piling atop another after a day full of them, like a cherry at the zenith of all her troubles. She dragged the keyring out of her purse and cycled through looking for her house key. Feeling more than a little buzzed from the after work drinks she'd had with Billie, she missed it the first pass around. Finally, she found the right one. Inside, she slammed the door behind her, making a point of entering the house noisily.

She stood in the gloom for a second, listening for her daughter, before flipping the light switch. Nothing. The kid wasn't home. Just perfect. That was worse than locking herself in. Where was she at this hour? Carol dreaded getting a call from a parent asking if it was okay if Harlow had stayed for dinner. *She and little Suzy-sweetheart were having the best time and we had stroganoff and Harlow says she loooves stroganoff. I just wanted to call to let you know I'm bringing her home as soon as they're through with dessert.* "Don't bother," Carol would be tempted to say. Except, it was a weeknight and she couldn't count on the unlikely mercy of a sleepover that'd make it easier to go out and have some fun—maybe bring someone home without having to sneak a guy past the kid up late watching something she shouldn't be on HBO. Not that Carol cared what Harlow watched, except when it came back on her at Parent Teacher Night. *Did you know that your daughter has seen the movie* The Entity? *We had to have a talk with her because she was describing it to the other girls, Ms. Sackett. It's inappropriate. We'd encourage you to take a greater interest in your daughter's viewing habits.*

And while we're at it, can we talk about her hair? And her clothes?

Carol hung her purse on the doorknob and plopped down on the sofa. She stared up at the blankness of the ceiling. She needed a bump to give her the energy to slip into character, and *then* she'd start phoning around to see where her daughter had landed. *Oh, I'm so sorry, Terri,* she'd say. *I hope she wasn't a bother. I got caught up at work and the time... well, you* know *how it is.* Of course they didn't know. PTA mommies who stayed home and drank chardonnay in the afternoon while she had to work—*had* to work because that asshole Stephen ran off. She glanced at her watch. "Jesus," she sighed. A quarter to ten. When did she get to ride off in a fancy red sports car and enjoy life? Hell, she was thirty-two and at her sexual peak and look at where she was. Cutting it off with Billie before either of them could really get a start on the evening so she could get back to her budding delinquent daughter—who wasn't even home!

She leaned forward and slid open the drawer in the coffee table, pulling out the glass vial and the plastic McSpoon next to it with the little arches at the end of the stem. *Fucking Stephen took the ivory one. Selfish prick.* She unscrewed the cap and dipped the spoon in, scooping out enough to take the edge off. Just a bump. She didn't get paid until Friday and this had to last.

A thump in the back of the house made her fumble the nearly weightless spoon as she inhaled. Carol replaced the bottle and spoon in the drawer and got up to take a look. Maybe Harlow hadn't gone to a friend's at all. She'd stayed home and, what? Gone to bed early? *Not* my *daughter.* It wasn't like her daughter to turn in before midnight, or to leave any room in the house dark for that matter. The girl was anxious about everything. Unlocked doors, the dark, silence, sleep itself. If Harlow was home, the place was ablaze with light and sound.

She stalked toward the bedrooms, feeling the numbness in her sinuses extend down into her throat, a touch of it tingling ever so slightly in her face. Billie always got her good stuff. Friday couldn't come soon enough.

She felt a breath of cold on her skin at her daughter's door, like standing in front of an open freezer. *The little shit left her windows open when she crawled out.* Carol decided she'd close and latch them. See if the little criminal remembered her key when she finally dragged her ass home. Carol reached for the knob and hesitated. She blinked, trying to clear her mind. Her head felt blurry and was getting blurrier. Standing in the hallway felt like a dream. Like she'd fallen asleep and woken up outside her daughter's bedroom. Something about the door. The darkness. Deeper here, like shutting herself inside a box. She turned and flicked the light switch. A dim illumination cut through the obscurity, but everything remained imprecise. She looked at Harlow's door and for a moment it seemed to blend into the wavering walls, like a shadow itself before resolving into a sort of solid clarity.

Carol rubbed her eyes. She'd overdone it. A little drunk and high as fuck. Not even ten and she was spent. Well, it'd *been* a day. She'd go shut and lock Harlow's window and go to bed. She reached forward and opened the door.

The darkness on the other side pooled and eddied in front of her like water. It drifted down and out of the room swirling around her feet, chilling her ankles. *Oh my god! Fire!* But the smoke was cold. So cold as it touched her. She took a step back. The darkness resisted her. It was thick and stepping back felt like walking in water. A small shriek escaped her lips and a booming noise invaded her mind like a sudden migraine. It pushed outward from inside her skull and she pressed her hands to the sides of her head trying to hold herself together against it.

SHHHHHHHHH.

Her scream died on her tongue and she struggled to take a breath. Tendrils of darkness reached out for her face. She batted at them with a hand and they broke and dissolved like smoke, but her hand came away a little blacker with each wisp she touched. She wiped her dirtied hand on her pants and the darkness smeared in a streak across the fabric. *Not smoke.* Where was the heat? Where was the crackling sound of it?

"Wha- what's happ—?"

SHHHHHHHHHH.

Carol dropped to her knees and the charcoal mist swirled around her legs, lapping up against her thighs and hips. Chilling her in intimate places she preferred to be warmed with breath and body. She shivered. It cascaded out of the room letting the light from the hall strengthen and enter slowly, touching the familiar shapes in the room tenderly, bringing them out of the shade. A dresser covered with girlish things—a music box, a stuffed mouse—the chair beside Harlow's desk with a leather jacket draped over the back, and the desk itself, lamp and cassette tape player atop it, books and albums on a shelf next to the record player. She saw the walls adorned with posters and clippings from magazines stretch away from her like she was backing out of a dark tunnel, until the posts of her child's bed emerged from the darkness, and beyond them Harlow lying on top of the covers, black boots, black tights, a white shirt and her bright crimson hair, face nestled up against... it. Another scream rose up from her lungs and threatened to emerge from her mouth, but died before it reached her lips and the black mist was reaching up from the floor and smothering her.

YOU'LL WAKE HER.

The pain of the voice in her mind made everything blur and dim before her vision resolved again and she saw the thing on Harlow's bed, her daughter on top of it, clutching it like a... like a...

"Mother?" the girl said, stirring. An onyx hand caressed the back of her head as she turned to face Carol. "That you?"

Carol struggled against the wisps. She brushed at her face and tried to push up from the floor. The mist held her down. Darkness reentered the room and shifted against the walls as the thing under her daughter extended its great wings, stretching them in the confining room. Harlow pushed up on its lap, and looked at her mother.

"G-get away… from it." Carol beckoned to her daughter.

The girl didn't move, except to turn and look into its face. "That's her," she said. "My mom."

The dark thing shifted and wrapped an arm around the girl. It whispered from a red mouth like a gash torn by a dull knife. "Your mother."

Carol's bowels felt tight. Her head ached and fear peaked in her, making her heart pound. If the thing spoke again, *in* her, the way it had shushed her, she thought she would die.

The dark thing sat up, heavy breasts and broad shoulders shifting as it righted. It cocked its head and a spill of writhing, inky hair obscured a shoulder. Its eyes were darker than anything Carol had ever seen. As black as not existing at all. The gash in its face opened again and it said, "Caroliiiiiiine." Her name oozed in the air like oil.

Harlow nodded. The thing pulled her back to its body. Harlow wrapped her arms around it. The girl turned her head and said, "You should get some sleep, Mom. You have work tomorrow." Her voice sounded like it came carried on the wind from a mile away. Everything was wrong in the way that dreams are. A gross distortion in a familiar setting, like being in her office but also out to sea. Her real daughter in the lap of a nightmare. Carol was too heavily embodied, too delicately conscious. Nothing was real, though everything felt it.

Another tendril of charcoal mist reached up and left a streak on the side of Carol's face. She felt the thing looking into her. Seeing through her to blood, bones, and organs—She felt it exploring her being, experiencing all the boundaries of her from the inside out.

And she despaired.

⛤

Carol awoke in bed, lying on top of her covers, still dressed in the clothes she wore the night before. She felt dizzy, her head throbbing. A queasy feeling in her stomach threatened revolt. Her daughter's record player blared shrilly from the far end of the hallway, making her head ache to a beat. *Identity! Identity!* She forced herself to sit up, and swing her legs over the end of the bed. After a moment to adjust, she stood, holding on to her nightstand for support while the room seemed to pulse before setting into fixed reality. Creeping to the door, she opened it a crack and peeked out expecting to see... what? The memory was hazy and all she could recall was that deep black haze.

And the woman-thing inside of it that *was* the darkness.

The bright morning and loud music assured her it was only a dream. A *nightmare*. Mercifully, in the way of dreams, mostly extinguished from her mind. By the time she finished her second cup of coffee, it would be all gone, except maybe the lingering unease.

Light shone from her daughter's open door, reflecting brightly off the polished hardwood floor. Carol squinted against its offense. She smelled breakfast. Eggs and toasting bread. Harlow was cooking. Her stomach alternately growled and lurched. She dragged a palm across her moist forehead and worked to keep her gorge down. She'd never had a nightmare like that. It had been so much more vivid than a normal dream. Someone must've spiked her drink at the bar. *Bad trip*. That was it. That guy with his friend—the one flirting with Bobbie—he'd dropped something in her glass and she peaked when she got home. Probably intensified it with the bump. She wanted to laugh, but felt like she might vomit if she took anything but short, measured breaths. *Stick to blow, Carol. It's safer.*

She stank of cigarettes and sweat. She shed yesterday's work clothes and wrapped up in her bathrobe. First, a shower and then a cup of coffee. If her stomach would take it, maybe she'd try to eat some of the toast Harlow was making too.

Carol stepped out into the hall holding her hands against her ears to deaden the song playing on Harlow's record player. It was familiar and despised. Too much for a rough morning. She fought against her disorientation and ducked into the child's room, slipping in the candle wax melted in a mess on the floor, kicking something solid and glass sounding across the room. It stank. *What the fuck was that? God* she wanted something to take the edge off. Get her to baseline. She staggered across the room and lifted the needle from the groove.

"Hey! I was listening to that," Harlow yelled from the kitchen.

Carol didn't care. She didn't like punk music without a hangover, and she *really* hated it with one. She stomped toward the kitchen, her reprimand about how rude it was to play obnoxious music before everyone in the house was awake already half out of her mouth. The thought went unexpressed when she saw the strange woman standing at the stove, cracking an egg into a skillet. It wouldn't do to yell at Harlow in front of another parent. *Oh Jesus. How long has this woman been in my house?* She blushed deep red at the thought that another mother had brought Harlow home and decided to linger until Carol returned. And then she, what? Stayed the night until Carol sobered up? Was making breakfast for her child. Who was this woman inserting herself into their lives as if she had the right to judge, let alone *interfere*? Carol held down her rage and said, "I'm sorry, but who—"

The woman turned. Carol lost her breath. The woman stood assured and steady, spatula in hand and wearing a cooking apron like some TV reflection of the woman Carol had never been. Never wanted to be. Hair, height, figure, face, even the clothes she wore. Everything about her was the same... but better. All except her eyes. They absorbed light. They stole her breath. Those unseeing, flat black eyes drove Carol back. Being seen by them felt like being captured, stolen from herself. The woman had to be blind, but Carol was beheld.

Harlow stood from the table and skipped over to the woman. "I'm going to be late for school. No time! Sorry."

It said, "That's okay, honey. Take this." The creature that was not Carol handed her daughter a paper sack, the bottom bulging with the weight of a can of Coke or an apple. The girl got up on her tip toes and the too-familiar thing bent down and they kissed. A chaste motherly kiss that smacked loudly and echoed against the Formica countertops and tile floors.

The girl turned to look at Carol. Her wide eyes narrowed. Carol wanted to shout that Harlow didn't get to judge her. That she wasn't the one who paid the rent and put food on the table and who gave birth to her. Her work, her money, her body. She didn't say a thing. Her legs felt weak and bile burned the back of her tongue.

The girl snatched up her skateboard from against the wall and skipped out of the room calling back over her shoulder, "Love you!"

Before Carol could process the sound of her daughter saying those two words, so rarely spoken or heard, the thing at the stove said, "I love you too! Don't be late."

"I won't."

The door slammed and the world darkened. The black char mist of Carol's nightmares cascaded off the thing like waterfalls, filling the room, eating light. Stretching out from her back like great black wings. It turned. An abomination in a silk wrap top blouse tied at the waist and a tan skirt. It still wore her face. But its mouth was redder. Lips crueler.

"W-what are you?" Carol managed.

It tilted its head and looked at her with its shark's eyes.

It spoke.

"I'm what she wants." The voice that had a moment earlier held a sing-song lightness, deepened to an unutterable depth that made Carol's bowels slack.

Carol bolted from the kitchen. She snatched her purse off the front door knob, whipped the door open, and flung herself out into the bright morning daylight. She flailed and stumbled as she expected to run through the open door, down the front steps and into the soft grass outside. Instead, she plunged into the growing shadow of the thing filling the kitchen. Her panicked mind tried to comprehend where she was. She dropped to her hip to avoid running into the thing's swirling darkness, kicking and trying to backpedal away.

It smiled.

Carol's bladder emptied.

"Why?" she sobbed.

"Because she loves you."

Deep in its words, Carol heard something she knew was as true as morning and appetite and fear. Her daughter had summoned this thing to what? Love her? To steal the love Carol deserved, that *she* earned. And be loved in return?

"She's *my* daughter. You don't get to love her!"

"I do love her." The thing in the swirling darkness seemed to take a moment, look up at the ceiling as if searching its damned mind for what to say. It looked back at Carol and a chill penetrated her. It gestured to its face, her clothes. Its smile was cruel and mean and red. "Though I don't love you." It reached for her.

And she fell into darkness, lost and thoughtless, loveless and alone.

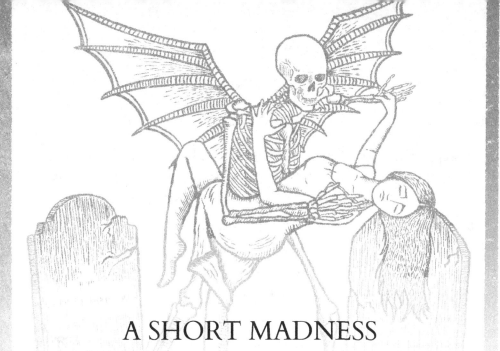

A SHORT MADNESS

"*It is difficult to fight against anger; for a man will buy revenge with his soul.*"
 —Heraclitus

"*Anger is a short madness.*"
 —Horace

"*Anger is a gift.*"
 —Zac de la Rocha

PROLOGUE

say, "This is my confession. I repent and ask for absolution."

✧

PART I: RECONCILIATION

WEDNESDAY

I stepped into the small, stuffy room and closed the door behind me. I tugged at my collar, trying to loosen it a little. It was likely no one would be seeing me for the next two hours, but I couldn't take it off. I walked around the screen and took my seat, flipping the switch on the wall that lit the green light outside the door, letting my parishioners know I was ready to receive their confessions. Ready. Though it was time, I never felt *ready*.

Other priests I knew felt enlivened by reconciliation. One told me that he saw it as evidence people were trying; they were seeking the grace of God and hadn't given up on their faith. Another said it gave him humility. Listening to people own up to their feelings of spiritual inadequacy reminded him of the work he needed to do to resist his own sinful nature. But what was a gift for others felt like a burden to me. No feelings of grace or humility kindled in my heart when I heard people lay themselves bare. Instead, those admissions felt like a burden. Just walking into the confessional reminded me of Giles Corey asking for more weight. Eventually, he knew the stones would crush him, but his conscience gave him no choice but to bear them. And the weight of these confessions grew heavier and heavier still, until I felt pressed nearly to death.

Someone entered the room. I waited to see if they'd walk around the screen to sit in the chair opposite mine, making their contrition face to face. When I heard the creak of the kneeling rail, I leaned back and settled in to listen blindly instead. Few people ever chose the chair over the rail. Anonymity was merely a mutually agreed upon illusion, though. I recognized all my regular parishioners' voices. I recognized them by their transgressions and anxieties *outside* of the Confessional as well.

I was jealous of my wife's accomplishments at work. I diminished them in front of her to make me feel better.

I had impure thoughts; I imagined making love to my neighbor while I masturbated.

I went a month without visiting my mother in the rest home. When I finally went, I resented her for being there.

I despair of God's mercy. I doubt that He will ever forgive me.

I took a breath and began the ritual. "May the mercy of God touch your heart, so you may know your sins and have the courage to confess them."

Margaret Fleming, kneeling on the other side of the screen said, "Bless me, Father, for I have sinned. My last confession was about three months ago. Last week, somebody was walking in the street and it was slowing down traffic a bunch. I was so mad, I yelled out my window at him." She hastily added, "I'm sorry for this sin and all the sins of my past life. I repent and ask for absolution."

I knew there was something else she wasn't telling me. Something that made *this* the sin she wanted absolution for. But, I gave her the benefit of the doubt and didn't press. "We all get angry sometimes. It's natural."

"I ... I called him the enword, Father Price. The effword enword."

A lawyer friend of mine (not a Catholic) confided in me once over a glass of whiskey that he only ever got to see people at their worst. Even when they were doing something constructive like buying a house or starting a new business, they still behaved badly because of the stress involved. He'd said that it had to be refreshing getting to see people who were trying to get into Heaven. There *was* a sort of truth there. I saw them laugh and dance at weddings, and weep and comfort each other at funerals. But then, at confession, I heard them at their worst. Their very worst. They admitted to being full of anger toward their friends and resentful of their parents. Breaking vows of marriage and professional honesty. They told me about stealing and fighting and fucking their neighbors' husbands. About abusing their children. It frightened me that they sometimes said the things they did with such calmness in their voices. And then they asked me for forgiveness, knowing that in most cases I couldn't refuse to give it. They accepted that *God's* forgiveness was unlimited, but it was me they wanted to hear it from, since I was God's instrument. That was my other conscious illusion. I granted them God's absolution, though I hadn't believed in any god for a very long time. They walked out of this room feeling reconciled with their creator, as though their souls were clean, but I knew nothing had really changed. They were still the same lying, cheating people they were when they walked in with heavy consciences. And I'd see them again, because if there was one thing I absolutely still believed from Catholic doctrine, it was that we all fall short of perfection.

I was glad that Margaret had chosen the rail instead of the seat after all. In years of sitting in a confessional, I'd heard all manner of sins, venial and mortal, and I was rarely surprised, but I hadn't expected this from *her*. I'd thought better of Margaret; she'd seemed truly nice. She *was* nice, and very often even kind as well. She made cookies and brownies for parish bake sales and donated hand-me-downs to the winter coat drive. She put money in the collection box and she said her prayers. But deep in the core of her, there was something cruel and bigoted. Her mother, Gloria, still complained about "forced bussing" in the Nineteen Seventies—that is, school desegregation. There seemed to be a piece of her in Margaret. If there was any glimmer of hope, at least she recognized that she'd done something wrong.

I said, "If you're ever looking for examples of wrath, look at traffic. We are so easily vicious behind the wheel. Did you try to make amends?"

"No. Of course not. I don't know who he is. He was just some… guy walking in the street." Her voice gained a hard edge. "I drove off. I had to pick up my kids. I'm not even sure he heard—"

"Have you made amends some other way?"

"What? I've prayed for forgiveness. I said the act of contrition and made my confession, Father. What else?"

I took a breath. I wanted to recommend that she volunteer somewhere she could serve people who might have once been hurt by the kind of word she'd said. Something to help her to get a perspective outside of her insular, white suburban community. But then, I knew how my congregation talked about me. The *liberal* priest from the city—a bleeding heart.

"I want you to read a book."

"A book?"

"Yes. I want you to read *Kindred* by Octavia Butler. It's a good one, trust me."

"How is that going to—"

"Every time you see … *that word* in the novel—nigger—I want you to say an Our Father." She gasped as if she hadn't just confessed to saying it herself. Though I hated the word, I said it so she couldn't have the bloodless confession she wanted. She had to face what she said, instead of some sterilized euphemism—the "enword." I continued. "And if you ever repeat it again in anger—or *at all*, for that matter—I want you to re-read the book—the whole thing—and do the same. You can find it at the library if you don't want to buy it, but I encourage you to get your own copy." I didn't say because I knew if she did what I said, she'd be reading the book more than a couple of times. I didn't know if she liked science fiction, but I made a guess that the book would be more personally meaningful to her than *Invisible Man* or *The Fire Next Time*. I *hoped* it would be anyway. That was more important than the prayer. "That is your penance," I said.

"But ... " she hesitated. Perhaps she caught the hard edge in my tone. For my first penitent of the day, she'd hit a nerve. "Yes, Father," she said. At that moment, I doubted she'd read the book. But I hoped she would.

"Now say the Act of Contrition." I listened as she did and then said, "Through the ministry of the Church, may God grant you pardon and peace. And ... I absolve you of your sins, in the name of the Father, and of the Son, and of the Holy Spirit. Amen."

Through the screen, I could see her crossing herself before she got up to leave. She didn't say anything else. I wondered if she'd be all smiles the next time I saw her after Mass. I took a drink of water from the glass on the table next to me and waited for the next penitent to come in.

The door opened again and another parishioner knelt at the screen. "Forgive me, Father ... "

Ugh. Anothony Tremblay. It was going to be a long two hours.

✵

I turned off the green light and drained the last trickle of water in my glass. Though I'd taken a break an hour earlier to go to the bathroom, I'd "broken the seal" as my lawyer friend put it and had to go again. I walked around the screen divider and left the confessional, almost running into a boy standing right outside the door. I recognized him, though he wasn't a regular church goer. *What's his name?* I thought. *Adam, Andrew, Alex... Aidan! His name is Aiden. Aidan Flynn.* He looked scared at first, and then guilty. He turned quickly and started to walk away.

"Hey Aiden. Can I help you?" I tried to sound welcoming and nonchalant.

The kid froze. His ears flushed red and his shoulders hunched up, like he'd been caught out doing something he shouldn't.

"Uh, no. Huh uh." He took a hesitant step away. I thought if he managed to take another, he'd build up enough momentum to break the spell of whatever had compelled him to come this far in the first place. I'd seen kids who wanted to come to confession but had trouble working up the will. No one wanted to admit to their sin. Least of all young teenagers like him, already struggling with doubts about personal worth that teachings about Original Sin planted like bitter seeds in fertile soil. I remembered being a boy, and how hot shame burned—how hard it was to work up the nerve to verbalize my slights, while imagining the most vivid torments of Hell. I could almost imagine this kid waiting in the pews, trying not to be seen until everyone else had gone and it was his turn to walk through the door, all the while, screwing up his courage to stand exposed before the judgment of Almighty God. And then, the time had passed. If he was like I'd been, he'd spend the next week agonizing over his unreconciled sin, afraid of being hit by a bus or some other freak accident that would send him directly to divine judgment. If he wasn't like me, maybe it wasn't that bad. But then, he was the *only* teenager who'd shown up that day.

"Aw, shit," I said, knowing the unexpected profanity would grab the boy's attention. I patted my pockets. "I think I left my iPhone in there. Sorry, I gotta go find it. Bishop'll hang my skin on the wall if they have to buy me another. See you later." Despite the urgings of my bladder, I reentered the confessional. The door clicked shut behind me and I walked around the barrier and turned on the green light. After a moment, I heard the click of the door latch. It clacked shut again and though I hadn't heard any footsteps, the kneeler creaked slightly under the boy's weight. I flipped the switch that turned the light outside from green to red and said, "May the mercy of God touch your heart, so you may know your sins and have the courage to confess them."

Aidan stammered. "Uh, bless me father, for I have sinned. I guess, it's been, like ... I don't know how long since my last confession. I don't really do it much, you know."

"It's okay. You're here now," I said, and settled back to listen. Though confession weighed heavily on them, I found young people's sins slight and their remorse out of proportion to the seriousness of the offenses they admitted to. If there was any joy I took in reconciliation, it was telling a child they had nothing to worry about—that their souls were not tainted.

I waited to hear Aidan tell me that he'd backtalked his mother or shoplifted something. I did my best to project a sense of calm forgiving through the screen. "What do you want to tell me?"

"I have kind of a question first."

"Okay. I'm listening."

"Father Price, is it a sin to, like, keep a secret? Like a *big* secret?"

"It depends, I suppose. If someone trusted you with something very personal, and repeating it would hurt them or your friendship, then I don't think so. That's what I do here. People tell me things in confidence, and I respect their privacy and their trust in me. If I didn't, no one would ever come back, and I would have failed at a very important part of my job."

"Yeah, but what if you're *not* a priest?"

"It's ... complicated." I paused for a moment to collect my thoughts. "If someone was planning on hurting themselves, for instance, it might be a good thing to tell someone else who could help, if that person wasn't willing to seek it out on their own. If you know a person who needs help—someone who might hurt themselves or someone else—it's not a bad thing to try to prevent that from happening."

The boy took a deep breath. I waited. After a moment, Aidan said, "What if someone already got hurt, like really bad, and the secret is about who did it?"

"Well ... that's different, isn't it?" My stomach knotted at the mention of secrets. I had once delighted in being the man my father couldn't be: a man people came to for comfort and spiritual nurturing. But my faith had *always* been delicate, like armor made of glass. I stepped into it, and though I could see right through it, I pretended it was thick enough, hard enough to hold me and keep me safe. And while cracks appeared throughout the years, it held. Right until The Boston Globe Spotlight reports shattered it, leaving me dressed in shards. I said, "If someone has asked you to keep a secret about something they've done that's illegal, that's not right, and it's not fair to you. I know it's difficult. But you can tell me, and together we can discuss what the right thing to do is."

"The Bible says to honor your parents, right?" He was taking the long way around to admitting what he'd done. I remained patient. We'd get there; I had to let him find the way.

"It does," I said. "That commandment *is* about obedience, but ... it excludes immoral actions. It's a direction to be a good member of society and a good Christian; you don't have to be obedient to a parent or any other authority who is asking you to do something wrong. Does that make sense?"

"I don't know. Maybe."

I heard Aiden shift on the rail. It sounded like he might be getting up to leave. I wanted to spring up out of my seat and grab him, say he couldn't go until he confessed what had been done to him, and by whom. I wanted to know so *I* could do the right thing. So, I didn't have to look in the child's face on Sunday and wonder if he was going to be all right, or if he was still in danger.

The boy blurted out, "I think my dad killed someone."

I stifled a cough. It wasn't what I'd thought—what I'd feared because it was what I'd been through. It was something else. I tried to relax, but my memories and my bladder had me perched on the edge of my chair. "I doubt it's as bad as that," I said.

The boy knelt quietly for another painfully long moment before saying, "You remember that lady and her kid on the news? The ones that got hit by the guy who didn't stop?"

I felt the bottom fall out of the room. Yes, I remembered them. I'd known Justine Neville.

I said, "They arrested someone for that. They caught the man who hit them." He had been an auto mechanic on the other side of town. Had a family—wife and three kids. People said he ran a good shop and didn't charge too much. But the talk about him changed once he was arrested. It got worse when they revealed he wasn't the man they knew. He'd said he'd moved to Ripton from New York, but in reality, he was someone else from someplace else entirely, living under an assumed name. Paolo something. Paolo was sticking in my head. Not that it mattered.

"It wasn't that guy. It was my dad."

"How do you know?"

"I saw him washing his truck with the hose. He never washes his own truck. He always takes it to the car wash. And he was like *really* washing the front, but not the back so much. Like there was something on the whatdoyoucallit?"

"The grille," I whispered.

"Yeah, the grille. And the bumper. Then, when he saw it on the news, he freaked the fuck out … sorry, Father. He, like, *really* freaked out, you know? He went out and washed his truck again. Then, they arrested some other guy with the same kind of truck. I saw it on the news, and it looks just like my dad's."

I remembered it wasn't long after the revelation about his immigration status that Paolo somehow "found" a loose piece of metal in his cell and sharpened it enough to slit his own throat. How hard it would be to cut your own throat? People slit their wrists all the time. But that didn't come with the uncontrollable panic of not being able to breathe. Blood was frightening. But if you got cut, you just slapped a bandage on it or went to the E.R. for stitches. A *throat*. How terrified would an innocent man have to be to do *that?* Of course, people would say he wasn't actually innocent. He was here illegally—he'd broken the law. But that wasn't running a mother and her child down in the street. And Aidan was saying he was innocent of *that*.

"I guess that means my dad killed *him* too, right?" the boy said, like he'd read my mind.

Finding the right thing to say was beyond me at that moment. I couldn't breathe.

Aidan started to cry.

I heard a sound in the room like someone else coming in with us. No one did of course; the red light was on. I tried to focus and tell Aidan it would be okay. But I didn't believe it. Nothing was okay.

✶

PART II: REVELATION

SUNDAY

I waited at the bottom of the steps greeting the people who'd come to Mass as they filed out of church. Some paused to shake my hand and make small talk. A couple mentioned how much they enjoyed my homily, though I knew not all of them really meant it—it was just a thing they said. There were always some who didn't like it when I touched on social issues; they'd rather hear about how wonderful the next life was going to be, than how they had to work harder to make this one livable. They were usually the ones who avoided me after the service. That morning, I'd been preaching to one person in particular. Though I knew that hint-dropping wasn't going to make Rory Flynn jump out of his seat and run to confess what Aidan had said he'd done, still, I wanted to see even a hint of something in his face. Whether it was remorse or guilt, didn't matter so long as I could see him wrestling with what he'd done. But the elder Flynn's glib expression didn't change at all throughout my sermon. Not even when I read Proverbs 28:13 aloud. I'd practically shouted it like some Baptist revival tent preacher. "He who conceals his transgressions will not prosper, but he who confesses and forsakes them will obtain mercy." He didn't react at all. Not even to nod like the other fakers. People who came to Mass to satisfy their spouses or grandparents often pretended to listen while they thought of sports or errands that church was keeping them from. Like them, Flynn had that practiced look that seemed attentive while his mind was somewhere else, far away. Most of the time, that look didn't bother me; I understood. I wanted to see Flynn sweat. But the man hadn't felt even a little heat.

Maybe he'd been unmoved because he hadn't done anything. I reminded myself that I didn't have actual *proof*—only the suspicions of an imaginative boy who'd seen his father washing his truck. But I *believed* Aidan. Unlike me, he feared Hell; he believed that bearing false witness against his father could send him there. Aidan had no reason to lie, and every reason in Creation to tell the truth. He was worried for his soul. And that made Rory's inscrutability more frustrating. His son was right there, filled with anguish, and he didn't feel a damn thing.

That made me want to climb down out of the ambo, grab his lapels, and shake him. That made me angry. Another parishioner took my hand and quizzed me about the upcoming yard sale. Her children, two boys, bickered with each other, shouting and tugging at her in an attempt to get her to intervene in their disagreement. She ignored them while she suggested much more deserving charities than the ones earmarked for the proceeds of the sale. "You know, people would bring better items to sell if they thought that the money was going somewhere they can *see* it doing good." I tried to listen to what she had to say but was losing patience. One of the kids shoved his brother and she grabbed his little arm and jerked it. The boy yelped and had to take a quick step to stay on his feet.

At that moment, Flynn came walking out of the doors, his wife and son trailing behind like an afterthought. He walked over to Rich Matthews and the two of them began laughing about something I couldn't hear. Only his obnoxious laughter carried. The swell of anger that had grown in me during the service came crashing down again.

"Are you listening to me? Father Price?"

I snapped back to the woman in front of me. She paled and took a step back. I wondered what my face looked like at that moment. I tried to soften my expression but wasn't sure I succeeded. My mind was clouded, though I remembered her last confession very well.

Sometimes I think about sending my kids to live with my ex. It's not that I want them to live with him—he's a terrible father—but I want them to push his new wife like they push me. I want her to feel as tired as I am.

"Yes, Margaret. I hear you," I wanted to placate her, if only to shut her up, but had no interest in hearing who she'd rather donate the money raised at the yard sale to. I told her, "We've already let the recipient organization know we'll be making a donation ahead of time. If you don't like them, perhaps you can take your boys to the park instead. I'm sure they'd love to have an afternoon with their mother's *full* attention." I looked at the children and added, "Wouldn't you? Perhaps a playdate with some friends from school. Wouldn't that be nice?" They immediately began barking names of kids that they'd like to play with at their mother, turning the idea of an intimate day in the park into a party. I ushered her away, giving the children the big smile I withheld from her. She walked off looking more than a little upset with me for putting the idea in her boy's minds.

I stared at Flynn and Matthews as they laughed loudly again. I wanted to go tell them to shut up. What I really wanted to say, was "Shut the *fuck* up." I wanted to shout in Rory's face about taking responsibility for the lives he'd ruined. But I couldn't.

I looked at Aidan staring quietly at his cell phone, waiting while his father socialized. He looked pale and shaken. While my sermon had no effect on the elder Flynn, it appeared to have badly discomfited his son. I took a step to go reassure the boy, but hesitated, unsure of what to say. I'd walked right up to the line of betraying the sanctity of the confessional by directing my sermon at his father. More importantly, I felt like I'd betrayed the boy's trust in me. What was there to say to fix that?

Out of the corner of my eye I caught a glimpse of a last, straggling churchgoer who appeared from the shadows of the doorway at the top of the steps. I turned, relieved to have another hand to shake instead of having to make amends with Aidan. Shame burned at the back of my throat. I told myself I could talk to him in a minute. Greet this person first. Use the time to think of something to say.

The woman stumbled, taking the steps too fast and off balance. Her ankle rolled and she tumbled down. I lurched forward to catch her but was too late and she sprawled flat on the path in front of me. Her black hair was a mess and hid her face, though she was unmistakable. Except, it couldn't be her. I knelt and reached out to help. With her open wounds and jutting bones, I couldn't find a single place where my hands wouldn't cause her pain. The blood on her skin was wet and bright in the sun. And there was more than there should have been after a fall down the steps—even one as bad as she'd taken. Much more.

I heard a loud laugh behind me, and I turned ready to bellow at whoever thought this woman's suffering was funny. But no one was looking at us. Rory and Michael were still joking, and their wives were chatting with each other and Margaret was gesturing with a thumb over her shoulder at me while talking to someone else, but not a single one of them seemed to have noticed what happened.

I turned back to the woman. She pushed up from the ground. Her arms trembled and one of her wrists shifted under her weight, distorting at an angle no joint could make. I grabbed her arm and helped her to her feet. She slumped against me, heavy. I wrapped an arm around her waist and held her close. Her head lolled back and she opened her mouth. Instead of speaking, blood cascaded from her lips, spilling down her chest onto her uniform and plastic nametag.

Her tongue probed at the gaps where her broken teeth had been. My stomach tightened and I clapped a hand to my mouth. She smiled with her split lips and caressed my cheek with a blood slick hand. It smelled like iron and the sweet perfume she always wore.

She whispered to me. "Conccceals his trans-gressionssssss."

I struggled to hold on to her, pull her closer, but she slipped out of my arms like smoke, and I let out a small cry of despair as I imagined her falling again. Falling under a truck as it mowed her and her child down.

She was gone.

Never there.

My chasuble and stole were stained dark with her blood. I touched my cheek where she'd caressed me and my fingers came away wet and red.

Aidan came over and said, "Are you okay, Father? Did you trip?"

I looked again at my clothes and hands and felt like I might be going mad. "She ... I was ... " He looked at me with concern, but not horror. Covered in blood as I was, it should've been *horror*. I cleared my throat and took a deep breath. "I'm fine, Aidan." I reached out and placed a hand on his shoulder, meaning to say something else, but the dark stain I left on his dress shirt stole my speech. He didn't seem to notice. "Everything's fine," I choked out.

His father stepped up and grabbed Aidan's shoulder, covering the bloody mark I'd left there. "It's time to go," he said. "Your mom wants to go get brunch. You hungry?" The elder Flynn looked at me and added, "Nice sermon; real inspiring," before pulling the boy away to go. Aidan stared over his shoulder as they walked toward the parking lot. I raised a hand to wave, knowing that I looked ... like I'd been hit by a car.

FRIDAY

I ran my toothbrush under the tap and set it on the counter next to my razor and comb. I rinsed and spat and lingered in the bathroom, not looking in the mirror, but straight down into the sink basin where there was no reflection to remind me what I looked like.

I flossed and stepped over to the toilet. I pissed, zipped up, and sighed at the knowledge that there was nothing left to do in the bathroom. Not unless I wanted to take *another* shower. I'd spent the week trying to wash her blood off. I showered and showered, and the red stains lingered. I could only get so clean and no more. Though it seemed like only I could see the blood.

I turned off the light and walked out of the bathroom.

My bedroom in the rectory was simple and didn't have space for deep shadows. The lamp next to my bed was bright enough to read by and cast what I'd once thought of as a warm glow. Now, it seemed like it invited shadows. Like the bathroom mirror, I avoided looking into the dark corner at the far end of the room. Where she stood. I blinked, trying to banish her. But she persisted. The darkness came with her, a spreading degradation that grew deeper and blacker. She wasn't a dream I could wake from.

Justine Neville had worked at the drug store over on School Street. She'd always been kind to me when I went in to shop. She flirted with me. While I didn't wear my collar out, she confessed that one of her co-workers had let her know I was a priest. She joked that I was going to either save or damn her soul—she just couldn't tell which one yet. "Would you like to give me your e-mail address, Father Price?" she'd asked me once, winking as she said, "Father."

"Please, call me David," I replied. "And it's already in the system."

"It is, but *I* don't have it."

I blushed and said, "You don't want to go on a date with a thirty-nine-year-old virgin."

She'd said, half under her breath, "You let me know if you decide you don't want to be a forty-year-old virgin." I skipped a step and stumbled toward the doors. Looking back, she was smiling. I kept walking, though I should've stopped. I should've turned around and gone back and given her my cell number. I should have done a lot of things. Instead, I left.

Off and on, I found reasons to go back. Buying necessities that weren't necessities, and picking up things for the rectory that were already stored away in cupboards and closets. I looked forward to seeing her and would wait in a longer line to be rung up at her register, waving other people ahead of me if another checker called out for the next shopper. She always made it a point to touch my hand when she passed me my shopping bag. It was a slight gesture, but it made me tremble inside. I shook a lot of hands, but no one ever touched me like *that*. As if I were a man first, and not a priest. And underneath the teasing and the flirting, there was something really there, maybe. Something that could've gone further, if I'd ever gotten up the courage to leave my job—and that's how I'd looked at it for years, not a calling, or a vocation, but a job. I didn't leave my job. I didn't call Justine for a date. I didn't do any of the things I dreamed about.

I hadn't known she was a single mother until I read about the incident in the paper. That's what they called it. An *incident* involving a truck and two pedestrians. Not an accident. She had been walking home from picking up her son at daycare when someone ran them both down. The media had described it as "road rage gone wrong," as though that ever went right. Witnesses said they'd seen a pair of men shouting at each other at a red light. When the signal turned green, one of them tore up the street and around the corner, hitting two people in the crosswalk before speeding off. The other driver had gone in the opposite direction. Other motorists stopped to help, but no one had gotten the plate—all anyone knew was that it was a red truck. The kind with a silver ram on the back gate. The driver never even slowed down after hitting them.

Justine's two-year-old son, Kerry, got to ride in a helicopter, though he never knew it. He lingered for a day in the hospital before dying.

After that, I never saw her at the store again.

Since Aidan's confession, the darkness had split open, and Justine stepped through. She lurked in the periphery of my vision like the aftereffects of a camera flash. I tried to ignore her in the pews during service, across the street when I went running … standing in the corner of my bedroom. Everywhere else, I could pretend that she was someone else. Not the image of a woman broken under a truck, but just another person out for a run, coming in to hear the word. But in my room, she was as exposed as I was. She was Justine. The woman I'd fantasized going on a date with. The person who flirted and made me feel like a desirable man. The woman who never needed a thing from me—not a prayer or a good word to a bishop. All she wanted from me was a moment of fun banter while she worked a dull job—a smile and a kind word. Now she wanted something else. What that was she couldn't say. Or wouldn't.

I tried to ignore her, pretend nothing was different. I draped my robe over the back of a chair and pulled back my bloodstained bed sheets. I climbed in, pulled them over me and turned out the light. But I could feel her looking at me. I took a deep breath. The air was stale and tasted like copper.

"Why me?" I asked the darkness.

She was silent. I knew exactly why.

"What do you want me to do?" I asked.

She slipped into bed next to me. Her arm across my chest was cold. It was what I wanted. I tried to hold her hand, but I couldn't find a way to grasp it.

"Kill him," she whispered.

PART III: WRATH

SATURDAY

Rory Flynn parked in the lot behind Hautala's Lounge. He climbed out of his red truck and headed for the entrance. He held the door open for a woman who came stumbling out. She said something to him I couldn't hear from inside my car. He laughed. It was the same obnoxious laugh he let out on the front steps of St. Francis, loud and broadly gestural. The kind of laugh you couldn't ignore or speak over. He ran his free hand through his hair. I could see his artificially white teeth gleam in the light above the door from a half block away as he smiled at her. She touched her own hair, mirroring his gesture before brushing past him. She passed into shadow and all I could make out was a dark shape in the distance, but I could tell she looked back at him. And he lingered, watching her. When her shade fully disappeared into the night, he went inside. I wondered how hard it had been to make the choice between craft bourbon and her. I wondered if he knew her. Their exchange seemed to be a continuation of something larger. I didn't know if he was having an affair—he didn't come to confession—but it wouldn't surprise me if he was. The kind of man who could run down a mother and child in the street wouldn't have any compunction about fucking around on his wife. But then, his buddies were waiting inside. He was faithful to *them* at least.

I waited a couple of minutes. When I was sure he'd found himself a seat and a glass, I got out of my car and tried to look inconspicuous. There was no way to stay in the shadows in the lot, though. Flynn had parked under a light, and his truck stood out like a big red beacon, like a warning—come no closer; there's danger here. I was beyond caring how exposed I'd be. Fuck Rory Flynn and fuck his big red pickup. I didn't put stock in Freudian interpretations of vehicle sizes, but it was hard to argue that Flynn wasn't compensating for something. I'd have said, self-doubt and character deficiency, but that assumed he recognized his own flaws. I hadn't seen any evidence that he did.

The behemoth was bright and clean. It wasn't a work truck. There wasn't a speck of dirt on it, and no chrome toolbox behind the cab suggested that the thing served any purpose other than plumage and intimidation. There was a step on the side for the driver to climb in. A step, because it was too big to just get inside. I had to fold myself into a contortion every time I got into my Kia Rio, and if I turned to look for traffic at a light, I hit my head on the door frame half the time. But he needed a God-damned step.

I leaned over to look at the grille. I didn't know what I was looking for, and knew I wouldn't find anything anyway. Still, I wanted to see it up close. There was no damage to the thing that I could see. Flynn's truck had a big, black grille guard on the front—thick steel bars like the business end of a battering ram. It was the sort of thing that made me nervous when I saw one in my rear-view mirror. I shuddered to imagine what something like that would do to a body. I doubted it was much different than what the front of a pickup truck like this would do without it, but it still seemed almost monstrous. I touched it. Nothing special happened. I don't know what I expected. There was no revelatory vision that showed me the truth of Rory's guilt or innocence. No flash of pain communicating what Justine might've felt as the truck barreled into her body. I got nothing from it but cold. Leaning closer, I squinted and tried to see inside the black honeycomb grille, hoping to catch a glimpse of a scrap of fabric from a Rexall Drug apron or a piece of fluff from a favorite stuffed animal. There was nothing there but plastic and steel. The truck kept Rory's secrets. There was no "evidence" to be found. That had been washed away long ago. So, what was I doing there?

I was doing what I told people to do every day: I was searching for answers that couldn't be seen.

I straightened up and turned back toward my own car. Unlike Flynn, I hadn't parked under a streetlight—purposefully so—but still, I could see a spot of deeper darkness sitting in the passenger seat. A shape like the one Flynn had lingered to watch walk away in the dark. Except this was no flirty blonde with an easy smile and an unspoken invitation to follow. My shade was silent and dour. She was angry and wanted blood. And, Heaven help me, I intended to give it to her.

A couple came stumbling out of the bar, laughing and leaning on each other. I jerked out of my paralysis and staggered an involuntary step forward, trying to get away. If they recognized me, or even noticed I was there, they didn't let on. The pair headed away in the opposite direction, continuing to laugh and carry on as they held each other up. I looked at my watch. Flynn wouldn't be coming out for a while. There was still time to back out.

I looked at my car again. The shadow still sat there, waiting. I took another step toward it. And another. Eventually, I made it across the street and found the shape in the passenger seat was just a shadow from a tree falling across half of the car. At least, that's what I told myself when I climbed inside. Despite that, I couldn't bring myself to look at the passenger seat. Instead, I stared through the windshield at the door to Hautala's, waiting for more people to come out. Waiting for one in particular.

I'd brought a Thermos full of black coffee, thinking it might be difficult to stay awake until closing time, but it wasn't. I didn't feel tired at all; I could have stayed up all night without caffeine, riding the energy of my anger. Of course, I didn't have to. The bar, like every other in Ripton, closed at two in the morning. I'd been following him since nine, when he walked out his front door. At around one a.m., I started the car and let the engine idle. After a while, when people started to leave, I put it in gear and pulled forward so I could see better. I didn't want to make a mistake. I didn't want to hurt the wrong person. I very badly wanted to hurt the right one.

He came staggering out at ten-to-two with a pair of his friends. They were laughing and roughhousing. Flynn gave one friend a shove and staggered back, taking a hard, unintended step off the curb. He nearly fell in the street and my heart raced. I almost put it in gear and jammed the gas at that moment, but his pals caught him before he landed in the gutter. I didn't want to kill all three of them. I doubted I could if I tried. And leaving them alive meant getting caught if they saw me and could remember the details of my car or plate—or my face. I cursed myself for not wearing a ski mask or even a hat. But on a warm late spring evening, it'd look more suspicious than just sitting in the car outside a bar all night.

They righted him and I could hear his laugh through my windows over the sound of the idling engine. I squeezed the steering wheel tight. I felt my knuckles pop, but didn't relax my grip. I wanted to be squeezing Rory Flynn's fucking neck. Throttling him until my hands hurt and his eyes came bulging out of their sockets and I felt him thrashing underneath me. And then I imagined holding on longer, squeezing tighter until I felt his windpipe collapse and the bones in his vertebrae grind against each other and smelled his bladder let go. I wanted to kill him with my hands because it was a cowardly fucking thing to run someone down in the street. But there was no other way. I didn't know if I could beat him in a stand-up fight. And I wasn't an assassin. I didn't know how to break into a house. I didn't know how to kill a person and get away without having to murder everyone else in it. I didn't know how not to leave a trace. All I understood was that Rory Flynn was never going to be punished in this world, and that there was no other. He'd live his whole life having gotten away with it if I didn't do something right now.

So, I put the car in gear and stood on the brake.

A cab pulled up to the curb next to them. Did the driver see my car and wonder why I had been sitting there for so long? I could've been competition—a MyRyde driver waiting for my app to summon me to pick up someone at the bar. It was too late to print out one of those company logo signs people put in their back windows and install it as a diversion. I'd failed again in even the most rudimentary kind of deception. I didn't look like anything other than a man who'd been sitting in his car for close to four hours, waiting. And when they came to find Flynn lying broken in the street, people would say things like, "There was a car parked right over there all night," and "It was there when I went inside and was still there when I came out again. And I saw a *man* sitting in it both times!" My master plan was less than masterful by a long shot. It didn't matter. Flynn deserved to pay for what he'd done. And if that meant I paid too, that was the price of rendering his judgment.

Flynn's pals got into the cab. I saw Flynn shake his head, "no." He wasn't going with them. They urged him again and I willed him to refuse. *Say no say no say no. Just refuse their generosity and walk away.* He held up his keys and I could read his lips when he said, "I'm fine." He slammed the taxicab car door too hard and a second later the cabbie pulled away, carrying his responsible patrons away. Flynn, alone on the sidewalk, swayed a little on his feet and then took a step toward the lot. Not falling-down drunk, but drunk enough to kill someone.

He hadn't been drunk when he hit Justine and her boy. Just full of rage. I wondered how his anger compared to mine. His had been deranging; mine was focused. He hadn't intended to hit Justine and her boy. I was pointed right at him.

I took my foot off the brake.

The car crept forward. My foot hovered over the gas pedal. I could jam it down, steer the car up onto the sidewalk and run him down. I could do this. It's what I'd hoped for—he was by himself, drunk and senseless, and I had a clear shot at him. I could hit him and get away. There might even be a moment to back up and run him over again before anyone could make sense of what that sound was outside and come running to see. And then it was home to wash the car. I thought of Aidan's confession. He knew what his father had done because he washed his car. I never washed mine by hand either. I took it to the drive-through. I enjoyed reliving the pleasure of being a child inside my mother's car when it went through the carwash tunnel like an amusement park ride. It never got the car quite clean enough, but the trip was worth it.

That's when I realized a washing wouldn't do it. I wasn't driving his truck or even a decent-sized sedan; I was in a low-to-the-ground subcompact that would hit him at mid-thigh and throw him up onto the windshield. It'd break his legs for sure, but unless I really got up to speed, chances of killing him seemed slim. And whether or not he died, the impact would definitely wreck my little car.

I watched Flynn take an awkward step, right himself, straighten his clothes, and then with measured intent, walk carefully toward his pickup truck. With purpose in his stride, he walked confidently into the parking lot and out of the path of my car. I'd waited too long. I'd failed. Though I imagined I'd have another chance to set up exactly this scenario some other night, I knew I'd never do it. I was plagued by doubt and hesitation, while he had the confidence of a man who knew that even when he did wrong, he would be just fine. He never felt like he had to atone for anything. And I had no ability to hold him accountable, because I was a coward.

I pressed down on the gas and steered toward home.

Behind me, I heard the roar of his V8 engine and a squeal of tires as he peeled out of the lot, taking the turn onto the street too fast. I pictured him rolling the thing and killing himself right there without me. Then his bright headlights filled my rear window and blinded me.

He rode up on my bumper and I braced for the collision that would ruin my car and my body and leave him without a scratch. At the last second, with his truck so close it felt like his headlights were shining out of my back seat, he honked and swerved around me. His engine roared like a monster and my shoulders tightened in response. My little car rocked in his wake.

Tears stung my eyes, and I felt weak and utterly vulnerable. I pulled over and breathed deeply for a few seconds, trying to calm my heartbeat.

Her voice whispered in my ear. "Home."

I knew where he lived; I'd followed him to the bar from his home. And the fastest way to get back there was straight ahead.

He'd turned right at the end of the block instead.

⛤

I turned onto Flynn's street, pulled over to the curb, and stared at his McMansion standing in the center of the cul-de-sac. It was a straight shot from the street into his driveway. If he'd beaten me, there would've been a light on, but the windows were dark. While it was possible that he was navigating his house in the dark to avoid disturbing his sleeping family, it somehow seemed more likely that I'd gotten there first.

He'd turned right instead of going straight when he left Hautala's Lounge, because he was following the call of the woman he'd run into on the sidewalk out front. I imagined her saying something like, "Swing by when you're done." After he'd drunk his fill with his friends, he took her up on the offer before going home to his wife and son. Because he could.

Or maybe he was already asleep in his bed, and I had missed another opportunity.

I pulled around the cul-de-sac and drove back toward the intersection at the end of the street. It was closing in on two thirty and all the houses were dark. I pulled up to the stop sign and rolled down my window. I shut off my engine and listened to the sounds of the nighttime. A soft breeze rustled the tree branches overhead and somewhere in the distance I heard a dog bark. I wondered if it was a stray or if someone was out walking it in the middle of the night, tired and anxious for the thing to do its business so they could both go home and get back to bed.

I'd give him an hour. If he didn't show up by three-thirty, he was probably already home and I was a fool. Except, whether he was sound asleep in his own bed or fucking someone in another, I was already a fool. I was a fool for thinking that I could hold him accountable.

Then, through the breeze and the calm of night, I heard a faint engine rumble. Throaty and loud enough to carry through the outskirts of the city. I listened for a little bit to make sure it was coming closer.

I opened the jockey box and pulled out the small flashlight I told myself I bought for emergencies. Most of the time, those emergencies were simply that I'd dropped something that had landed underneath the driver's seat. I clicked it on. A thousand lumens lit up the inside of the car like an explosion. I doused it immediately; a blue afterimage hovered in my sight like a ghost. The thing was brighter than I ever needed, but at the time I bought it, it seemed like a fun thing to have. A light bright enough to cast a beam in the sky, like a spotlight summoning people to a Hollywood movie premiere. It was an indulgence that seemed silly in hindsight, though at that moment I was glad to have it.

I restarted the engine and pulled forward. I turned the car to the left and stopped in the middle of the intersection. Then, I turned off the engine again and got out. The sound of Flynn's truck was growing louder.

While the low branches of an elm tree near the corner shaded the streetlight above me, the intersection was still lit up well enough. I took a few steps back and tried shining the flashlight up at the sensor on top of the light. Even with my flashlight focused down to a tight beam, the streetlight wasn't going out. I gave up and doused my light again. I went to hide in the shadows of the opposite corner.

After a few minutes, a truck turned the corner at the far end of Effdey Street and started toward me. With the bright headlights shining in my eyes, I couldn't be certain it was Flynn's truck; I put my faith in the now familiar sound of that engine. That sound had been roaring in my ears since he tore around me to get to his girlfriend's. It had to be his truck. It *had* to be.

I ducked behind an elm in someone's yard. The engine grew louder and more terrifying. This was the sound that Justine and her son heard the moment before he ran them down.

Come on, you fucker.

He was going fast and didn't seem interested in slowing down for the four-way stop. That suited me. I ran through my list of explanations. *I sometimes drive at night to think. My car died and I didn't know what to do. I'd gotten out to push it clear of the intersection when I saw him coming. He didn't even slow down, officer. I was barely able to jump out of the way before ...*

The woman stepped into the road without looking, pulling the child along behind her. She screamed, but the sound was nothing compared to the truck's howl, and I cried out incoherently, not mute but rendered speechless by what I saw. Just a long, loud cry of terror.

I lurched out from behind the elm and dashed toward her. The sound of screeching tires was shrill as a chorus of angels. My legs felt boneless and I stumbled into the road, half upright and entirely out of control. The headlights lit me up bright and white and cold like Heaven, blinding me to everything but it. I put up my hands, dark against the stark brilliance. They were worthless against the monstrous consequence bearing down on me.

I stood frozen in the street waiting to feel the push bar and grille slam into my body. I waited for the feeling of being hurled through the air, weightless and then landing, devastated, on unyielding asphalt. Or perhaps, I wouldn't feel any of that, but rather a merciful blinking out.

And then everything went dark. But not silent.

The screeching chorus of tires reached a higher pitch along with a racing engine suddenly flooded with gas and became a symphony of scraping metal and shattering glass. I heard a sound like the slamming of a great door. The percussive sound of it splintering and breaking and then another crash. The musical conclusion of the last cymbal trill of safety glass and the engine winding down like a sigh before dying. And then, the soft breeze returned and I heard the muted sound of rudely awakened dogs barking behind locked doors.

I opened my eyes to see Flynn's red truck resting on its roof, warped and ruined, and wrapped around the oak I'd hidden behind a moment earlier. He hung half out of the window, a dull white ball inside the cab pressing against him. The airbag hadn't done any good. He was contorted, arms reaching in impossible directions, and his neck turned at a right angle, unblinking eyes looking directly at me standing in the middle of the street, untouched.

I looked around in a panic for the woman and child but couldn't see them.

My legs still felt rubbery as I staggered toward Flynn. A black pool spread out from under him, glinting red in the streetlamp's glow. Windows in living rooms all along the block began to light up. I ran to my car. Despite wanting to stay and watch them pull Rory from the wreck—wanting to see them lay a sheet over his body and lift him into an ambulance that drove away without its lights flashing—I climbed in my car, started the engine and drove away.

In the distance, I heard a siren wind up. It reminded me of a single soprano voice intoning the first notes of Górecki's *Cantabile-Semplice*.

EPILOGUE: REUNION

I say, "This is my confession. I repent and ask for absolution."

The headstone is silent. I reach out and touch it. My fingers trace over the letters engraved in the granite.

Adam Linden Neville

Born, May 19, 2017

Taken, June 28, 2019

Beloved son, loved forever.

I set the small stuffed bear I bought at Rexall in front of it and wonder what happened to the one I left before. It doesn't matter. If this one vanishes, I'll buy another. And another.

"What are you doing?"

The voice from behind startles me, and I feel shame burn in the hot blush of my cheeks. I turn around to say "sorry," and freeze. She's shorter than I remember. Her face is different, uneven, but still beautiful. Her hair is cut differently, but the same deep black. Now framed in white at the temples.

Too young to be going gray.

"Father Price? Is that you?"

I swallow. "I, uh, I'm just David now. I left the priesthood. I'm sorry, Ms. Neville. I'm so sorry for your loss." I stand and take a step to go. She stops me with her free hand—the one not holding her cane.

"It's Justine."

I reach for her hand, expecting her to pull away. She lets me take it. Her hand is solid and I don't pass through. Her fingers are cold, and I wrap them in my hands to warm them, though mine aren't much warmer. They're finally clean though.

"*You're* the one leaving the stuffed animals?"

I nod. "They keep disappearing."

"He would've been upset if they got cold or rained on, so I've been taking them to put in his room." She laughs once, softly. It's not a happy sound. "He would have liked them."

"I'm glad you have them."

"I miss seeing you," she says.

"Me too." I let go of her hand and take another step to leave.

"Wait." she says. "Can I get your e-mail address?"

This time, I don't walk away.

MEMORIES OF ~~YOU~~ ME

"This is about the difference between the figure and the body ... About who gets what and who owns what. About who is remembered and who is forgotten. Here. In this place. This is about ~~you~~. I mean ~~me~~. I mean you."

—Barbara Kruger

You awake with a jolt, like being ripped from the void, light breaking nullity as lightning splits a starless sky. Sleep is blissful oblivion that embraces you too infrequently. Alive again and thrust into bodily consciousness, you rise and set foot onto the cold floor. The foot that touches it isn't yours. Though, it *was*. You feel as if it is a thing borrowed. Like the rest of your body, belonging to another. Many others. A sense memory of moist grass tickling the sole of your foot comes and goes, though you can't remember anything about the occasion that spawned the feeling. An arm harkens back to swinging a roque mallet. The other, cradling a baby unknown to you. Your legs had known climbing and the painful cramp of a prolonged squat. None of those feelings attuned to a place or time. Bodily memory divorced of lived experience, like a phantom sensation lingering at the end of a dream.

You stretch, arms up, reaching for the ceiling high beyond your grasp imagining the rough scrape of wooden beams against your fingertips. A sensation of a splinter emerges from the past. You let your arms down, absently rubbing your thumb where the reminisced insult lingers.

Smells of antiseptic and rot war for supremacy as you leave your bedroom. Moving creakily, reaching out with a hand against the rough wall to steady yourself, you slip past the washroom, not wanting to catch a glimpse of that woman's face in the mirror, whoever she'd been. Not you. Also you. So many women in that reflection, beautiful and terrifying and strange. With black eyes and ashen skin under a mane of curly red hair streaked with gray, your face seems wan. Makeup only emphasizes how like a dead thing you look. Still, pretty in your way.

Not you.

In the front room, you grab the fireplace poker and sift through the ashes of the previous night's fire. Dragging it back and forth in the soot and charred leavings, the metallic grind of the tip scraping on brick like screaming. A memory of ringing ears and stinging throat. You stack wood on the wrought iron rack and set some wadded paper under to help it catch. A gust of wind outside wafts the smell of old smoke and ashes into your face from within the chimney. It smells like home. Burnt and rebuilt on the char of its predecessor. You light a long match, savoring the aroma of sulfur before setting light to the starter. The fire catches quickly and slowly the room fills with warmth and pale, dancing light. A patch of skin on your thigh feels sun kissed, as if remembering tanning on a beach somewhere. Another piece of you tingles with the itch of a healing burn.

MEMORIES OF ~~YOU~~ ME

In the flickering golden glow, you turn and sit nearby in a highbacked chair next to a small table with a dusty lamp beside. The springs beneath you creak as you shift, trying to find a comfortable angle to still the ache in your back. Failing, you lean back and close your eyes. You breathe in deep and exhale, slow and long. Struggling to remember.

Anything.

A sensation moving across a breast, pinching punching pulling petting. You try to move elsewhere in the body that isn't yours to seek out another sense. Haunted from the inside by memories of long-gone women who you weren't ever and still are, your body a record of all the hurts endured in an eternity of being reduced to parts, the sum of which never quite equaling you. The *real* you. Your back aches from bending, your ass from a strop, thighs burn with rough friction, and wrists ache under the hands holding them fast. Your body filled with rising agony as all the lives you've lived collide in shared insult and indignity.

Your eyes snap open and you gasp a breath into burning lungs. How long since you've last inhaled? A minute? An hour? Forever? The fire dwindled in your reverie. You stand and set another log on top. The last. You'll have to go out and chop more. If there is more. You can't recall. Your arm feels weary with the sensation of swinging back and falling and being stuck and then free once more before up and falling again and again. Back aching with the burden of carrying a load.

A body.

Nails bend back as they claw skin, scratch and tear before peeling away. Hands grasping, squeezing, holding until they burn and cramp and feel like they might forever curl into fixed claws.

You sob.

When will you ever stop feeling?
When will you remember to forget everything?
Remember.

※

You twist the key in the padlock, feeling it pop open in your hand. A present sensation you savor as it fades from your palm. You slip the lock hoop from the hasp and let the thing fall on the floor with the dull thud of dense metal. The heavy door swings open on old hinges, the squeal of them making your ears ring ever so slightly. Another present sensation. This one less pleasing, but still yours. Descending the stairs into the hall below, you don't bother with a light. Your body knows this place better than it knows itself. You move through the darkness like a bat, knowing every wall and angle by the sound of bare feet on hardwood and breath bouncing off stone walls. At the end of the hall, you let herself into the room that stinks of decay and ozone. Here, you flip a switch, kindling the spark in the walls that ignites the bright light above. It makes you squint. A solitary white star in a dull sky of stone and rafter.

In the center of the round room stands the metal table where you first met him. Both dressed all in white, like matched dolls. Him shouting, you screaming inside, unable to find the air to let it out. His stained clothes are greasy now with the skin beneath stretched and blackened with rot. His teeth bared in amusement at a joke eternal.

Death.

You bend and grab his arms. Skin under lab coat sloughs and slides in your hands. Your stomach is still as a grave despite conscious disgust. No revulsion for the wicked. You drag him from the stain on the floor beside the workbench where he sat slumped and heave him up onto the steel table. Fat and oil and putrefaction cling to your

MEMORIES OF ~~YOU~~ ME

palms and arms and bare chest as you shove him onto it. You rub her hands on your thighs, trying to get him off of you. He clings. Again. Covering more of your body. Bits of him. Everywhere.

At the workbench, you look at the notebook. His handwriting is rushed and excited. A slur of sloppy scratches obliterating hastily chosen words, replaced with better expressions. You read, struggling to remember. You've read it before, you know. But none of it sticks. Every day fresh innocence claws forth from graveyard earth. None of what he'd written makes sense to you. He was a genius. Unparalleled in matters scientific and philosophical. The very best of men.

Rotting.

You were …

You glare at him. His lab partner—long gone—might've helped you. Except, he hadn't. So where did that thought come from? Hope? That isn't anything you can remember feeling in any part of your body. Not heart or brain. As unconnected to you as a wish on a distant star. No. you are hopeless.

You pluck a scalpel from the tray beside the table and admire its elegant clean lines, gentle and smooth in your hand. The metal remains cool against your skin. With a grip around the handle, you set a finger against the back of the blade and push it into his neck. An odor emerges from him like copper and rotten pork and something else.

You.

Death.

How did he die? You could examine him again. Look for the signs where you'd strangled him, or perhaps where you'd hacked at him with a cleaver or shot him with a pistol or any number of past confusions running through your body from finger to ear to nose and bowel. None seem right. Had you even killed him? You reason you must have done, since there is no one else with you.

Killer.

Murderer.

Undoubtedly, your body replies. Though about a killer of whom, it is coy. Babies smothered, old women poisoned, men in alleys offering you coin slashed and bled, and so on. All there with you, just out of sight at the edges of your memory, like something always just beyond the eye. Your history? Your present? When had you done these things or not done them? A dream of power? A wish? Who was the killer? Surely not *you*. Yet, in some part of you, the memory remains.

You slip the blade out of his neck. A trickle of ichor drains from the wound. Slipping down his mottled flesh onto the dull steel table and gathering, viscous and dark among his other leavings. The red, wet tip of it slips into your palm like a wary lover slipping into bed after a tryst. Quiet. Careful. The same black blood that oozed from the man's neck pools around the blade deep in your hand. You close her eyes and focus on the sensation of steel penetrating skin. The focused sting of it, warmth, and a radiant burn arcing from palm to wrist—the nearest suture scar. You take a deep breath of foul air and let it out, counting the seconds from full lungs to emptiness.

You pull the scalpel out of your palm and look at the instrument again. It possesses the same gentle elegance as before, though now imbued with the moment. Darkly red. A deliverer of present feeling all your own; it is a lover who won't balk, but only acquiesce to your needs and demands. You tilt your head to the side and run the point of it along the scar lining your jaw, listening to the soft singing of thin metal against your jagged edges. Almost imperceptible. You can hear the hushed voices of angels in the edge of the blade. Promising what? Death? You *have* that. Life? Yours as well.

The distant sound of the crash from the house above cascades down the stairs into the workroom. You spin and look back the way you came, toward the din of faraway footsteps and raised voices. You feel the shouting in your body. It is angry and you relive the fright of a lifetime ago in your belly in your ears in your limbs as they tense to flee, though there is nowhere to go except up toward the voices. You step back into a shadow behind a cabinet and listen as heavy bodies thud furiously back and forth through the house, searching. For you? No. For him.

The dead man's eyes gaze blindly at the stairway, as if waiting to rise and greet his guests when he glimpses them. When the first man appears in the doorway at the top, he remains still.

The man descends, a hand up to shield his eyes from the glare of the lamp hanging from the ceiling. It bathes the room in brilliance while creating deep pockets of black. He glares into those pools, searching. More men follow, barking questions at the first, at each other, not waiting for answers before barking again like beasts with mouths full of teeth and greedy throats behind.

The first man speaks. You struggle to hear, to understand, but his words are fast and strange and you don't have the ear for them. He gestures at the surgical table, and they all surge ahead as one body with many limbs like the spiders in the dark corner where you hide. A man raises a hand to his mouth and flees for the far end of the room. You hear him retch and choke. Another man shouts at him, while covering his nose and mouth with a cloth. The first man frowns as he turns the dead man's face toward his own. He peers at him and says, "Karl."

The word settles in your mind with oppressive weight as you recall the dead man stabbing a finger at his chest and saying, "Karl, Karl" over and again until you tried to mouth the word, find air to utter it and failed.

Hahl.

"No!"

Another word you know.

Galle.

"No!" He shook you and you wanted to cry and explain why you couldn't say it. Of all the disparate pieces of you, none remember what it is to speak. Your tongue isn't of the same woman your throat had been. It can't remember. None remember how to hear or say the words that would tell him to let you be. To let you die.

The first man stands upright and turns. He holds up a hand and his barking, puking companions quiet. He points toward shadows and makes sounds, which puts the other men in motion. They peer into corners and search the dark places and inevitably come to the place where you hide, crouched down and small.

More shouting, a dark figure above you pointing, reaching, grasping your arm and pulling you from darkness into light. You stagger after him, bare feet stumbling and scraping against stone. He lets go suddenly and you crash to your knees on the floor. More memories. More pain. The pain of now.

It's good.

The men huddle together, faces slack and eyes wide. The first stares agape and says, "Madelina?" You know the word. Not *your* word. But yours nonetheless. Your face tingles. Part of you. Other words like it were yours, too.

Your names

All you.

None of them, *you*.

You raise a hand to calm the man and he levels a black shape at you. You glance from your hand to his; shiny blade to blunt black rod and darker hole. Another man points at your hair and says something. You hear, "Valerie's!" Your scalp itches. What other names did your body know. Anne's arms. Una's legs. Your body bearing another and other names, the pieces of you a silent chorus of women's unheard voices.

The black thing erupts with light. You feel something punch you hard in the chest. Bad pain like burning. All here, all now. All yours. You lurch forward and it happens again. Another hit, another sudden moment in the now that silences the memories of others.

Yes!

Again!

You take another step and it blooms fire once more. Your ears hurt at the echo of the explosion in the stone walled room. Your eyes sting from the flash. The acrid smell of it sears your nostrils. This is new. This, whatever it is, has never happened to any of the women who are you, and you want more. So present in this moment, your body your own as it is punctured again and again by this thing in his hand.

He stops, and your mouth falls open. You want to speak.

More.

Instead, you hiss and spit. The men recoil. The first man says it again. "Madelina!"

Your face twists with frustration. You look at the knife in your hand. You shriek and raise it and he makes the explosions again and again, throwing you down to the floor. Hands fall on you at once, lifting. The room spins as if you are being whisked away. A grunt and the heavy thud of a dead body splatting on the floor. The room fills with the stench of putrescine and cadaverine erupting from split skin. They gag as they set you on the table where the dead man— Karl—had been. You feel your bare skin slipping in his grease. The straps fall over you. You scream, "No!" in an unfamiliar voice.

Yes!

The hands pause for only a second and then resume strapping you down. The knife vanishes from your hand. Taken.

The first man looms over you. He traces a finger along the long scar framing your face. Arcing around your jaw and running down to your chin and back around before rising up behind your ear and across your forehead. You know every one of these scars. Connections. Those around elbows and wrists. The ones at your hips and ankles and curving under your breasts. All the places where the *she* who was all of them met to be *you*.

He touches you again. Your cheek. Tender. Sparking memory. Making connection. You smell his breath, heavy with alcohol. The touch is familiar; his odor isn't. You don't remember him drinking. You try to speak again. Mouth stretching open, lungs filling, you sigh a sound. Long and low.

"Yeeeeess."

Your voice found, the missing piece, never sewn in because Karl didn't know how to place that part of you. Fit it in the being he'd pieced together to be for him. Another man speaks. Soft, like asking. The first man's face twists with anger and turns red. He raises the knife and slices at you, pulling the blade fast and sharp long the lines around your face not *your* face. He cuts and you feel the sharp careless tears in your skin and cool wet flooding over your ears and into your hair. You feel him grip your skin, fingers digging under flesh, and tug and rip and the first man backs away, taking part of you with him. A face like a mask.

The other men scream and you try to be heard among them.

"Yes! Yes! YES!" Lipless and wetly impassioned.

They run, leaving you there on the table where you were born. And you know the answer is no. At least for now. Perhaps they'll return and finish.

You wait.

And wait.

If they take all the pieces, all that will be left is that void where you really live. The deep place where you are only one woman no man can define who or what you are. Where you own yourself. You wait for them to come back and take you apart, piece by piece. Like Karl had put you together. Piece by stolen piece. The perfect woman, as he saw one. You long to be deconstructed, pieces severed, reunited with the real women you had been and never were.

The ones in the room deeper down the cellar.

Where he kept them.

Be patient and let them take it all away.

"Yes."

You wait.

THE GIRL IN THE POOL

The day was bright, and closing the door behind him felt for a moment to Rory like having a black bag slipped over his head. He waited by the front door, letting his eyes adjust to the gloom. Before long, shapes began to coalesce. In the room to the left of the hallway, he could see a sofa and an end table. At the far end was a standing chess board with oversized marble pieces and, next to that, a big floor lamp that resembled one of those outdoor sculptures you'd find in front of a bank or a hotel instead of inside someone's house. If it weren't for the small light fixtures jutting from the sides of it, he wouldn't have thought it had any function other than to cost money and take up space. So much of the stuff he found in these kinds of places was like that. A globe on a mahogany stand in a study or a life-sized porcelain wolfhound in a foyer had no purpose other than to justify the size of some interior decorator's fee. The chess board seemed like that. There weren't any chairs nearby where players could sit, just the sofa too far away to be of any use. He had friends who liked chess—they'd learned how to play in the Navy or in prison and their boards were cheap and fit in a box you could store on a shelf. The way this room looked, he doubted anyone spent more time in it than it took to tie their shoelaces on the way out the door. It was a drawing room, not a *living* room. Only the housecleaners who dusted it once a month spent any real time in there.

He followed Tod down the hallway past the dining room on the right toward the stairs. This was a second-story job. While he imagined there were plenty of expensive things on the first floor they could take if they wanted—Bluetooth speakers and nice silverware—the money in a place like this was always upstairs in the bedroom and the office. Places where people kept jewelry and watches and money. If he could find a checkbook, his girl, Gloria, could make it rain before anyone even thought to go looking for it. That sort of thing would be locked in a desk. As if a desk drawer lock could keep him out when the front door deadbolt had opened up for him like a panhandler's palm.

He followed Tod up. The stairs creaked under his weight and he held his breath, waiting for the sounds of barking and claws clacking on hardwood. He knew the dog was in the beach house on the Cape with its owners, but the smell was there and the scar on his forearm itched. Even if there was no dog, there was a *sense* of hound in the house and that got Rory's hackles up. Fuck man's best friend; he was a cat person. A cat scratch might get infected if you were lazy about taking care of it, but you weren't going to have to get twenty-seven stitches and have permanent tingling in your fingers because someone's housecat tried to bite your fuckin' arm off.

At the top of the stairs, Tod pointed to the left. "Marta says the office is that way. I'll check out the bedroom." He stalked off to the right. Tod was an okay partner; he didn't fuck around, and he didn't have any weird kinks that'd make the police worry the job was done by anyone other than run-of-the-mill burglars. Rory had worked with a guy a couple of times who insisted on taking a pair of women's underwear as a souvenir from each house they broke into. *That* sort of thing gave detectives incentive, imagining it might "escalate." Even if the dipshit never graduated from panty-raids to something worse, Rory didn't want the kind of heat that came with getting pinched coming out of a place with a woman's underwear in his pockets along with her jewelry. Prosecutors didn't like burglars, but they *hated* perverts.

Still, better not to get caught either way.

He walked down the hall and opened the door to what was supposed to be the office. He saw a treadmill and a rowing machine inside and thought Marta had gotten it wrong. Workout equipment was the sort of shit people set up in the basement. You saw that stuff, it usually meant there was nothing of value in the room. Nobody paid their bills while doing cardio. He let out a relieved breath when he saw the big partner's desk to his right. Okay, the guy liked to work out in his office. Marta hadn't let him down after all. He sidled over to the desk and went to work.

The thing was an antique, which meant the lock was sturdy, but simple. He had the drawer open and the contents dumped on the blotter in less than a minute. He started sorting through, trying to find anything of value. Credit cards, checkbook, even a notebook full of Internet passwords.

Behind him, outside, he heard a shout and a splash. He jumped up and put his back to the wall beside the window. No one was supposed to be home. Marta assured them that the owners went to the Cape every weekend in the summer. He'd confirmed that, casing the place with Tod for the last three weeks. The splashing continued for a minute and then settled down. Maybe it was a neighbor's pool. Sound carried. But it sounded like whoever was out for a swim was right there, like he was sitting on the back porch with a beer watching the kids play Marco Polo in the inflatable. He leaned out from the wall and pulled the sheers open enough to peek outside. Rory blinked, trying to make sense of what he saw.

The girl floated face down in the water. Sunlight sparkled on the ripples surrounding her body like stars. A halo of redness wavered around her head.

Marta said it was just the couple and their dog. No kids. But the person in the pool was a child. Skinny. Twelve or thirteen, maybe. Hard to say from a distance. Peering out of a gap in the curtains, he couldn't tell if it was blood in the water around her head or if she was a ginger. Not that it mattered either way; she was facedown and still.

He ran out of the office, nearly colliding with Tod on the landing. "What the hell was that?" his partner hissed. "What's going on?"

"It's a kid!" Rory turned to run downstairs. Tod grabbed a hold of his elbow.

"What d'ya mean, a kid? You said everybody was out of town."

"There's a kid in the pool. She's drowning." He shoved Tod's hand away and ran downstairs, taking the stairs three at a time. Halfway down, he missed a step that rocked his spine, turned his ankle and almost sent him sprawling the rest of the way down, but he kept his feet under him and a grip on the banister. He skidded on the hardwood floor in the hallway at the bottom of the stairs. Tod thundered down the stairs close behind him.

In the kitchen, he ran for the double sliding glass door that led out onto the back deck and beyond that, the pool. Half the pool was out of view and he couldn't see the girl, but she wasn't making any more noise. He grabbed the sliding glass door and yanked. Locked of course. The owners were away.

Tod's hand closed around his arm again, tighter this time. "The fuck you doing?" he said through clenched teeth. "Get your shit together. This ain't our problem."

Rory pointed to the pool. "What's wrong with you? She's drowning!"

"You don't know that."

"Get offa me." He shoved at Tod.

His partner's face turned a dark red. Tod grabbed the back of Rory's head and shoved his face against the glass door. "You see those houses back there? You see the second-floor windows all lookin' out into this fuckin' yard? You go splashing around out there for Christ and everybody to see and you're going to get us caught. Chill the fuck out, man."

"She's drowning." Rory's breath steamed up the glass.

"You hear her calling for help? You hear any splashing? She's gone or she's gone home. Either way, it's not our problem."

Rory kicked back with a heel into Tod's knee. It flexed back further than it should have and the bigger man grunted and staggered away. Rory turned and ducked low, jabbing three times fast into Tod's ribs. The big man fell backward on his ass, crimson-faced and breathing heavy. Rory stood over him, fists balled up and ready to knock him back down the second he stood up.

"You put your hands on me again and I'll fuckin' burn you down. Understand? I'm not Marta. You don't fuckin' scare me."

Tod's expression darkened, but he didn't argue. Rory grew up in the gym and was fast and hit hard. He was pretty sure he'd broken a couple of Tod's ribs, not that it bothered him. The guy deserved it. No one put their hands on him. No one. When it was clear Tod wasn't getting up to fight, he turned back to the sliding door. He flicked the lock and pulled again.

The door resisted and his hand slipped off the handle a second time. "Fuck!" He kicked at the door frame in frustration. He looked down and saw an inch-thick wooden dowel in the track, bracing the door closed. He yanked it out of the groove, threw it across the kitchen and slammed the door open.

Tod said, "You go out there, I'm taking the fuckin' car and leaving."

Rory looked over his shoulder. "I give a shit what you do."

"When you get caught, if you tell anyone that I was with you on this job, you will. *Gloria* will give a shit."

Rory felt the urge to lay into Tod a second time at the sound of his wife's name—give him a second helping of what he'd already dished out. A lot more. Rory wasn't a rat and he didn't like being called one, but he liked Tod threatening his wife even less. He wanted to show him exactly what threats bought. Except, there wasn't time to impart the lesson. Every second he spent punishing Tod was another that the girl in the pool spent dying … if she wasn't dead already. He resolved to pay his partner a visit at home if he was still a free man after this was all over. He ran through the doorway into the sunlight.

Outside, he felt blinded again; the sudden light made his head hurt. But Rory rushed forward anyway, a hand shielding his face, trying to block the sun glaring off the water. He looked around for the girl but couldn't see her. He'd heard her fall in—*seen* her from the window upstairs. Tod had *heard* her too. It wasn't his imagination.

He squinted and cupped his hands around his eyes, forcing himself not to turn away from the pool and go back inside where it was comfortably dim. And out of sight of the neighbors; Tod was right about those second story windows.

Then he saw her. A shape in the water, light, but not bright. Pale. And still.

The girl was too far from the edge and Rory couldn't reach her by kneeling and reaching out. He kicked off his Timberlands, took a deep breath, and dove in. Water-soaked clothes made him feel heavy and slow. He fought against his thick work pants and the mechanic's jacket he should've shrugged out of along with his boots and headed in the direction he remembered seeing her body. It felt like he'd swum the length of the pool, but couldn't have. He'd jumped in from the side, not the end. She'd been *right* in front of him. It would have taken only a single stroke or two to reach her. Not this much. He thought he must've come up on the other side of her, swimming away toward the other wall. And then his hand hit something soft and yielding. And cold.

He grabbed the girl's arm and pulled her toward him. He turned her over, slipped an arm under hers and began paddling backward toward the wall, pulling her along. Rory wasn't a strong swimmer, but she wasn't fighting him. While it had felt like an eternity finding her, he reached the edge of the pool in seconds. He scrambled out of the water and pulled the girl onto the patio after him, wincing as her back scraped along the edge of the pool. The tiles caught her swimsuit bottoms and pulled them down to mid-thigh. Embarrassment stung him, but he focused on what he needed to do most. Still, from one of those windows it had to look bad. He turned her head to the side to clear the water out of her mouth. She was blond, but the back of her head was crimson. He didn't bother pulling her hair away to try to find the gash. Getting her to breathe was his first concern. The cut would have to wait.

He turned her face back toward him, careful about her neck, jutted her jaw forward to open her mouth. Her eyes were open and staring blankly into the blue sky overhead. He leaned down and forced a breath into her mouth. He waited two seconds and blew again. He drew back and looked at her chest to see if it was rising and falling on its own. She was as still as the statue in the foyer. He blew again and again and still nothing. He checked her wrist for a pulse. Cold skin and tendons underneath; bone and flesh and no throb that signaled life.

"Please. Come on," he said. He leaned down to try again.

Water answered. It flooded out of her mouth into his throat and he lurched away. The water slipped into his lungs and he coughed and sputtered, spraying droplets in the air that sparkled and vanished like sparks in daylight. He felt her hand on the back of his neck and her lips and another rush of water flooding his mouth. He tried to resist as it filled him. In his throat and mouth and nose. He was drowning. He shoved at the girl. She was strong and held on. Stronger than he was.

Rory's mind raced. *No! Stop! I tried to save you. I tried to rescue you and I did my best and I'm sorry I was too late it was Tod not me I swear it was Tod who tried to stop me I would have been here faster if it wasn't for him oh I'msorryI'msorryI'msosorry!*

A cool burst of air rushed into his mouth and lungs and he gasped and scrambled backward across the patio, away from the pool and the girl. His back hit the edge of the deck and sharp pain arced from between his shoulder blades down into his spine.

In front of him, the girl lay on her back, pale and glistening like she was made of diamonds. She hadn't moved. Her eyes, wide open and white with cataract, stared at him as a red blanket spread out from under the wet splay of her straw-colored hair.

Rory coughed and took another deep breath.

"I'm sorry."

She didn't say anything.

He stood up, unsure where to go or what to do. His clothes hung on him like woven gravity. He took a step toward the girl. He waited for her hand to reach out for him, for the solid grip of her fingers—so strong—around his ankle and then the feeling of the bracing, cold water in the pool as she dragged him to the bottom and held him there while he died with her. Not *with* her.

She was dead already.

Open eyes.

Cataract-white eyes.

She didn't reach out for him. She didn't blink. Her chest didn't rise with a shallow breath and then fall. She was dead.

Rory took another step toward the girl. And another. He knelt beside her and pulled her swimsuit bottoms up from her thighs, covering her, restoring the dignity he'd taken, pulling her clumsily out of the water. He put a hand on her cheek and thought about the times as a boy her age that he'd dreamed of being a hero, of running toward danger instead of away, and of the faces of the people he rescued, thankful he'd been there when they needed him and he hadn't shied away, but had done the right thing. Except he wasn't a hero.

He was the villain.

He was the man who broke into your home and looked into your most private places and took your treasures. The one who stole the ring your grandmother gave to your mother, that she passed down to you in turn on your wedding day. He took special things because fuck 'em, they were rich and it was all probably insured and he needed to buy food and a new coat for the kid each winter. But not everyone he robbed was rich. He wasn't Robin Hood. Just a hood. He was the one who took that feeling of safety and left in its place fear and vulnerability.

He'd never wanted to be this person. He'd wanted to be a boxer, a lifeguard, a good father and husband. But lives didn't work out the way you wanted. And he had a better talent for locks than anything else.

Rory picked up his boots and turned to go inside and dial 9-1-1. He figured he'd set the phone on the counter and leave. They'd trace the call and come eventually and find her. The child from the neighborhood who'd snuck into the yard with the biggest pool while the owners were away because it was hot and she wanted to have some fun and cool off. They'd find the gash in the back of her head that came from slipping and bashing her skull against the side of the pool and the blood. They'd find so much blood. But not his footprints. Those would dry in the sun and disappear. He'd leave no trace, except ... her lying on the patio instead of floating in the water, and a phone off the hook.

He glanced over his shoulder at the girl, wanting to tell her one more time how sorry he was that he wasn't a hero. He half expected to see that her head had turned to follow him with those dead eyes.

Instead, she was gone.

I left her right there ...

He sprinted back to the edge of the pool and searched for her under the surface.

She couldn't have fallen back in. She was dead. The water below was as clear as the day above. On the bottom of the pool, he could see a stone and one of his lock picks that had fallen out of his pocket, but nothing else under the water. No girl.

He stood there looking around the yard, wanting more than anything to catch a glimpse of her slipping over the high stucco wall, returning home.

She was gone.

It wasn't a dream. He'd gone in. His wet clothes were proof of it. He had touched her. Dragged her out. Covered her up. His aching lungs and painful breath were witness that she'd almost drowned him while he tried to give her his breath. She hadn't been a hallucination. Why else would he risk diving in?

The raking tool at the bottom wavered and distorted in the water reminding him, he wasn't done diving.

He dug in his back pocket and pulled out the dripping leather folder that held the rest of his burglary tools. He didn't want to be the kind of man who needed them. That was an easier idea than a reality, though. He didn't have much to fall back on. He simply didn't have much at all, except for these tools and what they got him. He stood, walked into the house.

He made his way through the darkened place to the front door and slipped into his boots before stepping outside onto the front walk. He pulled the door closed behind him until he heard the latch click. The front path led between blooming rhododendron bushes and a large, well-manicured green lawn. At the end of the walk, he reached the tall hedges bordering the property, separating it from the street beyond. He heard a siren wind up in the distance. There were *always* sirens in Boston.

He walked through the lattice archway onto the sidewalk and turned toward where they'd parked the car. He knew both it and Tod would be gone, but that way led also to the Green Line train and home. He would've called Gloria to come pick him up, but his cell phone was still in his pants pocket. He doubted a bowl of rice would fix it. It was dead as …

Around the corner, he spotted the car, parked where they'd left it. Tod hadn't ditched him. Maybe he was having a cigarette, waiting for the sound of sirens to get closer before driving away. Rory started to run, ready to apologize for the work he'd done on Tod's ribs. People did things they regretted under stress. He slowed. He wasn't sorry he'd tuned Tod's ribs—the guy had it coming—but nevertheless, he was glad his partner had waited for him. It was something.

Water dripped out of the tailpipe.

It dripped from the trunk and the taillights and out the cracks of the doors. It stained the asphalt dark underneath the car.

Everything in Rory said, *turn and walk away*. He stepped closer and leaned over to look in the passenger window.

Inside, Tod's hair flowed in an invisible current, his arms floating up at his sides. He was pale and his face was bloated. Water lapped at the tops of the windows.

Behind him, he heard the quick slap of bare, wet feet. Like a child running toward the edge of a pool, ready to dive in.

EXTINCTION THERAPY

1.

The view of the city from the hotel room window was spectacular. Spencer looked down on the reflecting pool behind the Christian Science Center dome and watched the people gathered around it enjoying a sunny day in the park, small and insignificant from his vantage. That was the greatest joy he took from height—the relation of beholder to beheld in its proper ratio. Whether from his office, his apartment, or this room, elevation served to reinforce his vision of where he stood in relation to the city: high above it all.

Walker beckoned him to the leather chaise. Reluctantly, he parted with the view and joined the man. If one wanted a guided meditation session with Dr. Miah Walker, one had to sign up for one of his expensive week-long retreats at SkinWalker Temple outside of Seattle. Or, alternatively, one could make a healthy donation to his foundation and put him up in a luxury hotel for the week. Walker had explained that he didn't normally arrange private meetings, but the personal endorsement of their mutual friend convinced him to make an exception in this instance. He'd also told him that a single session wasn't likely to have miraculous effect, though it would start him on the path toward overcoming his mental roadblocks. "If this is beneficial for you, I'd like to see you at my Dream Dance Retreat in the fall," he'd said after the initial interview. "It's very exclusive." Spencer agreed that if the initial session helped with his problem, then he'd come to Seattle in November for the retreat.

Dr. Walker's public bio advertised that he had both Navajo and Cherokee heritage, and had spent many years studying with tribal elders from a number of different North American tribes in both the U.S. and Canada. It explained that he'd learned from many shamen—including his grandfather who'd been a Code Talker in World War II—the ways of spirit healing. Spencer's private investigator found instead that Walker had come from an ethnically unaware family of Italian extraction in northern Utah, and that his actual grandfather had been an insurance salesman and 4F during the war. But the testimonials from certain vetted people who'd received direct therapy were compelling.

Spencer was a skeptic; he didn't buy into energy fields and chi and other New Age bullshit. But he suffered from a crippling hesitance, and Dr. Walker's technique, however unorthodox, was highly lauded by trusted friends.

He sat and reclined in the chair. Walker let his hand hover over Spencer's forehead as he started to chant in some language Spencer didn't recognize. Chances were, it was less likely to be Navajo than some made up glossolalia. Whatever it was, he didn't understand a word of it. Dr. Walker was supposed to be guiding him in a therapeutic visualization. He thought it'd be more effective if he could understand what the hell the man was saying. Still, Walker's baritone jibber jabber was relaxing. Other than a little relaxation, however, he didn't feel much of anything else and started to fear that he'd wasted a considerable amount of money. *What can it hurt? Spend a little money and see. If nothing happens, then I know. If something changes ... if this first session works out, it was money well spent and perhaps worth a trip to Seattle to do more.*

Then, he felt it.

It was just a tiny push at first and then a little harder, right in the center of his forehead, like Walker was pressing the tip of a finger against his skin. He resisted the urge to open his eyes. Walker had assured him that at no point during the session would he physically touch him. Anything the patient felt was the power of his spirit being channeled through healing hands. Spencer played along and thought of the endorsements from people he respected. People who said that Walker had unburdened their spirits and set them free into a world they'd never known was so ripe for their appetites.

The pressure on his forehead increased and began to feel hot, like Walker wasn't touching him with a finger but with the melted end of a candle. Spencer shifted in the chaise. Walker said, "Shh. Let your body go and become a being of pure thought."

When had he switched back to English?

"Be mind, be spirit, be the eternal consciousness that can travel through time. The self of your mind is energy and cannot be destroyed. Since Creation, it has existed and you have been traveling through the ages from body to body. You have already been there. Go back now." Spencer felt the wax finger burn and pierce his skull, probing deep into his brain and sending sharp spikes of hot pain through his whole body. He jerked up from where he lay and opened his eyes.

He looked around the dark, low-ceilinged room in which he found himself. The hotel penthouse high above the city with the comfortable chaise lounge and the R. Carlos Nakai flute music on the sound system was gone. A fire pit built close to a far wall sat unused, blackened char piled in the center. A few clay pots lined another wall and a blanket made of some kind of tanned and bleached hide was laid out with what looked like the remnants of a hastily abandoned supper. Through a doorway in a separate partitioned room, he could see the bare legs of a woman lying on her side on another treated animal skin. The bottom of her ass was visible through the door, and Spencer still felt a stirring in his abdomen. Discomfort and desire. Repulsion and longing.

He stood and, ignoring the woman lying still in the other room, walked toward a hanging cloth haloed with bright light like a rectangular eclipse. On the other side of it, he could hear the distant sounds of people. Shouts and chatter. Calls of panic and screams of terror. His anxiety rose. He hesitated. But then the voice of Dr. Walker came drifting down to him from above, saying, "You are a consciousness which has lived a thousand lifetimes. You have always been welcome and will always have a right to live whenever you choose."

Spencer rubbed at his eyes. When he opened them again, he was still standing in the low, primitive pit house staring at a cloth door separating him from the world beyond. He grabbed the tapestry, pulled it aside, and stepped up and out into the daylight.

2.

Doug walked along the bike path beside Cary listening to her chattering about the mess that waited for her at work. He listened, occasionally expressing his sympathies. "How *does* someone get fired from that lab?" Cary groaned, "Right?" and went on with her story while they moved around slower pedestrians and dodged bicyclists flying by in neon spandex racing gear imagining themselves in the Tour de France and not on a two-lane pedestrian path to the subway. Despite the discomfort of walking in the early summer heat in a suit—it was already seventy degrees and humid—their time together on the bike path and riding the subway in the morning and the evening were his favorite parts of the day. There was nothing to distract them from one another—not work (though they talked about it), not dinner or the dishes, or work they'd brought home. It was just the two of them in a bubble of togetherness where no obligation or chore could distract them from each other. So, he walked, sweating through his blazer and listened to his wife talk about the day ahead of her.

At the station, Doug held the door open for Cary. She smiled and drew a finger along his cheek as she slipped through, followed by two other people who didn't acknowledge him or say "thank you" for saving them the second it would have taken to let him follow his wife in instead of barging on through. The sound of a train arriving at the platform below sent several commuters rushing for the escalator, furiously digging in backpacks and briefcases for their fare cards, risking injury on the slick escalator stairs for the sake of catching this train instead of waiting five minutes for the next. Doug and Cary kept their normal pace, stepping to the right side of the escalator steps as people flowed past them. *What's the hurry?* He knew none of them were hurrying because they loved their jobs so much they couldn't stand to lose five minutes of the work day. Maybe a couple of them did. But he saw the faces around his office. He knew his colleagues came to work for the same reason he did: to earn a paycheck. His salary paid the rent and his student loans and allowed them a little money left over for fun. But after only a year as an associate in the firm, he realized he was merely a billing unit doing document review, and work for Baylor, Hansen and Aaron LLP was no more than a way to finance his real life. Being on time was merely a step taken to keep a job he tolerated. And five minutes was nothing that would cost him. Not as much as *he* billed for the firm.

Unlike him, Cary enjoyed what she did. Not so much that she was willing to cut their daily walk short by running for a train, though.

On the landing halfway down, they scanned their passes and the Lexan doors slid open, letting them through. The couple walked down another flight of stairs instead of taking the escalator. The departure warning bell dinged and the subway car doors slid closed. Watching a train leave, Doug always thought about those plastic canisters and vacuum tubes people used to use to send their bank deposits to the teller at the drive-through, before direct deposit and online banking meant he never went to a local branch to do anything more than get quarters for the laundry. He watched as the train pulled away leaving him and Cary and a few winded commuters who weren't quite fast enough standing on the platform waiting for the next train. The pre-recorded female voice of the Massachusetts Bay Transportation Authority above them announced that the next Red Line train to Braintree was now approaching. *Not even a five-minute wait,* he thought, feeling cheated at its early arrival. The train arrived, brakes screeching, cutting off their conversation. Together, they stepped into the car and took seats next to each other.

Cary pulled a book out of her bag and gave Doug a big smile. Her daily acknowledgment that she was not ignoring him, but was now going to read. It was too noisy aboard the train to keep trying to have a conversation. He nodded and put his earbuds in and rested his hand on her thigh. He leaned back, closed his eyes, and listened to Freddie's trumpet drown out the sounds of the subway. Before he knew it, Cary's hand patted the back of his to let him know they'd reached her stop. She was getting off to transfer to another line that would take her to the lab. He took out one of his ear buds and said, "Think about what you want to get for dinner."

She winked and put her finger beside her nose. "Not it! I picked last night." She leaned over and kissed him. "Off to the arena!"

"Fight well," he called after her as she stepped through the doors. They closed behind her and he was swept off to help move money from one rich person's bank account to another. Hardly the glorious career of dragon-slaying he'd envisioned in law school.

3.

Climbing the rock hewn steps out of the low house, he looked across the red sand and rock yard of the pueblos carved into the side of the cliff. The morning sun shone in his eyes and he raised a hand to shade them. A shrieking man rushed past, naked and bleeding. He stumbled and tripped and another man fell upon him, swinging a rock maul down on his face again and again until the man's head was bloody, muddy pulp. The man with the maul grinned with excitement at Spencer and held up the dripping tool in acknowledgment before returning to his victim.

The mud and wood roofs of the other pit houses smoked and smoldered as more men war-whooped and swung clubs and axes at people trying to escape. A woman crawled through the rocks, her intestine dragging out behind her like a wet tail. She wept and her head lolled as her blood dripped out of her mouth and her stomach, splashing in black beads onto the dirt. She stumbled on her hands and knees, falling on her face. Behind her, a man followed, his weapon hanging lazily at his side in a loose red fist. He grimaced as she pushed up, and kicked her in the back. She fell again, her breath heaving up a cloud of dust. She coughed and lay still, not dead, but waiting. Her tormentor obliged her. He began to bash her like his compatriot had done to the other man.

"What is this?" Spencer said. His words sounded foreign, but familiar all the same. He reached up and touched his mouth, shocked at having spoken in a language he'd never heard before. His unanswered question was lost in the cries for mercy and whoops of ecstatic savagery. He looked down at himself. The familiar paunch he hid beneath his tailored Gitman Bros. shirts was bare and significantly reduced. His gray-haired, fish-pale belly replaced with a flatter, hairless, tanned midsection. He moved and felt the body he inhabited. It was energetic and powerful. Young and beautiful and vicious. A woman ran up and fell against him, smearing her blood on his smooth belly and begging for mercy for herself and her children. Behind her, another man stopped and waited, staring at Spencer, waiting for his answer.

"Please stop! Please don't hurt my children!" she begged. Spencer grabbed her arms and pulled her to her feet. He looked into her dirty tear-streaked face and listened to her plead for mercy a moment longer. He spat in her eyes, shoving her back toward her pursuer. She screamed as the man caught her. "Why?" she screamed. Her pursuer answered with a stone knife.

Two men held another in place as a third beat the soles of his feet with a club. Beyond them, a group dismantled the roof of the largest pit house in the center of the development, casting aside mud-covered branches to expose the shallow, round hole dug out as a community gathering place. As fast as they could remove the roof, other men pitched the remains of their victims into the hole. Spencer's mind raced as he tried to absorb all that was happening around him. He stood in the center of a village being razed, heart pounding and short of breath with the excitement of it. He watched as people were torn from each other, from themselves, from the world and thrown into a mass grave to lay together forever in their silence. The people killing them screamed "Witch!" and "Devil!" Their words fell on the bodies like rain on rocks. The smell of slaughter flew on the breeze and slipped into his body with every breath. He inhaled the scents deeply, imagining ghosts seeking to escape the horror all around penetrating him, coming to live in his heart where he could love their dying forever.

The odor of blood baking in the dirt under the scorching sun made him feel dizzy and he turned from the mass grave. He stepped out of the heat into a pit house to find more men working, removing limb from body, flesh from limb, breaking bones against stone anvils before scorching the ends in a hearth fire. They worked in silence while the screaming outside continued. Shoving past him, two more men arrived bearing corpses. They sat down in the dirt to set to work performing the same processing ritual. "What are you waiting for?" one asked as he hewed a hunk of meat from a slender thigh. He cut it into two smaller pieces and shoved one in his mouth, blood running down his chin and dripping onto his bare chest. The men pointed and laughed at Spencer as he turned and rushed out of the house back into the light. He ran for the house in which he'd awoken.

Around him, the voice of Dr. Walker chanted in the strange language he still could and couldn't understand. He rushed through the familiar door to find the young woman he'd woken up with. She was bleeding from her head, but was breathing and alive. He picked up the maul that lay in the dirt next to her and hefted it. Its weight and shape and balance all felt so natural in his hand, though he couldn't remember ever in his life picking up a tool like it. Wood and stone, lashed together, primitive and perfect. He swung it once in the air, getting the feel.

Looking at the woman, he felt a stirring in his guts. A pressure under his balls excited him and he felt his cock fill with blood and push against the leather apron hanging from his waist. His breathing quickened. His heart raced. He could hear it beat in his ears, deadening all the sounds of chaos around him. This *is what I paid for!*

4.

Cary sent Doug a text letting him know that'd she'd be leaving the lab in another ten minutes. He knew it'd be more like twenty; it always took her longer to wrap up work than she anticipated. Though she possessed this self-awareness, she never adjusted her estimates to reflect it. Both of them factored that lag into her messages. They liked being able to joke about her magic power that made time pass half as quickly as it actually did. *Teach me, oh master. It'd be great for my billable hours,* Doug would say. Today, though, she got out of the lab exactly when she said she would. She reckoned that meant she'd end up skipping a train or two to meet her husband on the deck so they could ride the rest of the way home together. It was that or head back to her desk to goof off on the Internet for a while. She preferred waiting on the deck. Underground, without a signal, she could sit and read her book without the distractions of social media or another lab associate cornering her to gossip. Or, she thought, if she got into Downtown Crossing early enough, she could drop in to her favorite bookstore and browse for a bit. *The day can't get much better than that.*

EXTINCTION THERAPY

She headed for the bus that would take her downtown. As she approached the stop, a trolley pulled up, no waiting. She contemplated sending another text to let Doug know how her luck had come in, but decided it didn't matter. *As soon as I do, we'll get stuck in traffic.* Cary wasn't any more superstitious than she was timely, but she liked to hedge her bets. Worst case scenario thinking was something both she and Doug leaned toward. They were so often pleasantly surprised when things went better than anticipated, they felt like it made them a perfect couple.

5.

Dr. Walker handed Spencer a glass bottle of sparkling spring water, careful not to let go until he was certain the man had a good grip on it. Often, it took new travelers time to get their shaking under control. "The first time can be very unsettling," he said. "And thrilling."

Spencer was sweaty and wide eyed; possessed of that charge Dr. Walker had seen so many get in a place like Sacred Ridge or Barkol during the Dzungar conquest. He'd actually been much more receptive to the suggestion than most of the others. If this man possessed a hurdle to his fullest penitential, it was low. He was going to be someone truly magical if Walker could get him to undergo the therapy again. This session had taken up the day, and he'd had to forego lunch and shopping on Newbury Street. Given what the client was paying, though, it was worth it. And from what he could tell from the look in the man's eye, maybe doubly so. Spencer was shaken and looked worried, but if Walker was right about him—and he was *always* right—he had a new convert. A moneyed disciple who'd broaden the circle.

"You didn't tell me it would be … like *that*."

"The Sacred Ridge massacre is a truly special event. It's a chance for you to push yourself to the limits of your ability to comprehend your own potential. Like I told you when we began, however, a single session isn't usually enough to overcome the totality of your reticence. Every journey begins with a single step, right?"

Spencer finished the rest of the water and gasped. "Was it real?" he asked.

Dr. Walker cocked his head to the side and held out his hands, moving them up and down like a scale. "As real as your mind. As real as time or any of your perceptions of it. What matters is how you chose to live the experience. What you took from it."

Spencer smiled, showing his back teeth. Dr. Walker felt something change in the air at that man's grin. A charge like he had become lightning looking for something tall to strike.

He looked at his watch. "Jesus Christ! I've been here for—"

"The meditation takes place in real time. But as you've come to know firsthand, it's what we take from time that matters."

Spencer set the bottle on the table next to the sofa, stood, and straightened his tie, buttoning the front of his sport coat. "It *was* something special."

Walker gave the man the same big wolf smile that graced the back of his books. "So, I'll see you in November?"

"That's a guarantee."

"Excellent. You should know, in the Invitation Only Group, we're going somewhere far better than the Dream Dance Retreat. Bank on it."

Spencer laughed. "If it's anything like what I just did, I'll break the bank for it."

Of course you will. Walker led his client to the door of the suite, ushering him out into the world.

6.

Doug rushed out of his office. He'd gotten distracted and only half-heard the chirp of his phone when Cary sent him a text letting him know she was out of the lab on time. Actually, *on time*. By the time he noticed the green light on the device, a quarter hour had passed. He scribbled down the last three six-minute billing increments of the day on a notepad and vowed to do a proper job on his timesheet tomorrow. They weren't due until tomorrow anyway, and he was ahead on billables for the week. So, it could wait. He had time.

He grabbed his suit coat off the hook on the back of his door and hurried past his secretary's empty desk. She left every day at five like clockwork, unencumbered by time that had to be counted in tenths of an hour. Where he counted minutes, she counted days. Three more until Friday. One more until the weekend. Two more before it was time to come back to work. He envied her. With her seniority in the secretarial pool, she made more than he did as a second- year associate and had less stress. She didn't have to justify her time to the partners.

The elevator seemed to take forever, stopping at every floor to gather more and more people leaving work. Halfway down from the 18th Floor, it was too full, and when the doors opened, no one else could get on. The stop was just a delay in their descent. The air was hot and Doug began to sweat again. What had dried out in his air-conditioned office, was freshly moistened, and the scent of that morning's perspiration wafted up to his nose. He felt embarrassed and clutched his elbows to his side a little tighter, trying to contain his body odor. He'd probably end up taking a shower both before and after he and Cary went to the gym. She'd laugh, but he wouldn't be able to deal with it.

Outside, he hurried along the sidewalk, not running, but walking briskly enough to dart around other commuters. He didn't run for trains, but he'd run for Cary. He didn't want to leave her alone on the subway platform for too long. This time of year, it was hot as murder down there.

He scanned his fare card and hustled down the escalator to find a train waiting. A small flood of people disembarked and he fought against their tide to reach the car doors before they closed. The signal bell chimed and the doors closed. He slapped a hand against one and shouted, "Hey!" The MBTA operator looking out the window stared right through him. The operator rang the bell again and the train started to pull out of the station. The asshole only had to flip a switch to open the doors to let him on. It would've only taken a second.

Doug stepped back behind the yellow line as the increasing speed of the train buffeted him with wind. He checked his watch and sighed, hoping that Cary hadn't been waiting too long.

7.

The driver held the limousine door open, but Spencer told him that he'd like to walk home today and stalked off without waiting for a reply. The man's face showed an expression of concern for a second before returning to its professional blankness. Whether his boss wanted to walk a mile and a half back to his house wasn't any of his business. Spencer set off in the wrong direction, and his driver remained by the car, waiting for him to change his mind. But he was set. He walked around the corner, toward Back Bay Station.

He wanted to go underground.

Once there, it took him a few minutes to figure out how to pay the fare. He hadn't taken the T in adulthood, and while he knew they had replaced tokens several years ago, he had thought getting a ticket to ride would be as easy as handing a person in a booth a certain amount of cash, and them handing him back a card. The booth he approached was unoccupied and didn't look like anyone had worked in it in quite a long time. Standing off to the side of it was a bank of self-service machines. He approached one and made his way through the process on the touch screen, buying himself a month's pass, though he only intended to take this single experimental ride. He hadn't ridden the subway in decades and wasn't about to start regularly. But if this experiment was successful, perhaps he would make it a more occasional indulgence.

The people waiting behind him in line were anxious and one was outright rude, but he didn't care. The rabble could huff and puff all they wanted; he was still tingling from his experience in the pueblos. Or, the illusion of it.

It had seemed so real. So, present. He still felt the touch of the sun on his bare skin and the weight of a stone club in his hand.

Descending the escalator felt almost like stepping into a pit house. It was dark and humid and the smells were slightly similar, though different enough to spoil the illusion when he tried closing his eyes to imagine.

A train arrived before he could get the real lay of the station. He stepped on board along with the other commuters. It was crowded, and he almost fell when the train began to move, because he hadn't wanted to grab on to a pole or a strap. A woman caught him and helped steady him as the car moved faster. She smiled with crooked, yellow teeth. He thanked her and reached out to hold the pole. It was cool in his hand and felt like it was slick with the residue of hundreds—thousands—of previous riders who'd grabbed onto it before him. Despite his strong desire to let go and wipe his hand on a handkerchief, he held on. Falling on the floor would be worse. Being double indebted to the woman with the idiot smile would be the worst.

Anxiety started to build up in him. His heart beat faster and it felt harder to get a breath. He hadn't had a full panic attack since he was a boy, but he remembered them well. Spencer closed his eyes and imagined the odors of blood and smoke. He tried to pretend that the acrid stink of the subway car was the smell of a pit house fire. The movement under his feet dispelled his best attempts at recreating the illusion. He needed Dr. Walker to return to Sacred Ridge. But the Doctor had said the next meditation would be different. It would be something *special*. November was so far away.

He rode for several stops until the mechanical voice announced they were approaching Downtown Crossing. That felt far enough. This is where he wanted off. This was where he wanted to see how Dr. Walker's therapy had affected him.

8.

Cary hustled down the stairs of the station, a plastic bag of books slapping against her hip as she dug in her purse for her Charlie Card. She'd found a first edition of one of her favorites and had spent a little too much time lovingly admiring it before finally settling on used copies of two other books she could actually afford. Looking at her phone, she'd realized that Doug would likely already be on the platform looking for her. She'd explain she saw the copy of *The Blind Assassin*, and he'd understand—he knew that she "lost time" inside bookstores—but that wouldn't mean that he wouldn't be worried. She kind of loved his little panics. Still, she wanted to protect him from that kind of misplaced anxiety when she could.

She turned the corner to find the train pulling out of the station. People leaving the station slipped past her like water around a rock. She moved carefully toward the wall, where she could wait for them to pass and then get a look to see if Doug had gotten there ahead of her. If he hadn't, she'd sit on the bench and flip through her new used books. The half-finished novel in her purse would have to wait this evening while she flirted with her next lovers.

The last of the riders filed out of the station, leaving her momentarily alone on the platform. It wouldn't be long—likely seconds—before other commuters came down to wait for the next train, though they'd be fewer than when she first got there. Rush hour was almost over. She had lost so much time in the bookstore.

She walked to the bench and turned to sit. Out of the corner of her eye, she caught the image of a man at the far end of the platform. Too far down to have just arrived—he hadn't passed her. He must've gotten off the last train. He just stood staring at her. That familiar feeling crept into her bones. That feeling that this man's gaze wasn't the same kind of gaze she met whenever she went out. It was something different. Something that made her skin pimple and her scalp tighten. He had a weird vibe. *You're being paranoid,* she told herself, and sat down on the bench. *Vibes aren't reality.*

That the man was wearing a suit was no guarantee that he wasn't a creeper, she knew. But she also knew that men in suits had jobs and families to protect. As soon as someone else arrived on the platform, she'd be safe. He wouldn't try anything in front of a witness.

Cary cracked open the copy of *We Have Always Lived in the Castle,* but didn't read a word on the page. She kept her eye on the man, watching her.

⛤

9.

"Hey, there you are!" Cary started at the sound of Doug's voice and fumbled her book.

"Jesus Christ! Where did you come from?" She bent over to pick her book up off the floor, frustrated that she'd just bought it, and now it was getting filthy.

He shrugged. "Sorry. Asshole conductor wouldn't let me on. Instead of waiting, I went back up and hiked to this station."

"Meanie."

"Right? Anyway, you been waiting long?" She held up her Brattle Bookshop bag and he nodded. "I'm sweating like crazy and you didn't even miss me, did you?"

She shrugged and set the bag next to her on the bench. "Books." As if that was all that needed to be said about it.

The man at the end of the platform started to walk toward them. Cary felt her skin crawl again, but Doug was there. The stranger wouldn't do anything to her with Doug standing right here. He'd abide by The Man Code and not objectify another man's woman. Especially not one accompanied by a man *in a suit*. Men in suits did not do things to offend another member of their tribe. Men in suits were well-behaved around each other.

Except when they weren't.

"Excuse me," the man said. Cary thought he looked familiar close up, like she might have seen him before, but couldn't place where. He definitely wasn't an academic. He was a lawyer or a banker or something. Maybe she recognized him from something at Doug's firm.

Doug said, "Can I help you?"

"I was wondering if you knew how often these trains run. I missed the last one and have been waiting here for a while."

Cary knitted her brow. That was bullshit. He hadn't missed a thing. He'd been standing there the whole time. He got off the train she'd watched pull away. At least she thought he did. She supposed he could have been standing there longer than that. Waiting. No. That was ridiculous. Of course he hadn't been waiting like that. Waiting for them, instead of a train.

Doug looked at his watch. He looked at his wrist even when he wasn't wearing it. Another neurosis born of law school. "Shouldn't be long. This time of day, they run every ten minutes or so."

"Thank you." The man turned and walked a few paces in the direction he'd been standing before. He straightened his arm and checked a watch that even from a distance looked like it cost more than Doug and Cary made in a year. She started to whisper to Doug that the man hadn't missed anything. But she only got, "Hon, that guy…" before he turned and came toward them again.

10.

The way that bitch was looking at him, Spencer wanted to break her fucking skull open with a sharp stone and make her cuckold husband eat what was inside. He wanted to scrape her scalp off and make the faggot wear it. He wanted to do so many things. But he wouldn't. More people were appearing on the platform and he couldn't touch anyone without being caught. His indecision had cost him. The last vibrations of the massacre had worn off and he felt like himself again. Except, now he was underground with these people, instead of high above. Up in his office building. On the hill where his penthouse stood. He was down and debased with all of them.

"I'm sorry to bother you again," he said. He wasn't. "Can you tell me if one can walk to Cultivar from here?" The man's face clouded like the woman's, though instead of suspicion, it was confusion. He didn't know where Cultivar was. Looking at his cheap suit, of course he didn't.

The voice from the speaker above announced that the next train was arriving. Spencer felt the advance of air pushed out of the tunnel ahead of it begin to blow. A damp coppery smell carried along on the breeze.

The man raised his voice to compete with the rising drone of the train. "I suppose you could walk. But if you get on the next train and ride to the State Street exit, it's right there. It's just one stop."

"Thanks." Spencer took a step back. The woman stood and she and the man walked toward the yellow safety line at the edge of the platform. He wanted to shove her so much. Wanted to put his hands on her back and push hard, so she fell on the tracks. Maybe she'd be electrocuted by the third rail, but really he wanted to watch her cut apart by the wheels of the train. He wanted to smell the insides of her like the scent carried ahead of the train but… more. More pungent. More vibrant. More real.

He wanted more.

That was the point of the therapy: to free him from the reservations of ordinary people and be the true elevated being he was. Someone who not only controlled fortunes, but lives as well. He could decide whether this person lived or died. Whether her man mourned or joined her. But he wanted to do it with his hands instead of with a memo or a policy. Not with a pen or in a dream, but with his own hands.

The headlight of the train flashed in the tunnel. It was coming.

The woman looked over her shoulder in a panic. Spencer followed her eyes. She was looking at her shopping bag. She'd left it behind. The man turned and darted in front of Spencer to grab it. He snatched it up and turned to rejoin her at the front of the platform.

Spencer extended his leg, like a playground bully. The man's foot caught on his and he stumbled. The woman screamed and tried to catch him. Spencer watched, enrapt, hoping against hope that they become entangled and would both go over the edge. He gritted his teeth holding back the smile.

11.

Doug saw Cary lurching to catch him. Her hands grazed against him and he intuitively reached out to grab her, despite his conscious desire to push her out of harm's way. His body did what it wanted, not what his mind did, and he latched on to her. She slowed him and pulled, preventing him from going over the edge. She saved him.

He hit the platform, feeling the raised bumps of the yellow strip pushing painfully into his ribs and elbow. He heard screams from other people on the platform.

He saw the son of a bitch who'd tripped him smile.

He heard Cary shout, "No!"

But she'd saved him.

He felt the impact for only a split second.

12.

Cary tried to pull him back from the edge, but he was too heavy. He hit the floor and she screamed and the train hit his head with a thump she felt in his body more than heard and then she was screaming more and more. Her eyes flooded with panicked tears and her vision narrowed down to a dark tunnel in which there was nothing visible but her husband's caved in head lolling on his broken neck.

She tried to right his head, cradle him and wake him. The crackle of shattered bones in his neck vibrated through her hands and she almost dropped him in fear and revulsion. Doug's eyes rolled back in different directions from each other. His mouth fell open.

Hers did too. But of the two of them, only she screamed.

13.

Spencer watched the EMTs cover the man's body. The police had dragged the woman away. She was screaming hysterically about Doug—his name was Doug—being tripped by *THAT MAN!* She pointed at Spencer. Another policeman came to talk to him and Spencer handed him his business card. The policeman read it carefully before handing it back. He didn't need to be told that he was *the* Spencer Cronin of Cronin Global Investments. It was right there on the card. It was there in the policeman's mind. In his deference.

Of course, he'd be happy to give a statement, he told the policeman. "Though I don't know what to say. The man was running toward the end of the platform, and he stumbled. People should be more careful."

No one countered his observations. No one took the woman's side and accused him of tripping a man. No one wanted the full force of his fortune and power levied against them. They took him at his word, and never questioned why a man of his stature would be down in the tunnels with everyone else.

The EMTs lifted the gurney the dead man's—*Doug's*—body rested on and wheeled it away.

Spencer climbed up out of the subway station after it, and called his driver from his cell phone. He wanted to have a drink at Top of the Hub. He wanted to look down on the city and dream about November.

NO ONE WHO RUNS IS INNOCENT

[The artist's] only justification ... is to speak up, insofar as we can, for those who cannot do so.
—Albert Camus

Every wall is a door.
—Ralph Waldo Emerson

The television in the other room was so loud, Pepper couldn't concentrate on what he was drawing. His grandmother's hearing aids were dying even though she'd just charged them. They were three years old and they wouldn't hold a charge for longer than a couple of hours anymore, but she was trying to draw out every last drop of life in them. Pepper understood. Replacements were expensive and she probably didn't have enough in her account to get new ones until the next LibertyCare qualifying period. Still, instead of sitting closer, or even better, not watching TV at all, she cranked the volume. When it was one of her morning talk programs it was alright, he guessed. But then, commercials were always louder; they paid to be a higher volume so you couldn't ignore them as easily. Except this wasn't an ad. The President was on TV again and his broadcasts were even louder than the commercials. Louder than everything. They had to be. That was the law.

The President was talking about borders and terror and America and all the things that presidents talked about, but wasn't saying anything he hadn't repeated a thousand times before. It was the beginning of the work week and that meant it was time for the Monday Address to motivate the nation. He came on twice a week, steady as a heartbeat. And Grandma never turned it off, though no one else in the house could figure out why.

Pepper tried to tune it out, but couldn't. He closed his book, stuffed it in his backpack, and grabbing the last of his toast, ducked into the living room where Grandma Claudie sat. He kissed her on the cheek and said, "Love you, Mémé," into the hearing aid like a mic. She nodded and smiled, though he was sure she didn't hear. The dim red light on the side told him the damn thing was already dead. That's why she had the set cranked so high.

He slipped out the front door, unexpectedly finding his parents on the porch. Mémé had woken them early; typically, they wouldn't be up for another hour, but there they were. His dad was leaning against the railing, looking at his phone. Mom sat in the ratty wicker chair across from him holding a cup of coffee like its warmth was a precious, fragile thing she needed to protect. Her hands were thin and bony like the rest of her and warmth *was* precious. Even a little chill got deep into her and made her bones ache. Pepper knew her knuckles especially hurt in the cold. Like Dad's knees. It was cool yet this morning, too early for the sun to have risen up over the trees and warm them. But it was better out here in the shade than inside with the television.

"Headed out already? Isn't it early, mon vilain?"

Pepper blushed. He hated when she called him that. "Yes, Maman. I mean. It's not that early."

His father looked up from his phone. "I thought school was canceled this week because of ... what happened on the North Side."

His mother's mouth tightened at the mention of it and her lips went pale. She looked down into her coffee as if it contained answers why what happened the week before had. There were no answers. Not in the coffee or in the manifesto posted online before the government took it down. There weren't any answers in the faces of the people responsible or in the official reports on the news. Still, everyone looked for them where they could, because at least the search for answers provided order of some kind. Even if there was no coherent reason why, there was reason in *asking* why.

Pepper shrugged. His backpack clanked softly and he forced a little cough trying to conceal the sound. His father's brow furrowed and he opened his mouth to say something, but Pepper's mom put her hand on her husband's arm and he let the thought die in the back of his throat where he kept all the things he wanted to say, but didn't.

Marielle turned to her son and said, "Where *are* you headed this early?"

"I'm meeting Jack at the library. We're gonna work on the comic we've been talking about. The monster one."

His father sighed. He knew better. Still, he held it in. He took a drink of coffee and Pepper's mom said, "That your Thermos I hear in your bag? You have lunch in there too or do you need me to fix you something?"

The President's voice carried through the closed windows and Pepper told her he had something to eat even though he didn't because he didn't want her to have to go back inside. Not until it was over. The President said something about last week and Pepper coughed again, trying to avoid hearing him utter it, but the word emerged like a black blemish in the sky, hovering over them, at once weightless and heavier than any pile of debris from the collapsed side of a building where people were lucky enough to die right away instead of being lost in the rubble for days.

He said it.

Townsend.

Their town. The latest on the list.

"I'm good, Maman. Got everything I need."

"I'll bet you do," his father said. "What else is in that backpack?"

"Just art stuff, Papa. For the comic. See?" He turned so his father could see through the clear pack, knowing that his hoodie obscured everything except his sketchbook.

"Rayan!" Marielle set her cup on the table between them and stood. She rarely said her husband's full first name, and never outside of the house, though the porch was barely *out* of the house. In public, he was Ray, just like she was Mari. No one looked twice at Ray and Mari. They passed, as did Pepper, as long as they played it right. She smoothed down her son's thick, unruly hair, placing a warm palm against his cheek. Her fingers were still cold. He leaned into her hand and she kissed him on the forehead. "The *library*, mon vilain. Then home. Nowhere else, you hear me?"

"Where else would I go?'

"*Nowhere* else, love. Stick to the main streets. You promise." It wasn't a question.

"Library and home. Main streets. Got it."

"Promise."

"I *do*." Pepper glanced past his mother at his father. The man was looking at him with a mixture of understanding and concern. He knew Pepper had just lied to his mother. The boy could see it in his old man's eyes. But he kept Pepper's secrets, even if he didn't know them exactly. He knew his son, and he remembered being a boy his age.

"Be careful," Rayan said. "And home before curfew. *Way* before."

"I will, Papa. Nothing's going to happen."

His father laughed. It was humorless. Sad.

Pepper's mother kissed him on the forehead again and waved him off the porch. "Go now. Before I change my mind."

He bounded down the steps onto the sidewalk and down the block in the direction of the library. "I love you, Maman. Papa," he called over his shoulder. His parents watched him go, saying nothing to each other but thinking the same thing. *Be safe.*

Behind them, the President finished his address. "God bless you, and God bless the United States of America."

※

Pepper ran past the library, the soft clinking in his backpack brash to his ears, like a rhythm in time with his pounding footfalls. *Thump thump tink thump thump tink thump thump tink.* Bass and hi-hat. A beat for running. He knew he shouldn't rush, but couldn't help it. No one who runs is innocent. Not in adulthood, anyway. Or even adolescence. Unless they're exercising, grown up people don't run for anything but escape, self-preservation, or evasion. And often those categories overlapped. He wasn't dressed for jogging, but Pepper counted on his small stature and smooth face to give him the camouflage of nonage. Someone for whom running was still play. Though, these days, not even little kids ran much. Their parents held them close, fists wrapped too tight around little hands and wrists. Still, he didn't want to get caught out on the street with what he had in his bag. So, he propelled himself on at speed.

Of course, running made him look suspicious, but even if he could bring himself to walk, the backpack was shady enough on its own. While it was his school-issued clear shoulder bag, no one could see through to what the black hoodie he'd stuffed inside concealed — what he hadn't thought to muffle as well as cover. He'd hoped the sweatshirt would've deadened that sound, but hadn't thought to slip his cargo in the hoodie's sleeves or stuff something in between them so they wouldn't make a racket when he moved. Carelessly, he'd just shoved it all in, pulled the hoodie around so no one could see, and then jammed his pens and sketchbook in next to it all.

He thought of what he'd been drawing, a portrait of his grandmother. He'd illuminated her name, *Claudie Laliberté*, in embellished script in an arc over her head as if the image were advertising a concert she was giving, though she hadn't sung in years. He'd shown it to her and she smiled that smile of hers. The one that made her look like the arty girl she'd once been instead of the old woman she was now. She'd put her hand on his and pushed the book in toward his heart. Not rejecting it, but having seen enough. They all lived with memories that were more beautiful than their present lives. All but Pepper. He'd been born to this.

Behind the library, he took a hard left and ran into the alley. It wasn't like an alley in a big city, a knife-wide valley between towering edifices of glass and steel, but still, the town buildings blocked the morning sun and cast him into the shadows he craved. He knew there were still cameras in alleys, but they didn't track. Not like the ones in the street. These were fixed, mostly pointed at recessed doorways.

He ran past stinking Dumpsters and steel bulkhead doors that opened to subterranean storerooms. Green scaffolding on one side forced him to the other, and he leaped over a pile of discarded boxes with black painted words on the side declaring them GOVERNMENT SURPLUS and NOT FOR SALE, though everything in them eventually found its way to a market of one color or another. Whether the trade was money or something else, nothing was free, not even disaster relief.

Then, skidding to a stop at the far end of the alley, he saw it, rising up on the opposite side of the road ahead of him.

The wall.

It stood, monolithic and impassible, topped with coiling concertina wire. It was solid without a break for as far as he could see. Pepper knew where the main gate was, with its guards and spotlights and cameras. Far from where he stood. He looked both ways and quickly crossed the street. On the other side, he climbed the berm and stood on the flat shelf of earth at the base of the blank wall. Looking over his shoulder, he searched the buildings behind him for a face in the windows. One perhaps with a phone pressed to its ear and lips mouthing the words, *I see him. The East Sector. Come quickly.*

There was no one watching.

Pepper swung his backpack off his shoulders and unzipped it. The pull sliding down the teeth sounded like a tear in the very air around him. As if he could drag it all the way down from his head to the dirt and step through to the other side of the wall without opposition. Free to come and go as he pleased without anyone questioning why his father was named Rayan, or where he might be from with a last name like Nasri.

I was born here. I'm from the New England Territory. I'm American.
Yes, but where are you from? How did you get here?
It's French. My parents are French.

Never Algerian. "French" got him looks that amounted to being beheld like a thing only slightly out of the ordinary. A fancy object, not an alien one. White. "Algerian" would make them *those* immigrants, even though he was naturel Américain né. They'd say those words. "Anchor baby." "Chain migration." "Emergency Acts." And, "Let me see your papers."

He pulled his sweatshirt out of the bag and shrugged into it. He slipped his hands into a pair of gloves, then tied a bandana over his nose and mouth before pulling up his hood. While running was bad enough, *now* he truly looked suspect.

The rest of his cargo now visible through the clear pack, he dumped the contents onto the ground, picked up the first can, and broke off the lid. The plunger cap was pristine. He held it up, pressed down with his forefinger, and a jet of black sprayed out, sputtering and hissing. A little paint dripped down into the valve cup, but most was propelled true. He threw a long line up on the wall high over his head, followed it with another at an angle, and then down again to the dirt. He filled a space inside with a swoop and a straight line, then dropped the can and grabbed the next. Red. A circle and then another line, a glow resplendent as sunrise behind a mountain. Next. Blue. Cool water and clean. Another. Green. Like the grass that should've grown on the berm on which he stood — but they killed that with chemicals because this wasn't a park or a greenbelt. They didn't want people walking here. No one was supposed to get close to the wall.

Color after color he projected onto the barrier until it all began to take shape, resemble the image in his mind, his heart. The one he'd drawn in his sketchbook under the covers lit by his cellphone. He ducked and leaned, almost dancing with the hiss and stop of the spray paint. The smell of it blew back in his face, but it was the act of creation that made him feel lightheaded. His small human rebellion in the kingdom of deadly gods with rifles and badges and laws. Mon vilain. My villain. No villain! He was the creator of the world on the other side of this amalgam of streaks and colors, having opened the door for all to see. What *could* be. A better place, if only imagined, still possible.

The faint hum descending behind him was almost inaudible — would've been if it weren't for the pause he took to admire his work — but Pepper caught it, sent to him on the breeze. Small propellers and a muffled motor. He spun and sprayed paint in the direction of the sound. The drone shifted and the blast of the gun barrel at the end of its extended arm rang out in the quiet morning along with Pepper's scream of fear. The bullet streaked over his shoulder, so close to his cheek he could feel the heat of it, and slammed into the wall, sending a small hail of concrete shards into his back. But the boy's aim was true and the paint obscured the thing's camera. It pitched to one side before righting itself, the barrel twisting toward where he had been a second ago, but not aiming true. A voice erupted from the speaker on the side.

"Don't move! You're under arrest!"

Pepper swung the can at one of the small propellers and the thing veered off wildly to the right. He spun around and threw one more line up on the wall. His piece wasn't finished, but it had to be enough. He dropped the can, not yet spent, but incriminating along with the others on the berm, snatched up his pack and ran. He sprinted along the length of the wall, away from the gatehouse a half mile behind him and toward the town common with its trees and deeper shadows and cameras obscured by branches green with spring leaves yet to be trimmed.

He couldn't hear them, but he knew other drones would be responding soon. They were likely already overhead, following, filming, and waiting to descend.

He jumped off the rise into the street, making for another alley. As he ran, he slung the lighter, silent bag back onto his shoulder and pulled the hood down over his forehead as he ducked around more waste, pallets, abandoned pipes, and tarpaulin-covered shapes concealing what he couldn't begin to guess. He darted around and through and stopped in a recess in the wall, slamming his back against a windowless steel door. In the distance, he heard a siren. Far-off now. Getting closer.

He hazarded a glance up to see if there was a camera pointed at him. If there was, he couldn't see it. Still, this was no place to lose the bandana or hood.

His heart thundered in his slender ribcage. He breathed in short, rapid gasps. Sweat dripped into his eyes, and he knew if he emerged into the street now, blinking blind and breathless, he'd be caught. He looked like he'd been running. And no one who runs is innocent. Not in America.

Pepper closed his eyes and tried to take slower, deeper breaths. He imagined the country Maman and Papa had come to as children, their parents so proud to have landed in the place of their dreams, far from anyone shouting, "Sale race!" or "Les émigrés!" In the breath of time before alien registration and relocation and the walls. Pepper tried to project himself into the liminal moment of tolerance and welcoming in a land of plenty — plenty for you and me and everyone who dreamed of things like freedom and equality. He imagined Fourth of July parades with old men throwing taffy to children from paper floats and their fathers following in tiny cars, wearing fezzes like silly Ottoman jesters. The sound of fireworks cracking that made no one flinch or look for shelter, but instead to the sky with awe and delight. He imagined a place that hadn't existed in his lifetime. A place he only knew from Mémé's stories and the movies.

The place his painted doorway led.

The hum at the end of the alley ripped him out of the fantasy. Faint and distant, but deadly familiar. Another high-altitude sentry drone. He pressed back into the shallow alcove as far as he could, sucking in a breath, trying to become thinner. His backpack pushed against his shoulder blades and he wanted to shed it, throw it behind a dumpster and come back for it later. But he couldn't. It had his RFID chip in the strap. They'd scan it and know everything. His name, age, where he went to school. Where he lived and who his parents were. He shoved harder, crushing it, clenching his teeth, listening for the soft sound of the drone propellers to echo in the alleyway as it came closer.

It faded.

He hazarded a peek out. Clear. As far as he could see.

Pepper stepped out of the doorway and pulled off his bandana. He couldn't throw it away. They could collect his DNA from it, and he was in the registry. Instead, he pulled the bag off his back and stuffed it, along with his gloves, inside. He walked away from the door, resisting every urge in his body to run. Though he moved smoothly enough, it felt as if he was stumbling along, his limbs thrashing in exaggerated jerks and spasms. His muscles wanted to move with an urgent volition of their own. Self-preservation at war with itself. He breathed deep and walked as deliberately as he could. *Just keep it together. Stay calm and don't run.*

At the end of the alley, he swept nervous fingers through his hair, brushing the hood of his sweatshirt back to flop behind his neck before slinging the bag over a shoulder and jamming his hands in his pockets where no one could see how badly they shook. He turned right and walked calmly away from the East Sector. Pepper ambled along the sidewalk trying to look like a kid dawdling on his way to school. Though there was no school today.

A car sped past, lights flashing and siren screaming, and Pepper flinched but didn't freeze. The driver flew past him and he kept walking. A couple of men emerged from a café and craned their necks to see what the commotion was. "What is it?" one of them said. "Another attack?"

"I hope they hang 'em all on the fuckin' wall so everyone can see. We need to stop coddling — Hey!"

Pepper moved a little quicker, hoping to slip past them without being noticed. He'd taken a risk doing what he had in the early morning instead of sneaking out after dark. But the risks were even bigger at night. Using a light to see what he was doing would've meant the drones or guards found him before he had a chance to draw more than a single line.

"Hey kid, you comin' from that way? You see what's happening?"

Pepper stumbled as he slowed. His breath caught. He turned and shook his head. "Huh uh," he said. The men turned away from him now that he was useless. He was glad to be dismissed and moved on. He wanted to go home, but couldn't. Not so soon. What would he tell Maman and Papa? That he'd heard sirens and got scared and came home? It was the truth, however incomplete. But he wasn't away yet, and no matter how confident he felt in his story, he knew if he was followed home ... He pushed the thought down.

He turned again at the end of the block, heading for the library where he was supposed to be meeting Jack. He should at least get his pack scanned in or check out a book or something to make it look like he'd actually done what he'd said he was going to do. The library was nearly halfway to home, and he felt comforted at least that much when he saw it standing at the end of the street. He picked up his pace and trotted toward the building. He pulled the bag off his shoulders to scan it at the doors, and panic hit him as fresh as it had at the sound of a drone descending behind him. His sketchbook. The one with Mémé's portrait and her name written in it. Where was the fucking book?

Pepper yanked the zipper open and snatched his bandana and gloves out, dropping them on the sidewalk. He swept his hand through, feeling for the thing even though he could see there was nothing else in there. It was gone.

He'd upended the bag at the wall, spilling all the spray cans onto the berm. The sketchbook had to have fallen out with them. As soon as real people on the ground reached his painting and searched the spot, they'd find the book with his sketch of the painting he'd done on the wall and the portrait of his grandmother with her full name illuminated above. They'd *know* her. She was an immigrant. They'd know where she was registered to live and go to ask her how it was that a book with her picture in it came to be at the bottom of a pile of spray paint cans at the base of the sector wall, and that would be the last time he saw home, Maman, Papa, or Mémé. Because they'd know it was him. He'd *have* to tell them he did it, because the alternative was unthinkable.

He spun around and sprinted back the way he'd come, unconcerned with how guilty it made him look. He angled sharply into the alley and pushed himself as hard as he could, dodging the same obstacles as before, each one newly threatening to trip him, slow him, stop him before he could get back to the book. He was sweating and panting and his chest hurt at the effort mixed with terror.

At the end of the passageway, he skidded to a stop, clutching at the brick of the building beside him, and peered out across the street at the wall. Unlike before, it was no longer blank. The sun was higher and the day was brighter and his painting erupted from the grey façade with color. An open door, leading through to a verdant world with blue skies overhead and reflecting water at the bottom of a rolling hill. And in the center of it all, a tall tree topped with all the colors of life reflecting through its leaves. What up close seemed abstract, at a distance appeared so real Pepper felt like he could run through and escape. Just the way he'd hoped it'd look to everyone who came to work in these buildings or even just drove by. People would look out a window and see, if only for a single moment of a single day before it was power-washed and painted over, the doorway to a better place. And the passage, once opened to their minds, never to be closed again when they looked and saw the space where it had once been. All the ambition and hope of a boy in color and movement, indelible in memory. Whether or not they'd ever actually beheld such a place.

And at the bottom of it, a small tan rectangle, sitting at a tilt in the dirt, its true nature too distant to be known. But still he knew, because it was his.

He leaned out from behind the corner and looked for a drone or someone from the Department of Haven Integrity. He saw no one. The blind machine likely called back to base, the others looking for him throughout town — their operators confident he wouldn't be foolish enough to return here — he crept out of the alley. It took effort to stay upright. He badly wanted to hunch over and make himself small, like a mouse in the kitchen trying to avoid the housecat. Instead, he strode across the street and hustled up the berm to where his abandoned spray cans lay. He bent, picked up his sketchbook, and stuffed it hurriedly inside his sweatshirt. The book was stiff and wouldn't bend against the curve of his body. Its corners jutted out under his hoodie. Pepper pressed his arm tighter against it and turned to go.

The man that stood there was looking up at his painting, not at him. He hadn't seemed to notice Pepper at all until he said, "It's nice." Pepper didn't know what to say. Responding at that moment seemed as alien as … a future. "You like it?" the man asked.

"I … uh, I …"

The man nodded. He opened his coat, revealing a DHI badge clipped to his belt and a handgun in a black leather holster. He dug a cellphone out of his pants pocket and looked at the screen. He swiped the face of it with his finger and raised it up. Pepper flinched as if it was a gun barrel. "You mind?" The man said. "Step aside." He pointed at a spot in the street a couple of feet from where he stood. Pepper complied, feeling held as fast as if there were hands on him.

The man took a picture of the imaginary door. He looked at what he'd snapped for a second before replacing the phone in his pocket. He didn't let his coat fall closed again, but stood with a hand resting on the grip of his gun. "This your work?" he asked.

Pepper stood frozen, wanting to run as badly as he wanted to not be shot in the back. He looked at the asphalt.

"It's good. But, why a door? I mean, why a door leading *into* the Migrant Development? The door should be on the other side. Have you seen it in there?"

Pepper shook his head. "Have you seen it out here?"

The man smiled with half his mouth. He nodded. A tinge of humorless laughter rattled the man's speech like a shudder. "Yeah. All the same, better to be on this side of things, don't you agree?"

Pepper reluctantly nodded.

"Thought so." The man checked his watch and looked to his right, up toward the corner where he was parked. "Why didn't you run?"

"I did."

"Not far enough." He looked at his watch again, as if he hadn't reckoned the time correctly the first time. "My guess is you've got about thirty seconds to get off this block before my backup arrives and I have to pull this weapon. I know there's no school today, but I'm sure there's *somewhere* you should be. *Home*, perhaps."

"You aren't going to …"

"Twenty seconds."

"Thank you."

The man looked up and said, "Don't thank me. You aren't out of this yet."

He sprinted past the man into the alley and away. He cast a look over his shoulder and saw a black car pull up. The DHI agent pointed and the driver turned away, looking at the wall instead of into the alley.

Pepper ran.

The drone high overhead followed him all the way home.

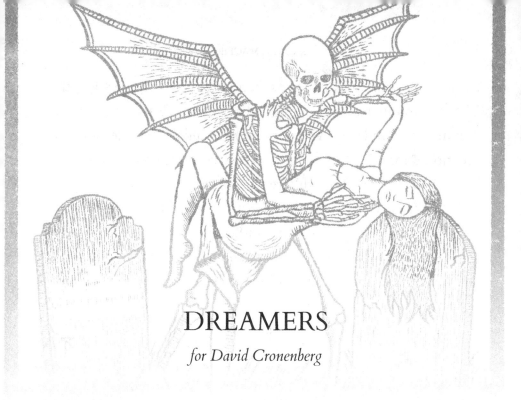

DREAMERS

for David Cronenberg

1.

He worked at the cuff securing his wrist. Without one free hand, he couldn't release the other restraints. What was it Carl Sagan had said? *If you want to make a pie from scratch, you must first invent the universe.* This wasn't as difficult as that. Before he could get out of this room, he had to get out of this bed, and in order to do that, all he had to accomplish was undoing a single buckle. Before *it* came back.

Might as well invent the universe.

The cuff holding his right arm in place was fastened with a simple strap and buckle. No lock or complicated mechanism to outsmart. Just the kind of something he'd manipulated a million times in his life, getting dressed or using the bathroom. A single buckle was all that stood between him and … not freedom exactly.

His neck hurt from craning it around and seeing wasn't helping anyway. The problem wasn't sight; it was reach. No amount of observation could make his wrist bend more or his fingers lengthen. These restraints had been designed for this very purpose—holding him in place—and there was nothing he could do to undermine their function. Not from his side of the transaction. He took a breath and decided to try something different.

Tucking his thumb as close to his palm as he could, he tried to slide his hand through the cuff. Without that digit, he imagined he could slip free with little effort, even though the strap across his chest and upper arms limited his movement, he only needed a few inches of motion. Once out of that, everything else would fall into place in easy sequence. Undo the chest restraint, move to his left arm, then his legs and ankles. And then, the floor and the door. But for a thumb, he would be free.

The door at the far end of the room opened. No sound of the slide of a key or clack of a deadbolt. He was immobilized; no need to bother with securing the room. He closed his eyes, tears fighting their way through the tight slit between his lids and escaping down the sides of his face. They caught in his hair, and he sympathized at them having been ensnared. Heavy footsteps approached. He dared not open his eyes, knowing what he would see. The smile. Those eyes. The knife.

The odor of decay settled on his face in a gentle, warm exhalation. His stomach cramped like it wanted to turn inside out. Another breath descended on his bare skin. This time, on his chest, as it turned its head to appraise the meat on the metal table. "Mr. Koenig. Shall we?" it said, low and gentle as if to assure him everything would be just fine.

He closed his eyes tighter as he felt the sharp edge of the knife tip lightly touch his belly just below his belly button. A hand followed it, holding his panicked belly steady as it drove the tip in and pulled up. With a sharp, hot stinging, he felt his skin and flesh separate. Warm blood flooded down his sides, running off his back onto the table. He tried to buck, throw off the hand and the blade, but his ruined stomach muscles wouldn't comply. The knife edge continued apace on its journey up his body, opening him like a garment bag.

Breathless, he tried to scream, instead letting out a whimper.

"Now, Mr. Koenig. What will that accomplish? Shhhhh." Like a parent calming a child having a nightmare, it patted his chest, before making the final cut and reaching deep inside of him. Fondling, feeling, caressing.

A nightmare.

He focused on his own hand. Slowly raising it, without resistance and drawing a palm down his face as if pulling away a shroud laid over him.

He sat up. Straps all gone. He got to his feet and felt the slide of his insides threatening to spill out onto his feet. He wiped again with a hand down his chest and belly and the line of severance ripped into him vanished.

It stood, staring at him, jagged mouth turned down in a scowl, its conjunctival gaze weeping redness. "Mr. Koenig?" The stink of its breath drifted to him. He turned and walked toward the door. "See you again soon," it said. He glanced over his shoulder at it. Long arms hanging at its sides, red knife tip dripping on the floor. It cocked its head and smiled like a gash. He drew another hand down his face, and when he opened his eyes again, it was gone.

Maxim Koenig walked through the door.

2.

The woman leaning over him winked as she detached the wires from the sensors stuck to his forehead. Her breath smelled like tea and honey. A man behind her was typing into a keyboard on a standing table beside the bed. He glanced over at Max and said, "Welcome back. Your readouts were all over the place. That one was pretty intense, yeah?"

Max nodded. His mouth and throat were dry. "A drink, please," he rasped. The woman disentangling him from the sensors leaned past him and retrieved a salmon-colored plastic cup from the steel rolling table opposite her. She aimed the straw toward his lips.

"The compound does make your mouth dry, doesn't it?" she said. "Sorry."

He sipped at the water like someone trying to burn the length of a cigarette in a single drag. She pulled the cup away and told him to take a breath, promising another drink once she removed the last of the leads. Her partner typed more, his fingers quietly clacking the keys.

The door at the far end of the observation room opened and in walked a silver-haired man in a white lab coat. Two younger people followed him in, each holding clipboards. He checked his hair as they passed the two-way mirror. He smiled and slid up beside the bed. "Hello Max. Given what we could see, that looked like considerably intense one."

"Yeah. It was a doozy."

"Was it the same dream?"

Maxim nodded. "The Corpse Surgeon." It felt like a small charge of electricity passed in a wave over his skin as he thought about what he'd just woken up from. The thing had been haunting him for nearly two decades. A spindly, cadaverous man with a scalpel and desire to plunge his spiderlike fingers into Maxim's insides.

One of the interns beside the man said, "You mean a coroner?"

"No. Mr. Koenig's recurring nightmare is of a living corpse who performs surgeries on him. Isn't that right?"

"Yes, Dr. Zeifman" Max said.

"And how did it go?"

"At first, it was the same. I was tied down and couldn't move. But then... I just... did things. I thought about my hand being free, and it was."

"Excellent. And this is your ..." He checked one of the intern's clipboards. "Third dose of the Lucidity Compound. Excellent."

"I just wiped it all away. Except ..."

The doctor and his wingmen stepped closer. "Yes?" he said.

"It ... the Corpse Surgeon—it seemed to realize what I was doing. It was there until the very end, watching."

"I see. Your dream experience differed as your took control?"

Max shook his head. The nurse removed the last of the wires connected to him and helped him sit up in bed, tucking a pillow behind his shoulders. He gestured for the water again, and she gave him another sip. "I guess. It was like it was *observing* me. Like you are now. Taking mental notes."

"Curious. Possible, I suppose, that's the influence of the clinical setting. Your subconscious recollected you were under observation and added that detail to your dream. It's an unsurprising development. Your nightmares are ..." he looked around the room, "already rooted in a clinical setting. That your sleeping mind would adapt is to be expected."

"It sure didn't feel like my subconscious. More like, *it* was figuring out how to ... adapt."

Zeifman turned to his intern and tapped the tablet, silently commanding her to record that feeling. "Well, Max, we anticipated that the process of moving you from passive to lucid dreamer would involve ... odd developments. Side-effects, perhaps, of the unconscious mind resisting having to cede control to an active dreamer. It *seemed* like your monster was plotting, when in reality it was emblematic of your dream state accepting the shift of power. You had control. In there," he said, tapping Maxim's temple, "that's threatening to the dreamed entity." He let out a quick sigh, straightened his back and added, "I think it all sounds very positive. You were able to purposefully engage with your recurring dream and change the narrative." He nodded at the woman at his bedside and added, "Once Mr. Koenig is certain to be clear of any sedative effects, please make sure to let me know.

"In the meantime, Max, I am heartened by your success here. I look forward to hearing a play-by-play about what you experienced, once you've fully awakened." The doctor turned and exited the room, his two followers on his heels.

Max looked at the woman still holding the water carafe and asked, "Do you think that's what it was? A shift of power?"

She smiled. "I don't know. But I agree it sounds like a good thing."

"Yeah," the researcher at the keyboard said. "It didn't try to come at you, right? Just stood there and watched you go?"

Max nodded.

The man grinned. "You were in control. You beat it."

"The Lucidity Compound beat it."

The woman put a light hand on his chest and his stomach clenched for a second. "The drug gave you the tools to stand up for yourself. *You're* the one in control, Max."

3.

Maxim sat in his room trying to focus on the book he'd downloaded. He read the same paragraph a third time, feeling as if he'd not forgotten the language as much as become interiorly deaf to it. He could see the words on the screen, but they weren't getting through. He closed the cover and set the device on the desk next to his chair. There was no bed in the room. He was only permitted to sleep in the observation room, like all the other volunteers, though, the drug—the Lucidity Compound—made him feel drowsy most of the next day after he received a dose. He would've liked to have a nap. At the same time, a nap brought with it the possibility of being sliced open by it again.

Over the years, he'd tried a half a dozen things to avoid dreaming. Prescription sleeping pills, Benadryl, alcohol, pot, and meditation. They all worked differently on his sleep, but not one touched his dreams. Most nights, he didn't remember his nocturnal adventures, but three or four times a month, it came to visit him. The Corpse Surgeon. Unlike any other nightmare he'd ever experienced, those dreams felt extra real. Almost as if he weren't dreaming at all, but existing in some other space parallel to this one. Though he always woke up without injury—*physical* injury—in his own bed.

When he'd seen the subway ad for the sleep study—RECURRING NIGHTMARES? YOU MIGHT BE ELIGIBLE TO PARTICIPATE IN OUR PAID STUDY—he figured it was worth a try. At the very least, he'd make some money. If he was going to have nightmares anyway, why not scan the code and apply? Lately, he'd been regretting that decision. The drug they gave him every few days made him feel nauseous. And his visits from the Corpse Surgeon were more frequent since getting it. Except today, he'd been able to take control and wipe it all away. Next time, maybe he could do it faster. Before it cut him open.

He wiped his moist palms on his pajama pants and stood to look out the window. Though the view was nice enough, there wasn't much going on. A parking lot and a fence separating it from an expansive wetland. A crane lived out there, but he only saw it occasionally. Otherwise, it was still. And dull. Like everyone else, he'd agreed to live in the research facility for the six-week duration of the experimental trial. The team insisted it was for his safety. Their drug, while shown to be safe in lab animals, had yet to be tested on humans and they wanted to have all their participants onsite, in case. Of what, he didn't know. Between what they were paying for the study and the potential of stopping his chronic nightmares, he was happy to be ... not a prisoner ... *sequestered*.

Signing up for the study, he'd agreed to have no outside contact. He hadn't counted on that meaning not having access to his phone, laptop, or even a tablet. His cellphone was secured in another room, where a volunteer accessed it twice a day to check messages and texts for emergencies. They said it was to ensure no leaks of their proprietary research. He imagined everyone, like him, had signed an NDA, but then, again, they were paying him enough to cover six months of rent on the outside. Fine. Only the preloaded e-reader they provided was allowed with him in the room. No horror or crime. Nothing that might influence his dreams. He read some literary nonsense about a brother and sister in love with each other out on the prairie and jerked off when he could get the image of them out of his head.

A loud sound in the hallway outside startled him out of his reverie. Excited voices. Not everyone was adjusting to the isolation well. A lot of the participants played board games and hung out in a common room watching television. It felt a little too much like a different kind of institutional setting he'd had experience with before. *I'm not crazy, I just have a problem with my drea—*

Another shout, followed by heavy footsteps hurriedly thudding past his door. *Gotta be Monty again. Guy's got a bug up his ass, I swear.* He crossed the small room, pulled open the door, and stuck his head out.

A pair of men in blue scrubs, hands extended out in front of them, stood between Maxim and whoever it was they wanted to calm down. He rose up on his tiptoes to see.

"Just put it down, Misty. We're all friends here," one called out.

Misty Hill! He'd laughed when she introduced herself in their introductions circle, thinking it was a joke—or a porn name. She deadpan stared at him and he felt like an asshole. She was nice and was one of the few people who liked to talk to him about things other than the study and their nightmares. He hoped to see her again on the outside.

The men ordered her to "put it down" again. Maxim couldn't see whatever it was she needed to let go of, but reckoned it wasn't a feather duster. He stepped out into the hall, joining a small group of other test subjects who'd gathered to watch the spectacle.

"What's going on?" he asked.

Gunnar Nilsson jutted his chin at the woman and said, "Fucking Misty's gone off her nut."

Maxim leaned to the side to get a look around the hulking Niveau Institute security officers to see. Misty stood with her left arm extended, palm out. In her right hand, something narrow and familiar glinted under the fluorescent lights.

"Don't come any closer! I mean it! I just need to get this off of me."

Maxim wondered what she meant. She was wearing the same PJs they all were and while—

She raised her arm and drew the scalpel across her forehead at the hairline. Blood spilled down her face. She pulled the knife from left to right along the length of her brow with a shriek that echoed through the facility like a siren. Maxim's mouth hung open silently and he blinked, trying to banish the image from his eyes, while Gunnar and Paula beside him shouted. The security men closed on her, one lunging for Misty's scalpel hand while the other tried to pin her other arm to her body. She disappeared for a moment in the mass of bodies, until one of them screamed and staggered back holding a hand to the bloody flap dangling off his face. She slashed at the other and slid the sharp edge along his forearm, opening him up. He joined the chorus of wails filling the hall, redness wetly gushing from him, splashing with hers and his partner's on the floor in a growing pool. He let go and staggered back, gripping his arm. He slipped and his head hit the floor, sounding like someone dropped a wooden ball. He stopped screaming.

"Get it off me!" She reached up again and with a hand gripping at her hair, cut along the length of her forehead again. She pulled and lifted a portion of her scalp away from her skull. A fast curtain of red descended down her face and she blinked and sputtered and staggered against a wall, continuing to saw at her skin. She tore and pulled and slid down the wall sitting in a pool of her blood, crying and choking and ripping at her slippery skin. A trio of unbloodied men appeared behind Maxim, shoving him into Paula and Gunnar as they passed.

She tried to slash at them but was growing weak as her blood cascaded down her face, staining her purple pajamas glistening black. They tried to haul her up, but she was wet and slipped out of their grasp, flopping on the floor, banging her head against the slick tiles. Another slipped and fell after her. She lashed out at him and Maxim lost the sense of whose body and limbs belonged to whom.

All their blood was communal.

An alarm in the building sounded, making his ears ring. Shouts of "Get them to their rooms," and "The fuck out of here," floated under the repeating buzzer and more orderlies and security arrived. A tight grip settled on Maxim's arms and he was whipped away, thrown back toward his room. He fell through the doorway as it slammed behind him. A deadbolt clacking shut.

Sequestered.

4.

"Mr. Koenig, would you like to talk about what you witnessed yesterday?" The study counselor regarded him with a neutral look. Surely, she'd been having sessions with Misty as well. Knew her. They were all supposed to talk about their dreams, for the record and their well-being. At least that's what they told him at the start. So how could she be so … unaffected.

"What I witnessed?"

"Yes."

He shifted, flannel pants catching at the seat fabric. "What I *saw* was someone I knew fucking skinning themselves. What am I supposed to say about that? How it made me *feel?*"

She blinked. "That's a good place to start."

"It made me feel like I want to get the fuck out of here." He looked at the door behind him, knowing on the other side waited the man who'd brought him from his room to the counselor's office. Standing sentry with a can of pepper spray on his belt until it was time to escort him back.

"I understand the impulse, Max. You agreed to the residential provision of the study, and—"

"I didn't agree to *this*." He gestured toward the closed door. "To watching someone rip her fuckin' scalp off!" Without realizing, he started to rise out of his seat. The counselor gently gestured for him to relax, waving at him to sit. It made him feel ever more agitated. He stood. "You *know* she had nightmares about ripping her hair out. So, why the fuck would she do *that* to herself?" he shouted. "What are you people doing to us?"

"Mr. Koenig, please sit down so we can talk—"

"I am fucking done talking. Fuck your 'study' and fuck the 'residential provision. I didn't agree to be a prisoner. I'm leaving." He turned and took a step toward the door. The counselor pressed a button on her desk. The door ahead of him clacked.

"Mr. Koenig, I am doing this for your own good. You need to sit down and calm yourself before things get out of hand." She gestured again toward the chair he'd vacated. "Please."

"Are you fucking kidding me?" He turned. "Unlock it. UNLOCK IT!"

The cellphone on her desk buzzed once. She pressed the button on her desk again and the door behind him unlocked. Maxim yanked it open before she could change her mind and lock him in again. He felt the heavy thud in the center of his chest before his eyes registered what might've delivered it. He struggled to catch his breath as he staggered backwards, deeper into the counselor's office. Faintly, behind him, he heard her say, "Take him to the dream center." Hands fell on him, gripping his arms and legs. He felt his body lifted off the floor and whisked away as he struggled to breathe. He tried to writhe out of their grip, tried to protest. The fluorescent lights in the hallway ceiling passed above him like glowing white lines on a bright highway. His head swam and his head fell back. Following, upside down, Dr. Zeifman strode behind.

The men carrying him, deposited Maxim roughly on the bed in

which he'd slept for the last week and a half. He weakly tried to roll over and out, but they pulled him back into place. His mind suddenly cleared as he felt the first cuff close around his wrist. Then his ankles and other wrists. "No," he shouted, thrashing at the restraints. "Don't! I won't go, I promise. I'll do anything you say! Please don't do this! Don't tie me down."

Dr. Zeifman appeared beside him. "Mr. Koenig. Please try to calm yourself. You are not in a nightmare, but this is for your own good."

"Fuck you!"

Zeifman turned to the woman who always hooked him up to the machine leads and said, "Give him fifteen milligrams of midazolam and then start him on a ketafol chaser. Hook him up. I'll be back in…" he checked his watch. "An hour to establish his fourth dose of the Compound."

Maxim thrashed. "No! No! I want out of here. Let me go!"

"Will that take him off the schedule?" the technician asked.

"No. He's due to get it tomorrow anyway. A 24-hour bump won't have an effect on the results." The doctor glanced at Maxim. "If you calm down everything will be much easier, Mr. Koenig."

"I revoke consent. Yeah! I revoke my consent to participate in this study. You have to let me go. If you give me anything, it'll be assault and you'll all go to jail." Maxim frantically searched the faces of the people in the room, looking for a single expression of appropriate concern or even simple agreement. The people surrounding him went on with their tasks as if he hadn't said a word. "Do you hear me? You can't perform medical experiments without consent. I want out of here, now. You'll be hearing from my—OW!"

The needle slid into his right thigh as he looked left at Dr. Zeifman. A wave of dizziness and disconnection washed over him. The room blurred and he felt as though he was going, after all. "Zei … ffff. Do … not … cons …

5.

He stared at the swinging doors knowing he should turn and walk away, seek instead whatever world existed outside, if any. Something moved him forward. He felt compelled to push through.

I'm in control. I am.

The affirmation didn't lower his arm or still his step as he entered the operating theater. Bare and stark as always; it was not yet reddened with his spilled life. The steel autopsy table stood next to a metal rolling tray of gleaming instruments and... the Corpse Surgeon beside it all. "Closer," it said, curing a long finger, beckoning him. Its voice was broken glass grinding with a resonant deep bass below, almost as if there were two voices speaking in concert, one comforting, the other the sound of suffering. Its breath drifted across the room to him.

"I'm fine right here." Maxim glanced back to assure himself the doors behind hadn't vanished in silent dream logic, replaced with a blank wall. They remained.

"Please." It took a step toward him.

Maxim stood his ground. *I can wipe it all away, like clearing a whiteboard.* "I don't want to."

It tilted its head, looking at Maxim with an expression approaching sympathy. Its reddened, bulbous eyes considering him with almost sad pity. It said, "Max, I invite you to talk." A viscous line of saliva slid out of its mouth as it uttered his name.

Maxim almost laughed. That it wanted to talk was absurd. His belly twitched at the memory of its knife. Its hands. He watched its sinewy body for a sign it might lunge. It seemed at rest and stood out of reach of its tools, though not by much. "What do we have to talk about?"

"Our relationship."

"We don't have 'a relationship.'"

Its thin slash of a mouth curled up all the way to an ear, lips cracking and weeping red as they stretched. It bent an arm and stared at its own hand. "What a thing to say after how often I've been inside you. Touching your heart."

"That's not intimacy! It's a violation."

It nodded. "Complicated, isn't it."

"Not from where I stand."

The Corpse Surgeon lowered its hand and looked at him again. The smile faded, and a hint of its cruelty played in its eyes. It said, "You rarely stand when we're together."

Maxim took a step back.

It reached out. "Please listen. I'm … I'm afraid."

"What are *you* fucking afraid of?"

"What's happening to you. Out there." It pointed to the doors behind him. I can't protect you from… that."

"Protect me? You cut me open."

"To hold your heart. Max."

"Stop saying my name. Stop it!"

It cast its gaze at the floor. "I am the barrier holding back the flood. I am—"

"The monster that's been torturing me my whole life!"

"The coherence of incomprehensible pain. I am what stands between you and the thing that would destroy you. Without me, you are naked in the thresher of memory."

The muscles at the back of Maxim's neck tightened. He didn't want to think about it. Wounds from his past crept at the margins of his thoughts waiting to be opened like…

"So, you're my protector now? And what am I to you?"

"You are everything. Without you, *I* do not exist."

"I don't want you to exist. I want you gone!"

It held out its rawboned hands, fingers splayed out. "You'll get your wish soon enough. When they kill you, we'll all be gone forever. Your memories along with us both."

"They're trying to help me. Help me escape you."

Its laugh was a box of broken glass tumbling along a drumhead. It thudded in his chest and made his stomach sour. The Corpse Surgeon's gaping mouth drooled freely, splattering the floor with grey wetness. It drew the back of a hand across its chin and flung the dull slaver away. "You are a lab rat with an open skull waiting to be harvested. They'll dissect your brain to see where and how the Lucidity Compound found a home and write up the results before throwing your cadaver in an incinerator to be forgotten ash."

The mention of the Compound was an intersection of nightmare and reality that frightened him worse than the autopsy table and scalpels. It cocked its head quizzically at him again. "You wonder how I know. Of course, I know. The Compound was made to bring me to the surface. Make *me* live behind your eyes instead of deep in the palace of your repressed thoughts. It is the mechanism by which I will become the driver, leaving you a passenger deep in *my* mind. Observing all, helpless to stop what I do."

"Bullshit!"

"What do you think happened to Misty Hill? She of the lovely locks who feared most of all losing … her … top. Her exchange was inchoate, and she awoke to a nightmare."

"You don't *want* to be in control?"

"Don't you listen, dear boy. I am what you created to protect you from the darkness deep inside. The focus of fear not midnight fumblings and liquor-scented threats of retribution if you make a sound. I hold your heart so nothing else can touch it. What am I if you are lost? A demon without a purpose. The idle damned in a stale Hell."

"I don't ... what do we do?"

It held out a hand. Maxim stepped closer. He hesitated. The Corpse Surgeon didn't snatch at him, but waited. He reached out. The Surgeon's hand closed around his, cold and dead—a loose suit of skin that might pull right off with a strong tug. "Good boy." It guided him toward the table and the tray of instruments, picked a scalpel off the table, and pressed the tool into his palm. "*We* can't do anything. It's all up to you."

"What can I do?"

"You must wake up."

6.

"Wake up. Wake up," the voice hissed at him as he slid from the grey twilight into bright white. The light stung his eyes and his head pounded and in front of him a shadow whispered, "Wake up."

He shook his head trying to clear away the fog. Nausea swelled and subsided. A pair of cool hands slipped behind his back and pulled him upright. "We have to go. Do you hear me? We have to get out of here, right now. My partner will be back any minute with the doctor."

"What ... I ..." He blinked and the face of woman who'd been his sleep companion for the last few weeks came into focus, framed in tight black hair. She looked at him with kind, but urgent, dark eyes.

"I was supposed to give you another round of sedatives before they come back with the net dose of the Compound, but I brought you out instead. And if you're serious about wanting out of here, we have to get moving. Now." She helped him swing his legs off the bed, holding him behind the knees. For a moment he felt off balance, ready to fall, then he found himself. He steadied a hand against the mattress before pushing off onto uncertain feet. He stood, wobbly but upright. The cold of the floor infiltrated through his no-slip socks. She guided him toward the door. Everything was dizzy, like waking up still drunk.

"Why ... are you ..."

"I took this job to help people. Not watch them cut their own faces off and bite people's throats out."

"Wait. What? When did—"

"No time," she said softly. She shoved a bundle of clothes at him. Not his. Scrubs. "Get dressed. My car's right outside, but we won't make it anywhere if you don't look like you're one of us."

He stripped out of the pajamas, embarrassed by his feeble nudity, and stepped into the blue hospital clothes. She slid a pair of rubber sandals on his feet and opened the door. "Don't say anything. Just stay close behind me." She stepped out into the hallway and marched toward the secure door separating the patient wing from the rest of the Niveau Institute for Dream Studies. She swiped her badge and the light on the lock turned red. A low buzzer sounded audible failure. She glanced at him, wide eyed and a bead of sweat forming on her upper lip. She swiped again. The light turned green, and a click echoed in the hall. She pulled the door open and held it as Maxim shambled through.

She led him into a side stairwell. The world swooned as he stood on the high landing looking down. She said, "It's okay. I've got you." She held his elbow and they descended together. At the bottom, she pushed the bar to open the door and peered out. "We're good. Come on." She hurried out onto the ground floor.

In the plant lined hall, they passed offices and paintings on the walls and the waiting room where he'd first registered for the study. Several people waited inside and he wanted to run into the center of them and scream for them to get away before they were—sequestered—taken prisoner. She pulled at him when his step faltered. "You have to go to the media. Tell them what's being done here."

"Why not you?" he managed as she pulled him out the automatic sliding doors into the parking lot.

She stopped and looked him in the eye. "People will listen to you. If I try to come out as a whistleblower, they'll ruin me. No one will believe me. But you. You can bring it all down. Tell everyone what they did to you."

"Come with me. Verify."

She shook her head. "I can't. They know where I live. Where my kids go to school. Where my parents are. They know everything and can get to everyone I love." She clicked her key fob and a car a dozen yards away gently beeped.

"And I've got nobody."

"You have to do it fast. The rest of the subjects, the people in that waiting room. They're all depending on you." She opened the passenger door and gently guided him with a hand as he slid in.

"I've got nobody."

She ran around the car and climbed in behind the wheel. The engine purred to life and she pulled out of the parking space she'd backed into without looking. A long angry horn sounded. She raised a hand in quick, dismissive apology and tore off. He looked behind them waiting to see security guards come racing out of the building, jump into cars, and speed after them. She slowed for the stop sign at the exit, but rolled through. He saw someone help a child out of a car in the lot before disappearing.

He turned and leaned back against the seat. Head swimming, still full of fog. He closed his eyes.

Just a minute's rest. So tired.

7.

He looked down at the mess. Red and glistening wetly in the light of the bedside lamp. He watched his hand reach forward and shove aside intestine and organs while his other sliced a long tear in the woman's diaphragm.

No!

He watched as his hand set the paring knife beside her body and then returned to pull the rent in her body wider. Her wide, dark eyes stared at him. He saw a silhouette of himself reflected in them. His hands plunged into to her and disappeared. He felt nothing.

Please stop!

His voice rattled in his throat like gravel. "I wish you could feel this."

And he didn't know whether the speaker meant him or her.

It's a dream. A nightmare. I'm asleep and must wake up and this is all a dream it can't be real. It can't!

"Hush, Max." his voice replied. "Be still and see with me."

PAREIDOLIA

It's a trick the mind plays. Lying in bed at night, staring at the pattern the streetlights make on the ceiling, and seeing a man in a wide-brimmed hat or the Virgin Mary in the center of an MRI brain scan when the doctor is trying to point to the tumor killing your mother. So, when he saw the first face in the side of the plowed snow drift, he dismissed it as an illusion of light and a mind that seeks patterns where there are none. And outside, there were plenty of snowdrifts in which to see faces.

Winter had come on late and hard, and the plows shoved it up as best they could on the side of the road until they stood taller than the stop signs. Because of the oil and other chemicals from gasoline exhaust, road salts, and whatever else spilled on the road, they were filthy and toxic. The snow couldn't be dumped into the Charles or the Harbor, and there simply wasn't anywhere in the greater metro area to haul it off to, so the drifts remained, growing higher with each storm until there was nowhere for the kids waiting for the school bus to stand except in the street or blindly behind them.

Cold weather seemed to arrive later every year, but when the nor'easters swept in toward the middle of February, it felt like winter had come all at once. An unrelenting nine feet of snow fell in six weeks, and the piles grew ever taller, darkening with streaked grime until they resembled miniature simulacra of the great peaks in the Himalayas, jagged black rock ridges jutting from snow-swept glaciers. Everest in the Trader Joe's lot, K2 by the Dunkin over near Brattle and Church. They only looked pristine after a fresh snowfall and only briefly at that.

When he saw the first one, he'd been scrambling aside to let a couple and their baby stroller pass in the narrowly plowed sidewalk channel. He climbed onto a low drift and found himself looking into the placid face of a frozen woman. In the early morning light, a shadow fell, so her eyes, nose, lips, and chin seemed so very obvious. He pulled his sculptor's thumb and loop and ribbon tools out of his bag and began tracing around the edges of indent and bulge, stripping off his gloves so he could feel his tools, refining what he thought he saw until it was undeniably there.

She seemed to frown at him less with annoyance than concern, he thought. As if she wanted him to put his gloves back on, climb down off of a filthy snowdrift, and not be late for class. He glanced at his watch.

Shit.

His students would have left by now, and his advisor was going to be pissed about another missed class. The graduate teaching assistantship was the only way he could afford this MFA. If he lost that, he was fucked.

He carefully descended the slope and shrugged deeper into his coat to ward off the chill he only now noticed had slipped inside with him like a cozy lover with icy feet. It occurred to him he ought to take a picture of his work. Something for his socials. He snapped a few shots and stuck his phone back in his pocket. A bus roared up to the stop with a grey belch of exhaust. Its hydraulics shrieked as it "knelt" for disembarking passengers stepping down onto treacherous ground. He boarded and rode to Porter Square, where he went down away from the soiled snowbanks into the grimy puddles and tracks of other underground commuters. Waiting for the T, he reviewed his pictures. The sculpture was good. One of the best he'd done, he thought. Very lifelike.

⛧

He scrolled through the comments on his Pixta app, marveling at the compliments he received for a spur-of-the-moment dalliance with a pile of snow. Single word exclamations like, INCREDIBLE! and WOW! weren't what he envied. When someone posted that the face haunted them or that it made them want to know her, whoever she is, he felt at once elated and deflated. His actual work didn't elicit anything like those kinds of comments from his professors. He chased that feeling of creative admiration like a child after a lost balloon. This piece was exactly that. Ephemeral and gone as the audience floated away to the next thing.

Anonymess: Too bad it's going to melt. LOL

Tremor_NOahhh: wish there was a way to save it

Komoda: SO ZEN!

He'd shown his advisor the pictures that afternoon while apologizing for missing his class. Her response had been, "You had time to do that, but not be on time?"

"The buses were all running late," he lied. "I did it while waiting."

She skeptically accepted his story, admonishing him to call next time the T was running off schedule. Then, as a final kick in the soul, she critiqued the piece, telling him while it was technically proficient, he should be striving for much more, not playing in snowdrifts. "Can you put it on a stand? Does it fit the theme of," she paused, closing her eyes that infuriating way she did as she mentally called up the words from his artist statement, "the artificiality of mass-produced experience and the deadening of participatory ritual?" The fact that she was right hurt the worst. If he was going to have his thesis show ready in the spring, he was far behind where he needed to be, and this dalliance did nothing to move him closer toward that goal. But when he saw that woman's face in the snow, nothing seemed to matter as much as her, not grading papers or working in his studio. Nothing had been in his mind except her.

He kept scrolling his post, searching for new interactions. A few commenters accused him of Photoshopping or using A.I. to create the image, but shots at different angles seemed to satisfy most of them that it was real. As he looked, a new comment appeared on the screen like a gut punch. A user named MonikaAtomika wrote,

OMG! she looks like my sister who died last year!

He'd felt a little in love with this woman in the ice, wanting her to be real so he could know that beautiful, sad face would persist longer than a season. A muse of flesh and blood out there, who he might someday meet. He'd dismissed the thought as a fantasy, but she *did* exist. Or used to. He told himself it was probably just wishful thinking from someone who missed her sister and wanted to see a familiar face in his work, the same way he'd seen a vague face-like pattern in snow and brought her likeness out of it. *A* likeness; not hers.

He clicked through to Monika's profile to search for the unnamed sister, to see the resemblance for himself. Her feed was mostly food shots and selfies in different dressing room mirrors—Monika seemed to have a thing for jumpsuits and sticking her tongue out. Then, he found it. A picture of the woman flashing peace fingers outside the Middle East club. A selfie with her at the Pit in Harvard Square. Another of her in a heavy coat with an ice cream cone on the sidewalk in front of Toscanini's, a broad smile on her face, her tongue protruding like her sister's. The similarity *was* strong. Scrolling back to the pic at the Pit, he switched between Pixta and the phone's camera app, comparing faces. Both had the same slender jawline leading gracefully to a pointed chin. High forehead above almond-shaped eyes framed with carefully sculpted arching eyebrows. She had a prominent but elegant nose that ended in a gentle scooped upturn. She and his snow woman could be ... sisters.

He scrolled until Monika finally tagged her. Gillian. She didn't have any socials he could find. Just Gillian living in the moment, occasionally captured in an image eating ice cream, going to a show. He tried searching up "Gillian Cambridge death." Too many results. He added "MA" and tried again. Fewer hits, and none that seemed right. Either wrong picture or wrong age. Reluctantly, he gave up. But not before taking a screenshot of a somewhat pensive-looking Gillian staring straight into the camera. Monika's caption: "I miss you."

☆

His hands ached from breaking the newly cast sculpture from its mold. Staring at the thing, he wanted to smash it, but it was long past the time for that. He should've taken a hammer to the mold or wadded up the clay sculpture and started over. Instead, he looked at an extravagantly expensive hunk of stainless steel that would break him long before he made a dent in it. On the floor in front of him, Steamboat Willie hung crucified on a ship's wheel holding a cross-topped orb—a globus cruciger symbolizing his dominion over the world—in one minstrel-gloved hand while in the other, he clutched a child's heart. He knew his advisor was going to hate it. It was too on the nose. It didn't help his case that the Steamboat version of Mickey was in practically *everything* the undergrad art students had made since it entered the public domain. But he was desperate and had a lot left to do before the show. Messiah Mouse would have to do.

He sighed and locked up his studio early. *Go home, get some rest, and start fresh tomorrow.* He had another piece molded and ready to pour that was probably just as uninspired, but better to sleep on it than do shit work because he was off his game and forcing it.

The wind outside bit. He plunged his hands into his pockets, shrugged deeper into his coat, and forged ahead. More snow had fallen while he was working and he should've gone home hours ago. But he'd had the forge time booked.

Fuck you, Mickey!

Turning a corner, some toy dog in a little plaid coat and tiny booties skidded on the ice in front of him, yapping and snarling as it tried to skirt around him. A woman further up the sidewalk rushing toward him shouted, "Grabbim!" He ducked to scoop the dog up, but the vicious little monster snapped at him with its sharp needle teeth before darting between his legs, its trailing leash painfully whipping one of his shins as it snaked past his legs. The woman barreled past, ripping out a "Thanks fah nothin'," as she rushed by. He slipped, trying not to collide with her, and tipped backward into a bush. Fresh snow fell into the back of his collar, sliding down his back like a frigid snake.

"Fuuuck!"

He pushed out of the hedge and brushed himself off. "Crazy bi—" His breath stalled at the sight across the street. The spectral figure froze him in place. He wanted to look away, run away, but he couldn't. He was transfixed by its stare. Another snowdrift with an unmistakable face looking at *him*.

He crossed toward it. A car horn blared, and he scrambled in the slushy salt grit toward the drift, trying not to get mowed down in the street by a bombardier cabbie. The figure faded into the mound, less present as if backing away the closer he came. "No, come back!" he said, dragging his fingers around the snow, finding the face he'd seen. Eyes reemerged from the pile and apprehended him, leaving him feeling both seen and seized. He kept working until it fully emerged. This time, a man's face stared back at him. Square jawed and sharp angled in contrast to the soft girlish features he'd sculpted a couple of days earlier.

Pulling his phone out of his pocket to get pictures, he caught a glimpse of the time. Over an hour had passed without him noticing. He couldn't remember the last time he'd been *that* in the zone. Years, maybe. It was intoxicating.

With shivering hands and numb fingers, he took pictures from every angle, finally ending with a masked selfie next to it for scale. The piece was magnificent. He despaired afresh at the realization he couldn't mold or cast this. It was as fleeting as the breeze that suddenly cut into him again as if it had been held back while he worked and then let loose like a held breath.

More work with nothing to show for it.

Like everything he did.

He forced himself to move on and head home. At least he could put it online. Though pictures didn't do either piece justice.

⛧

His phone kept blowing up. Every time he set it down, it chirped immediately with new notifications. Despite having thought a second earlier *I need to get up and make dinner,* he picked it up again and scrolled to the new praise populating his replies.

Boden_Says: its earie how lifelike this is like hes my dad lowkey judging me

wheezybreezy: what an amazing artist you are! Jealous!

BeatHoof: Bruh! This is straight up witchcraft! You summoning demons and shit! LOL!

A small but persistent voice from deep in that ever-doubting part of him whispered he should drop out of school and ride this wave. "What wave?" he mumbled. Two pieces, neither of which he could display in a gallery, let alone *sell,* were barely a ripple. *And* it was almost March; the snow would be leaving before long, and with it, his muses.

His phone chirped with its direct message tone.

LennyCollinsWBC5 wants to contact you. Accept. Deny.

"The hell?" he whispered as he opened the D.M.

Good afternoon, "Katastropher." I'm a reporter for Channel 5 News, and I'd like to talk to you about your work and inspiration as part of a piece about people dealing with the winter weather. Please DM me so I can get in touch and get a comment for our broadcast later this week.

"Holy shit!" A reporter wanted to talk to him about his work. *And not that Mickey Mouse bullshit; your* real *work,* his doubt whispered.

This could be it. This is the break he'd been looking for. If he could convince her to give him a whole segment, who knew what might come his way? This was what he'd been working toward. A chance to break out of group shows and student art gallery exhibits no one but other students visited. What if a gallery owner saw him? What if?

You need more. They're out there. He filled a musette bag with sculpting tools and headed out, barely remembering his coat and gloves. At the door, he lurched back inside, snatching his cell phone off the sofa, the DM still open and unanswered.

"Give me a minute, Lenny!"

⛧

He prowled around the city for hours, looking at piles of snow, searching for the patterns his mind would reshape into something recognizable. A ghostly portrait emerging from a frozen limbo. Nothing appeared. The only faces he saw belonged to red-cheeked commuters rushing to get out of the cold before the biting air did more than give them a flush. Despairing, he ducked into a black-walled corner bar called The Plough and Stars. Inside was small and noisy, but warm. He commandeered an empty stool and nodded at the middle-aged woman behind the bar. She came over and asked what he wanted. He ordered a beer. She asked if he wanted food too. His stomach rumbled at the thought of a burger and fries, but he could barely afford bar prices for a drink. Deflated, he shook his head and said, "Just the PBR, please."

"Comin' right up, hon." She turned away and pulled a can out of a cooler below the bar. She popped the tab and set it and a glass in front of him. He lifted the can and took a long drink. His phone vibrated in his pocket. He ignored it. No point in working himself up again. One drink, he promised himself, then he'd go home and get some sleep. Then, tomorrow, go back to the studio and do *real* work instead of chasing ghosts.

After his third, he finally kept his promise to himself, settled up, and stood unsteadily from the barstool. He left the best tip he could manage and stepped back out into the dark. After warming up for an hour or so and thinning his blood, the cold bit harder. He shrugged deeper into his coat and marched off toward the T.

Under a streetlamp, she spied him, catching his eye with a flirty side glance and smile. He stood, staring for a full minute before reaching into his bag for his tools. "There you are," he said, approaching her slowly, careful not to send the wrong signal. "I've been looking everywhere for you."

⭒

Lenny Collins's voice had a touch of vocal fry from years of reporting. She told him on the phone that she didn't do an art beat and had reached out just for the winter blues piece, "But your work is something else. That last one especially. I want to do the segment. I think we can easily fill three minutes on 'Snow Banksy." He couldn't help grinning like a fool on the other end of the line. That single comment on Pixta that had sent him soaring making the doubting voice speak louder and more insistently: *this is your shot!* So, he'd DM'd her with the new pictures and username as a pitch. She bit. The only problem was she insisted he hide his actual identity to really lean into the pun title of the segment. It'll sell. Without an agent, he wasn't sure how he could parlay this into bigger and better, but he'd figure it out. First steps first. In any case, it was a better brand than "Katastropher."

He left his apartment in his best mysterious artist cosplay, including a spray paint respirator mask, despite not being a stencil street artist. He arrived at the sculpt ready to fine-tune it if needed—sharpen anything that might've melted or pack in some new snow and rebuild. It was as fresh as the night he'd carved it. The woman in the drift looked at him as he slid up behind her. Like his first, something about her made him wish he could meet the real person.

His phone vibrated in his pocket. "What's up, Lenny?" he answered. She'd *insisted* he call her Lenny.

"Change of plans. I want to do the segment over by your other piece. The one of the guy, Michael."

"But this one's better. And newer! This is the one that—"

"Trust me S.B." He felt lightheaded when she called him S.B. "This'll be better. Tell me where you are and I'll send a MyRyde driver."

"Nah, s'cool. It's just a couple of blocks up. I'll be there in a minute." She said, "excellent," and hung up. "Wait! Michael?" he asked the dead line.

He walked as fast as he could on the snowpack in his Chuck Taylors without slipping and falling on his ass. Dressed in art drag, he was freezing in a hoodie and camo cargo pants instead of his heavy winter coat. He rounded the corner and his heart beat a little faster at the sight of the news truck in the distance up ahead. He quickened his step and started practicing his act under his breath. As he came closer, his excitement muted as it all started to look wrong.

There were new things around the drift. Items left behind, surrounding it like one of those roadside memorials. A cross with a wreath of plastic flowers had been stuck in the snow along with a few other offerings: a toy bicycle and miniature artificial Christmas tree were stuck in the snow next to a framed picture of a young man. The man he'd sculpted.

Lenny and her cameraman climbed out of the van. She stared

right in with, "So I figured we'd get a shot of you next to the piece before pulling back to reveal," she gestured with black-gloved fingers splayed, "all of this! Then I'll ask you what it was that made you want to do memorial pieces."

"What?"

"Memorial pieces for these three people."

"Three!" He turned and looked at the offerings left under his carving.

"Well, yes. Gillian Florez, this man, Michael Landry, and Lorinda Taylor."

He shook his head. "I don't know what you're talking about."

Lenny frowned with an expression that said call me Lenny was about to change to Ms. Collins. She tucked a fallen dreadlock over her ear and subtly nodded to her cameraman that he ought to start rolling. "All three of these people died in the last twelve months. Gillian Florez was found drowned in the Charles River last April, Mike Landry was killed on his bicycle in a hit-and-run in July, and Lorinda Taylor's body was discovered in a Dumpster behind the Plough and Stars six weeks ago. How did you select these people to memorialize? Do you know any of them before they died?"

His hands went numb as he struggled to process what she was saying. Realizing the light on the news camera was on, he fumbled with his respirator mask, trying to fix it into place. "I... I didn't know them. But..." he looked at her, wanting help. By the look in Lenny's eyes, none was forthcoming. "I wanted to make a statement about how life is, uh, ephemeral. I used to work in metal—steel mostly—but it's inauthentic. This will only last a while. Like us," he bluffed. His stomach cramped as he waited to see if she'd buy his bullshit and roll with it. The look in her eye told him she'd come out to do a puff piece, but thought now she might've landed a whale.

"Did you talk to their families ahead of time to let them know you had planned this art project or to ask even permission to use their likenesses at the places they died?"

Run! Delete your socials and go back to school. Forget all of this. Save yourself. Instead, he said, "No. I, uh, understand it might be hard for them, but winter is a fleeting season—they all are, I guess—but with warmer weather on the way, I don't have the time to ask permission."

"*Don't* have time? You intend to do more of these, I take it. Will you involve those people's families in the process or continue with a guerilla-style approach, Mr. Derderian?"

RUN!

"I uh, I..." He looked at his feet. "Could we stop for a minute?"

The cameraman peeked out from behind his eyepiece, asking a silent question. She nodded and he lowered the camera.

"How do you know my name?"

She cocked her head and, with a smirk, said, "You're not a difficult person to find, Kris."

※

He snapped awake in bed, sweating, head aching, room spinning. The sunlight piercing through the curtains hurt almost as much as the insistent knocking at his door. He hadn't planned on polishing off an entire bottle of whiskey the night before, but how often does one get to celebrate being exposed on the news as a freak? And now, it sounded like not only had his chickens come home to roost but that they'd forgotten their key and were trying to break down the door.

He rolled onto his side, trying to slide out from under the covers, but they stuck to his flop sweat moistened legs and he dragged them halfway off the bed as he slunk out. The knocking continued. He shouted, "Gimme a minute," and held a shaking hand to his head. Upright, his stomach threatened revolt. That bottle had definitely been a bad idea. But not as bad as the one to trust Lenny Collins. To dream of the future.

It was a struggle to get into a pair of sweatpants, but he managed without falling over. Shrugging into a hoodie, he looked through his peephole at whoever was banging on the door. A pair of men in suits stood on the other side. He called through the closed door, "What do you want?"

"We'd like to speak to you, Mr. Derderian," one of them said, holding a gold police badge in front of the fisheye lens. The urge to vomit swelled and reluctantly subsided.

"You got a warrant?"

"Do we *need* to get one? We only want to talk."

He unlocked the door and slowly pulled it open. He hadn't realized how he must smell, but the face of the second suited man told him all he needed to know about the subject. He stepped back to let them in. They lingered in the doorway, not entering, like vampires. *Why not?* "Please, come in." They slipped inside with practiced ease, entering the space quickly and positioning themselves to ensure he couldn't "try anything funny," as he imagined them saying. He didn't have it in him to try anything at all, funny or otherwise. "Mind if I sit down?"

The taller one said sure and gestured toward the sofa as if he was not the guest in this apartment. "I'm Detective Braddock. This is Detective Dixon. We're here to talk to you about your art." The way Braddock said "art," he might as well have been naming an actual pile of shit in the middle of the carpet.

Kris fell onto the sofa limply as Braddock took a seat opposite him in the worn Ikea Poang chair acquired off the sidewalk one

Allston Christmas. Dixon stood behind him. Or was it the other way around? He had already forgotten which was which. The seated one—Dixon, he guessed since his voice seemed different—said, "Do you go to The Plough and Stars often?"

"No, I... wait. How'd you know I was there?"

The detective smiled. "I could say I didn't. But I did. Since your portrait of Lorinda Taylor was near where her body was found, I figured I'd ask around. The bartender recognized you. You're a bad tipper, Mr. Derderian." The man didn't ask if he could call him Kris.

"I already told Lenn—Ms. Collins, everything I know."

The other detective said, "Tell us too. We came all this way."

He let out a breath, smelled alcohol hovering around his head, and said, "I didn't know any of these people. I was bored and waiting for the bus, and I saw this face in the snow."

"Saw a face?"

"Yeah, like, you know, that face on the moon and shit. Random shit that looks like a person. So, I sculpted around what I saw to make it into an actual face. It was random."

"A coincidence," Braddock declared.

"Yeah."

Dixon added, "Three coincidences. In a row."

"Y'know, When you say it like that."

"What? It sounds as bad as it seems from where we're sitting?"

He nodded. "I guess so."

"Walk us through it. Tell us how you *'found'* each face and where."

"First one—"

"Gillian Florez."

"The first one, was at the bus stop, like I said. Just looked up and saw it."

"Her."

"What?"

Dixon frowned. "She's a her, not an it."

"Whatever. The second face in the snow. It was in a snow pile." He rushed his words, not wanting to let the detective interrupt him again and catch him in some linguistic trap. "The guy's likeness, whatever his name was, I found after some lady shoved me over chasing after her ratdog. I looked up and *it* was just there. So, I made another sculpture. And then, this Lorinda person's face I found after getting a couple of drinks at *The Plough and Stars.* I'd been looking around the city all fucking day trying to find a drift with a face in it. I was kind of drunk and—"

"You're a heavy drinker." It was not a question.

He felt nauseous. "I'm *not,* actually."

"Despite appearances."

"Anyway, I was looking for someone to carve so I could convince that reporter to do a whole piece on just me." He regretted saying "*someone* to carve" as soon as the words fell out his mouth like dead pieces of meat. Too late to take them back. There they were.

Braddock leaned forward in the chair. Those curvy Ikea rocking chairs had a tendency to slide out from underneath the sitter if you leaned forward too far. He didn't warn the detective. Let him figure it out on his own. The man said, "Why?"

"What? Why do you think? I'm an art student with a mountain of debt and nothing to show for it except a bunch of bullshit nobody wants to buy." He looked around at the various pieces he'd created over the years, collecting dust on shelves and leaning against walls. "Why? Because I wanted to be famous, successful artist, and somebody called me 'Snow Banksy' on Pixta and I thought, fuck it! Why not lean into it if it gets me some exposure." He stood to get a glass of water. Braddock rose abruptly along with him, his hands at his sides, a bit forward as if ready to grapple. "Water. I just want to get a glass of water. I'm fuckin' hungover as shit."

Braddock nodded and Dixon went to the kitchen to fill a glass from the tap. Kris figured it was better to sit down than get shot for trying to get a Polar out of the fridge and have it mistaken for a gun or something. The detective returned and handed him the glass. The water was room temp and flat. He gulped it down anyway. The men asked him a few more questions about where he was and who he was with and if he could prove any of it. It all made his head ache, but he showed them a bunch of selfies and emails and texts. Braddock finally declared, "That's all we have for now."

For now.

"We'll be in touch."

"Yeah, sure. Don't be a stranger, okay?" Kris said.

The detective stared at him with a coldness he felt deep in his bones. A revealed contempt kept hidden behind a mask of aloofness until that moment. "Kid, I'm pretty sure you didn't kill any of these people. Good for you. But I think you know more than you're letting on. Let me tell you, going on T.V. like that gets noticed by more than just murder cops. If someone thought you were a rat or maybe you just couldn't keep your fuckin' mouth shut because you wanted to be the hipster Sylvia Brown on Xitter or whatever, they might come looking to ask you some questions too, Krisander Derderian of the very-easy-to-search name."

The men left him standing in his doorway with an entirely new terror rolling around in his poisoned gut. He shut the door behind them and ran to the bathroom to throw up.

He filled the cardboard box with sculpting tools and sketchbooks and a few odd pieces of his that would fit, knowing he'd have to get a friend with a car to come back later and help him with the bigger projects. A university police officer watched him pack from the studio doorway, blocking his exit in case, what, he tried to make a run for it with someone else's crucible tongs? His advisor had said in her email that his was a "temporary suspension" pending review by the department chair and administration, but it felt final enough. They sent a fuckin' cop to see him out. He finished up and turned toward the exit. The man stepped aside to let him through.

No one talked to him or even made eye contact as he slunk through the hallways of the Ciaramella Building, his humiliation in full effect. That girl, Ania, the one he'd drunkenly made out with at a Halloween party, looked at him like she always knew he was a piece of shit. Maybe he was.

With the heavy box in his arms, the UPD officer led him to the elevator and rode to the ground floor with him. The guy even held the door for him as he stepped out into the white, glaring day. Full service. He blinked in the light, blind. His sunglasses were in his coat pocket, but there was nowhere to set his box down to get them without it getting covered in snow and soaked. He squinted against the daylight as he made his way toward the T. He could make it a couple of blocks to get underground.

He stared at the sidewalk ahead, only glancing up to try to see if it was safe to cross the street, idly wondering if it was even worth raising his eyes. He noticed it in a drift near the corner. A hint of a cheekbone and ear. He looked away and continued up the sidewalk. A few more steps and he had to hustle out of the way to sidestep a trio of people heading somewhere three abreast on the newly plowed sidewalk. It looked at him from a pile in between a trash can and a bicycle rack. A high forehead and big eyes. He gritted his teeth and moved on again.

At the entrance to the T stop, he had to shuffle the box to one side to see the steps ahead. He lost his grip and it tumbled out of his hands, spilling its contents in a splay of creative tools and created work. A final indignity that made him choke with a stifled sob as he chose whether to collect his things or just keep moving on without them. A person stopped to ask if he needed a hand. "Nah, I'm good, thanks," he said to the figure already moving on after "N—."

On his hands and knees, he scrambled all of his things together, putting them back in the banker's box with less care than before. All that mattered was getting home. He'd likely throw everything out once he had a moment to reflect. And there, in front of him, it stared. Straight out from a low pile of grey and gritty snow. Insistent. Unrelenting. He dug his fingers into the oily, rough snow and began clearing away everything that wasn't chin and cheek and nose until it emerged. The face of a child. Terrified and terrifying, he sat back at the look of it.

His phone let out a shriek, followed a half second later by a similar sound from dozens of other cell phones around him carried by people passing by without looking down at the man kneeling in the grime. People pulled their devices from pockets and purses, if not already staring at them. He glanced at his own cell.

AMBER Alert

An Amber Alert has been issued for 7 year old Sadie Clarke taken this morning at 11:00 a.m. on Beacon Street in Cambridge, MA. She is 4 feet, 80 pounds, blond hair, brown eyes, last seen wearing a pink winter overcoat, Paw Patrol tee shirt, and pink pajama pants. Suspect is a white male, age 40-50, 5'10" 180 pounds with dark hair and glasses driving a white Kia Rio.

A photo followed.

"No," slipped from his mouth like thick saliva, slow and hanging. "Why?" He closed the alert and jammed his phone into his pocket before tearing at the face with raw, aching fingers until there was nothing recognizable of it left before anyone else could see what he'd done.

☆

He lay in bed, shivering, knees pulled up to his chest. That girl's face lingered in his eyes like the afterimage of a bright flash. Hovering in the middle of his vision, she haunted him. They all did. He wanted to forget their names, but they were all there, like the face of the child seared in his retinas. He didn't dare search her name to see if there was a follow-up for the phone alert. He knew she was dead. *All* of them were.

It's not your fault, he kept telling himself. All of them were gone *before* he pulled them out of the snow. The last one—Sadie—she had to have been missing for hours at least. How long does it take to process and issue one of those alerts? He thought about looking it up but chose to stay curled up under the covers instead. No point. Stay in bed. Sleep forever. Of course, he couldn't stay there forever. They had to be writing the letter dismissing him from the program that very minute if it hadn't been done and sent already. Once they kicked him out of the program and fired him from teaching, his stipend would stop. Even *with* that money, he could barely afford food after paying rent and utilities for a third-floor studio in the city. Eventually a Notice to Quit and an eviction summons would join other letters jammed in his mailbox. He couldn't even stay there until the snow melted. It was barely March, and sometimes it snowed as late as April. Eventually—before next month's rent was due, in fact—

he'd run out of ramen and coffee and gummies and all the other things he depended on to get through the day.

And then what?

Go home, he reckoned. What else was there? Move back in with his mom and dad and listen to them lecture him about art school and employability and responsibility and adulthood until he couldn't take it anymore.

And *then* what?

He rolled over. There was no "and then what." This was it. He'd taken his shot and come out of it looking like a creep and a fool, without an MFA, but with so much debt, he knew he'd never be free from under it.

His phone rang. He let it go to voicemail. There was no one he wanted to talk to. And anyone who wanted to talk to him wasn't on his side anyway. Another hard lesson learned. He pulled the covers over his head.

And there ...

He shoved the covers away with kicking feet and thrashing arms and yelled "No!" into the empty room, loud enough to draw the neighbors ire from downstairs. The sheets landed in a heap and he tried not to look, but couldn't help himself. Just a pile of white cloth that needed cleaning a month ago or more. That's all.

An eyelid.

A brow.

Nose.

Mouth.

And chin.

He climbed out of bed, gathered up the sheets, threw them in the closet, and slammed the door. "I won't. You can't make me. I don't want to know and you can't fucking make me." He slumped to his knees and sobbed. "Make it stop. Please. If I do one more, will you make it stop?"

No one answered. He pushed up off the floor, gathered his boots, coat and tools, and left his apartment.

Outside, the late day was calm and bright. For once, the wind wasn't howling and the air didn't feel like needles. He walked to the corner toward a drift of fresh snow and held a hand up to it. There. He saw it. His fingers traced the contours of the shadows and shapes and pulled out feature after feature with care, making sure not to add his own interpretation but only to reveal what was already there. Not a what. *Who.*

The work was quick. There was little to actually do; the face practically sculpted itself. Something lodged in his throat. An acorn or an apple or the whole damn planet because he couldn't swallow or breathe or cry out. All he could do was look into his face.

"There you are. I've been looking for you."

He turned. "What did you sa

PAREIDOLIA

BACK SEAT

for Tony Tremblay

The cold made her feet hurt. She was wearing the same sneakers she'd had since before the beginning of the school year, even though her feet had grown and her toes were pushing up against the ends. They were thin canvas and the flat soles were slippery on the black ice coating the road, but they were what she had. To combat the cold, she doubled up on socks even though that made the shoes feel even smaller and crunched up her toes more. Layering her socks worked at first, but the cold still crept in like needles slowly being pushed through the canvas and into the layers of cotton underneath.

There was snow on the ground on the side of the road, but it wasn't deep, not like the year before. She didn't have to slog through it like then. This was that dry, powdery kind that you couldn't make a snowman or even a ball out of—it just sifted through your fingers like weightless sand when you tried to shape it. It was the kind of snow that fell when it was so cold the condensation from her dad's breath froze tiny icicles in his mustache and beard. When that happened, she used to laugh and try to pick the little pieces of ice out of his facial hair. He'd smile and bat her hands away, telling her to keep her paws off his beard diamonds. But the novelty of it wore off after the second week of record low temperatures, and neither of them acknowledged the tiny icicles anymore. They were headed into the second *month* of frigid temps now. That's what they said on the radio. Record lows, not felt in New England in a century. At nine years old, a century was a mythical length of time. Like "once upon a time" and "happily ever after." One hundred years only existed in stories. Though plenty of things in New England were much older, she'd never met a *person* who'd lived a hundred years. She knew she wouldn't be around in a century to tell anyone how numb her toes were. Cold wasn't supposed to last like that.

They walked along the side of the road toward the next house. She didn't want to leave tracks, but the ice on the road was too slippery to walk on. She'd fallen a couple of times when they first got out of the car and her dad told her it was okay for them to walk in the snow on the shoulder. That was tricky because it was dark and there were no street lights out here to illuminate something in the shallow snow that might trip them. Just a faint, unsettling glow from the reflection of the moon behind the clouds. Hidden roots or not, if anyone came driving along, neither of them wanted to be *in* the road.

The snow crunched softly beneath her feet. Her dad's footfalls were louder, though he did his best to stay quiet—he couldn't help his size. He walked in front of her and she tried to step in his footsteps. Though the snow wasn't deep, it still got in over the tops of her shoes and froze her ankles along with her stinging toes. Walking in his tracks kept that from happening as much, though it still did.

She made a game of it, pretending she was a ghost stalking him, walking in his tracks so when he looked behind him, he couldn't see where she'd been. She'd stand in his footsteps and he'd see right through her and shiver at the thought that something was following him. What could it be? The spirit of a tragically lost girl he once knew? She thought it might be fun to be a ghost. Then, she could sneak into some of these houses—pass right through the doors and walls—and sleep in an empty room all by herself. Instead of in a car.

The shelters in the city wouldn't take them. A single man with a child was bad enough, but they definitely wouldn't take in a single man with a *girl*. Men and women were kept apart for safety reasons, they said. Her dad argued that she was his daughter, and they said it was policy. She couldn't stay in the men's area and he couldn't go in the women's. We're sorry, they told them. So, they had to sleep in the car. Her dad turned on the engine every couple of hours to run the heater. The sound of it turning over woke her up every time, but she pretended to sleep through the noise. She knew he wanted her to get good sleep so she could be alert in school. But then every few nights, they had to go for "The Walk."

She moved quietly behind him, pretending to be a spirit until they reached a driveway and he turned to remind her with a raised finger to be extra quiet. She didn't need reminding. She knew.

Stepping around her dad, she glanced at the mailbox, as if it mattered whose address this was. Most people bought those brass-colored metal numbers to stick on the side of their mailboxes, but this one had been carefully hand-painted. It was hard to read in the dark, but up close she could see. The person who'd done it hadn't painted the street name, just the numbers five and seven. That was enough. She remembered they were on Summer Street. That had made her smile at first. It was nothing like summer out that night, but it was nice to think about warm weather. She was ready for some.

Her father leaned down and whispered in her ear. She wanted to pull back her stocking cap to hear him better, but her ears were as cold as her feet. They hurt in the biting wind, so she leaned closer and turned her head, but left the hat in place.

"You know the drill. Don't forget the cup holders."

She nodded. She never forgot, though when she came back without anything in hand, he worried that she wasn't looking hard enough. She tried to find what he wanted everywhere she could think of. Sometimes, she even checked under the floor mats in the footwells.

She crept up the driveway. It was clear of snow, though there was some salt spread out. She tried not to crunch when she stepped, but couldn't help it. She was small and the noise was slight. Still, it sounded loud to her. At this time of night, every house on the street was dark; everyone was asleep. She knew how tiny little sounds outside of the car made her wake up all night long. She tried to move as silently as a ghost.

She hesitated beside the car and looked back at her dad. He'd melted into the shadows of the trees beside the driveway. The shadow he'd become nodded at her and she turned back to the passenger door and pulled up on the handle, gritting her teeth, waiting for the electronic chirp that would tell her to let go and run for the shadows. The door clicked faintly and popped out an inch. No alarm. She lifted and pulled hard and it swung open. And *that's* why they were in the town they were, instead of Manchester or Concord. No one out here locked their doors.

She jumped inside and pulled the door shut to extinguish the dome light overhead. It was still cold with the door closed, but the breeze couldn't get in anymore. She wished she had the keys so she could start the engine and let it idle for a little bit and heat up—take some of the chill out of her feet and hands. That was as sure a way of getting caught as leaving the dome light on or just standing out on the front step and ringing the doorbell. No. She had to wait. The drive back to Manchester would be warm. She'd snuggle up under her blanket and get some sleep when they were through. And tomorrow was Saturday. No school. She could sleep in. Though she never did.

She opened the center console, knowing she probably wouldn't find any quarters in the coin slots, but still hopeful for something. No one out here locked their doors, but they didn't need meter money either. Free street parking in small towns meant no one kept quarters in their cars. The best she ever seemed to find was what someone got handed back in change from the Drive-Thru window along with their Whopper and Coke. That ended up in the cup holders most often, as her dad reminded her. But she checked everywhere. Her mouth watered at the thought of a hamburger. She loved Whoppers so much! They were better than a Big Mac or those dry, square burgers from the other place with the girl on the sign.

She gasped when she saw the roll of quarters wrapped in one of those paper bank sleeves in the console. Ten dollars! Whoever drove this car must go into a city a lot. Maybe even Boston if he needed that much change. She'd never found a whole roll of change before and her heart started to beat fast with excitement. Dad would be so happy. Maybe he'd even let them quit early tonight. They could be out for hours on any other night before she found as much. She tried to imagine what his face would look like when she showed him. How the crinkles at the corners of his eyes would deepen and that one eyebrow would arch up the way it did. She loved that eyebrow. It only went up when he really smiled. It was how she could tell when he was faking.

Still, there was more looking to do before she could go back to him with her treasure.

She stuffed the coin roll in her pocket, closed the console, and started feeling around in the cup holders. Nothing. As if she hadn't found enough. She popped open the jockey box and felt around inside. Once, she'd found a checkbook and had taken it back to her dad. He'd gotten excited at first, and then his face fell and he told her they couldn't keep it. He didn't say why, he just said he couldn't write bad checks. She didn't know what made them bad. If they were filled out they were good, right? Still, he'd thrown the checkbook in the garbage and told her to focus on cash and anything they might be able to pawn.

Once, she found a toy. Nothing big. Just a tiny fashion doll of a blue skinned girl with bright pink hair. It had little removable bracelets and a belt that she was careful not to lose and the blue girl was beautiful even though she had little fangs. She knew it was a Monster High figure, though she didn't know the character's name. She'd hidden that find from her dad. She didn't want him to accuse her of having bad toys and throw that in the garbage too. When he found it in their car a week later, he'd asked where she got such a thing and she lied to him and said that her friend at school, Holly, had given it to her. She was ashamed to lie to him, but it wasn't a bad toy; it was a good toy and she wanted to keep it. The kid she took it from had a big house and her parents drove a big SUV and she didn't even care enough about the figure not to leave it on floor in the back seat like an empty wrapper. She loved that monster girl better than that other kid had.

There was a book in the jockey box. Who kept books in a place like that, she wondered. It was some grown up book with a pair of bare feet on the cover. She thought for a minute about taking that too and giving it to her dad. She didn't know whether he liked books, but maybe it was like the figure. Something he could love better than whoever had left it in a car. Sometimes, they went to the library and she sat and read while he looked at his e-mail on the public computers. He never checked anything out. He never had time to read, he said. This book though, stuffed in with the car papers like it wasn't anything important, could be his and he could read it and not worry about it being due or late fees or anything. He could take all year to finish it if he wanted. And he could love it like she loved her blue girl.

It was probably a bad book. Like a bad check. He'd throw it away and then no one would have it. She put the paperback novel with its one-word title back and closed the jockey box.

Her dad would be getting impatient soon. He didn't like her to take too long. She had to hurry. She checked the floors under the mats and stuffed her fingers deep in the cracks in the seats, but she knew the quarter roll was all she was going to find. It was enough. Still, she turned to crawl into the back seat and look for other treasures.

The boy sitting there stared at her from the shadows.

A shout she couldn't control escaped her lips. She clapped her hands to her mouth. She lurched away from the boy, hitting her back against the gear shift and then the dashboard. Another cry escaped her lips at the sudden insult of the little knobs that jutted out of the dash jabbing into her back between her shoulder blades. If she'd been in the driver's seat, she would've honked the horn and they'd be caught. She arched her back and her foot slipped. She fell face-first into the passenger seat, dragging her cheek down the cold leather. The quarter roll in her jacket pocket pulled heavily, like a weight, but didn't fall out.

She whimpered at the pain of her neck craning back against the upright seatback as she pushed up. The side of her right leg hurt where it scraped against the plastic of the center divider. She wanted to cry and call out for her dad, but she had to keep herself together. At least until they got back to their own car. She sniffled and gritted her teeth and got up on her knees.

Peeking over the back of the seat in the dark, it looked like a doll. Pale and still and small. And for a single second, an unwelcome thought about how much she'd love to have a baby doll intruded in her mind. But this wasn't a toy. It was a boy. He sat in his car seat, the harness over his shoulders holding him upright, head tilted to the side on a thin neck. His skin wasn't like a piece of plastic painted to look like a real kid; it was pale in the moonlight and looked unreal. His eyes were open, but they were dull and unfocused. Not like sharp plastic eyes that looked alert and had bright irises. His eyes weren't any of those things.

He had on mittens and a snowsuit with little built-in booties. She didn't want to know what his tiny fingers and toes looked like. She didn't want to know anything. Tears blurred her eyes as she struggled not to scream. But ... the boy. The tears in her eyes made him waver in the dark, and it looked like he might be wriggling against the straps of the car seat, trying to get free, trying to reach for her and close his tiny little fingers around her throat and squeeze. Once, she'd seen a part of an old movie about dead people coming back to life and they were a horrible blue color that made her laugh because it was so fake-looking and how could anyone be scared by a blue person? And then they bit people and the crazy extra-red blood squirted out and she got scared. Even though that was fake-looking too—like a living cartoon—it was terrifying. Because it was blood and nobody lost that much blood and stayed alive.

In the diffuse moonlight, this boy was blue like that. The thought of him biting her and crazy bright blood spurting out of her body onto his round baby face made her breath hitch and she pushed away from the seat back.

The boy didn't move. He didn't look up or cry or even breathe. He sat there in the dark and looked somewhere, a million miles away—maybe in a whole different world. Looking at her from the ghost world.

She pulled off one of her gloves and leaned forward to touch his cheek with the tip of a shaking finger. She didn't know why she wanted to touch him, but she did. The boy terrified her, but she *needed* to touch him. Needed to know he was real and not a ghost. It felt like he needed her to touch him.

He was so cold.

The car moved, and she heard laughter and loud talking. She tumbled into the back seat as the car took a corner too fast and she heard a woman say, "Take it easy, Louis." The driver replied, "I'm fine. It's fine," and he gassed the engine. The baby in the seat next to her sat there, his head dropping with heavy sleepiness until his eyes closed and he slumped down. The grownups in the front seat kept talking and it sounded like when her own Dad and Mom had wine and their words got mushy. She could smell wine and bad breath like when her own mom would kiss her goodnight. They turned another corner and the car stopped too fast and the woman snapped at the man and he repeated, "It's fine. I'm fine." She said, "Go open the door and I'll carry the baby in," and he replied, "Let him sleep for a minute." He pawed at her chest through her coat and she shoved at his hands and said, "Your hands are cold," but he insisted and started kissing her neck and she moaned and let him put his hands back inside her coat. They kissed and then got out of the car, laughing and she heard the woman say, "I should get the baby," and he said, "He'll be fine for ten minutes." "Ooh, I get *ten* minutes, huh?" She fumbled at the man's pants and he unlocked the door to the house and they nearly fell inside. They kept laughing and then the door slammed. And the baby woke up and began to sniffle and then started to cry. She tried to comfort him, saying, "Shh," and "It's okay; they'll be out in a minute." But they didn't come out. Not in a minute, or in ten, or in an hour. They stayed inside and she knew they fell asleep like Mom and Dad used to sometimes after too much wine and she saw the baby's breath in the car and he started to cry harder and harder and she got more worried and tried to get out of the car, but she couldn't move. She was frozen. It was cold. So cold. And the baby cried more, until it started to lose its voice and then his head began to bob again like he was tired and he sobbed and looked at her with glassy, accusing eyes she didn't want looking at her. She wanted to look away and be anywhere but in this car, but she couldn't get out. The baby boy looked at her and his lips were turning blue and then his head bobbed down and he stopped crying.

Everything was quiet for a long time while she watched the little puffs of breath from his mouth grow smaller and less frequent, until they stopped altogether.

Then she blinked and was back in the front seat reaching out to touch the blue boy's cold cheek. She drew her arm back like her hand had been burned and fell against the dash again. She started to cry harder, unable to control the hitching sobs that were building in her chest and her throat. She let them out and it was wrong because they could get caught but there was nothing she could do to stop it. She was only nine, after all. So, she cried.

The door to the car swung open and the dome light lit up the night and she screamed and stiffened, waiting to hear the angry shouts of the owners of the car, demanding to know in that way angry grown-ups did *what the fuck* she was doing. Instead, the dark blur in the door was her dad, and she lurched toward him, wrapping her arms around his neck.

"Daddy, daddy! There's a boy back there! He's in the back seat and he's blue and—"

He shushed her a little too sharply. Angrily. She repeated herself, trying hard to keep her voice down. "There's a boy in the back seat. A baby."

He shushed her again, softer, and held her tightly, pulling her out of the car and turning away. "It can't be," he said. "I'm sure it's just a doll."

All she could manage was "no" and "no" and "no" again. She said it and he replied with "Shh, it'll be all right," and "calm down," as if she could. Not after what the blue boy had shown her.

Her dad looked at the house at the end of the driveway. Her crying was noisy and they had to be quiet…like ghosts. *Ghosts don't cry*, she told herself and tried to stop sobbing. But they do cry. They were sad and lonely. That's why they were ghosts on Earth instead of souls up in Heaven.

But being a ghost meant being dead.

Like the boy in the back seat of the car.

He's dead.

He froze *to death, because his parents left him in the back of the car and they went inside and fell asleep.* She'd seen them do it. The blue boy had shown her. He showed her the things she didn't want to see. The man's hands on the woman's chest and her hands in his pants, each other touching their private places, and then laughing and going inside while their baby froze to death in the back of a car. Now he was a ghost and he was sad, and he gave her a little piece of his death and now she was a ghost, too, like him. Except not a dead one. He killed her inside. It felt like she'd never be happy again.

She tried to calm down, but her heartbeat and her breathing were beyond her control. Instead, she put a hand over her mouth, so at least she wasn't sobbing out loud. Snot slipped out of her nose and she felt ashamed for being a baby, but she couldn't help it. She wiped it away with the back of her glove and sniffed hard. The sound was loud and she gritted her teeth when her dad flinched at the noise of it in his ear.

Her dad whispered, "Are you sure?" She nodded. He set her down on her feet and dragged his hand down his mustache and beard the way he did, smoothing it down. It was the way he moved when he was feeling troubled. Even when he said he wasn't, if he did that, she knew he was. And that worried her. If the grownups were afraid, what hope was there for a kid?

"You go stand over there in the trees, okay? Go wait for me over there where it's dark and I'll be right over."

"Don't leave, Daddy."

"I'm not leaving. But I gotta have a look, okay?"

She drew in a long, wet sniffle and pleaded quietly with him. "I'll be good, I promise. I won't shout or cry or anything, I swear. Just don't go. Don't touch him!" Her heart thundered in her little body. She didn't want him to get in the car with the blue baby. She didn't want him to be frozen with the sadness like she had been. If he did, then they'd both be ghosts and nothing would ever be right again. She had been so wrong. The blue boy gave her what she'd wished for and it felt so bad.

It's a dream. I'm in the car and I'm dreaming we're out for The Walk. We're sleeping and the boy is blue because I found that stupid blue girl toy in the back seat of a car and I'm having a nightmare about her and that movie and none of this is real, it's all a nightmare. I have to wake up!

A chill breeze rustled through the trees and it hurt her face and made her eyes tear up more and convinced her she wasn't asleep and dreaming. The wet lines the tears had traced down her cheeks stung and she wiped at them with the glove she hadn't wiped her nose with. "Can we just go? Look, I found money." She reached in her pocket and pulled out the roll of quarters. She held it out to her dad, trying to press it into his hand. "I'll stop crying and be good if we go. I promise."

Her dad got that look, the one when he was worried. She knew it because his eyebrows came together and his eyes looked bigger somehow and his lips got so thin and tight they disappeared in the hair on his face. He looked like that a lot, so she knew it very well. He looked like that now. She knew *all* his looks.

"You *are* good, honey. You're the best. And I'm not leaving. I just want you to go stand over there and wait for me so I can have a look."

"I'll stay with you. Right up next to you. I can be brave." She wasn't sure if that last part was a lie, but she wanted it to be true, so she meant it even if she couldn't actually do it. *That* wasn't a lie, was it?

"Oh, honey. You don't need to look again, okay? Let me be brave for both of us." He put his hands on her shoulders and gently turned her toward the tree line at the edge of the property. "Go wait for me over there. Don't move. Just wait and be brave over there. I'll be right over."

"Promise you won't touch him." It wasn't a question. "Don't touch him. Promise."

He blinked. "I promise," he said, and nudged her away. She did as he told her and walked toward the darkness in the trees, wanting instead to hold on to her father and hold him back. She hadn't wanted to touch the blue boy. But then, she had. Something moved her arm like she was in a dream and what she wanted to do and what she actually did were two separate things. Before she realized what was happening, she'd reached out, and there was no way what she *wanted* was going to stop what happened next. Just like now that her dad had sent her away, and all she wanted was to make him come with her instead, leave the car and the boy in it alone. What if he made her dad do it even if *he* didn't want to? She wanted to plead with him to just leave. She could show him the roll of quarters again and say "breakfast is on me," the way grownups did on TV, and he would smile and kiss her forehead and they could go out for a eggamuffin and stare into each other's eyes because it was the weekend and she didn't have to go to school and they could go window shopping at the mall the way they liked to do and look at all the things they'd buy if they had the money to buy anything and she'd promise to get him a big leather chair he could put in his own room of the big house they owned in her dream and she would sit in his lap while he read her books all her own and not borrowed from the library or anywhere else and fall asleep and he'd carry her to her room where she'd lie in a warm bed with cozy Monster High sheets and on a shelf nearby would be a whole collection of beautiful dolls that would be her friends because she would buy all of them so they'd never be lonely or sad ever again. Except for the blue one. She didn't want the blue one anymore.

Except, that was only a dream.

Her feet crunched in the snow in the dark of the trees. She turned and waited. It was cold, standing still. Her breath billowed out in front of her face and hung there for a half-second before blowing away.

She watched her dad open the rear passenger door and he gasped and said, "No," loud enough for her to hear, even though he'd never made a sound before on any of the nights they went walking on the road. She looked at the house. No lights went on. No one emerged with a shotgun or phone in hand already dialing 9-1-1. There was nothing. Like the night had swallowed everything up, leaving them all alone.

Don't touch him. Don't touch him. Don'ttouchhim!

He leaned into the car. She watched his broad back convulse once. Twice. Was he crying? She'd never seen her dad actually cry. He'd look like he might feel bad for a second and then he swallowed it up. She knew he swallowed it up for her. That's why she tried to be brave, so he wouldn't have to eat so much sadness.

Her dad backed out of the car and closed the door. He turned and walked toward the house. She said, "Daddy." He held up a finger to shush her and climbed the front steps. The door was unlocked. He walked inside.

The girl wanted to run after him. This was the worst thing to do. They'd be caught. And if they were caught, people would take her away from him, because it was mommies that raised girls, not daddies. She knew they'd send her to live with someone else and then she'd be a real ghost—sad *and* alone all the time. She stayed put. Her feet were numb and felt frozen to the ground, and she was too afraid to follow him into the house. She tried to picture the people inside blue like the little boy. As if they were all dead and this was the end of the world like that movie and she and her dad were the only non-blue people left alive. They weren't though. She knew they were pink and warm and asleep.

After a few short minutes her dad walked out of the house. To her it had felt like forever, the way time feels to a child. Long and uncrossable, like an ocean. Or a hundred years. He came walking out, wiping at his eyes and joined her in the dark. "Time to go," he said. She wanted to ask why he had to go inside. What he'd seen. But she didn't say anything. Instead, she grabbed his hand and they walked up the driveway to the road.

In the distance, she heard a siren wind up.

They turned back the way they'd come, in the direction of their car. The weight in her pocket made her remember and she pulled her hand away and dug out the roll of quarters and held it out to him. "Here, Daddy." She wanted to see him smile. Ten dollars was a lot. It would make him smile.

A tear rolled down his cheek. He didn't bother to wipe it away. He said, "That's yours. Maybe you want to buy a new toy. A new monster doll."

"No. It's for breakfast."

He shook his head. "Huh-uh. That's yours sweetie. We'll go find something you can buy with it this afternoon." He paused. The siren was getting louder and she wanted to run. But he stood there. He crouched and more tears dripped down his face. "I'm so sorry, baby. I'll never make you do that again."

"It's okay. I understand."

"No. It isn't."

"How will we eat if I don't go look in the cars?"

He shook his head. "I don't know. We'll find a way. But you don't ever have to do that again. Not ever."

Her dad picked her up like he did when she was six and carried her the rest of the way back to the car, walking slowly so he wouldn't fall on the ice. She held on to the roll of quarters.

When they got over the hill and were on their way down the other side, she saw the flashing blue and red lights appear behind them. The sirens were loud now and lots of lights were coming on in the houses along the road. People were looking out their windows.

They reached the car and he tried to put her down so they could get in, but she didn't want to let go of him. With her chest pressed to his, she felt her dad's heartbeat. She held him tighter and never ever wanted down. But she had to get down to get in the car. "Can I sit in the front?" she asked. He nodded.

"We'll both sleep in the front tonight," he said.

"Did you touch him?"

He shook his head.

"Are we going to be okay?"

He nodded. "We're going to be fine, hon. Everything'll be okay." She let go and climbed in ahead of him, dragging her blanket out of the backseat up front with her. He climbed in behind her, started the engine, and turned the heater on full. Cold air blasted out, but soon it'd be warm.

For a while, anyway.

EVERYTHING WE LOST IN THE FIRE

"En los sueños no se siente dolor."
—Mariana Enríquez, "Las cosas que perdimos en el fuego."

SATURDAY

Some people in town called them the Speakeasy Steps because the stairway leading up the hillside was said to have once led up to a Prohibition-era dancehall at the top. Legend went that the place had burned down because it wasn't just a dancehall, but also a speakeasy nightclub. A local preacher and the sheriff were of a mind to shut it down for good, so one night they *burned* it down. With all the sinners inside. A hundred and fifty souls. Except, there weren't any old newspaper articles or anything else at all about it. Just talk. Old timers in town kept repeating the stories as if that might keep the kids away. It just made us want to go up there more.

We never found any proof there'd ever been a building there. No cellar or slab foundation, old plumbing or anything else that'd come with a building like they described. Just the crumbling concrete steps up the side of a hill, leading to a bluff overlooking the town. We didn't care if *any* of it was true.

From the top, you could see all of Ripton from the UMass campus and Wellington College to the steeple of the Old East Path Church stabbing skyward at one end of the common and Town Hall at the opposite end with the statue of Thaddeus Palsgrave in the middle. North, the Cabot Woods Scout Reservation was next to the up-and-coming richy-rich neighborhood being built, while the smokestack of the Whitehead Mill on the old south side of town stood as a reminder how this town had come to be. Nothing had come out of that chimney in maybe ten years. There was a sign out front advertising that it was going to be converted into luxury condos. We wondered what it'd be like if that ever happened. The mill was where the gearheads went to drink beer and talk about muscle cars or whatever it was they did there. We didn't really know what went on because if any of us slipped through the gap in the fence into that parking lot, it was well known, they'd kill us.

They had the mill; we had the hill.

Two abandoned houses, both alike in dignity, in fair Ripton, where we lay our scene.

Hardly anyone but us ever came up there. There was nothing at the top except the view and the wind. That it was haunted by the ghosts of the burned dead was icing on the cake for us. We imagined ourselves partying with them, toasting with funny old-timey cocktail glasses while jazz played too loud in the background. We called ourselves the Ghost Club.

Dany, Julian, Maia and Dustin would show up at my house and we'd walk a half mile along the road to the steps and hike up,

Jules bitching the whole way about how steep and long they were, though we climbed them all the time until none of us felt any burn in our legs anymore. We'd bring backpacks with blankets to spread out in the dirt and a bottle or two of wine if we could sneak it. My uncle Colin taught me to cup the ember of my cigarette in a palm so nobody could see it in the dark. He said he learned that in Vietnam. I didn't know about any of that; it was before my time. But I taught my friends to do the same with their smokes. It made our hands smell like clove smoke, but that wasn't bad. Better than being caught because some bored cop with a need to fuck with somebody saw a bunch of embers glowing in the dark like little orange stars at the top of the hill. Looking the way we did—black clothes, hair, nail polish—the town cops always gave us a hard time. You couldn't get away with shit if no one ever took their eyes off you. But up there, alone, we were invisible. Free. So, we climbed up those stairs any clear night we could.

In the daytime, Ripton looked like any other New England town, old mills and older churches, ranch homes on one end of town and big old colonial-style mansions all the way at the other, over by the hospital and the new high school—the nice one where the rich kids went. Not us. At night, the town changed into a living starfield. Headlights wound slowly along the cruise, through the illuminated streets, past houses and stores lit up like the actual stars overhead no one could see because of the light pollution from below. A world inverted. No above; only below. As much as we hated living in tiny, go-nowhere Ripton, we loved the way it shone after dark. Beautiful like diamonds on a black velvet.

But I always preferred to look at her.

Dany would sit next to me on the top step and hold my hand; she'd lean against my shoulder and her bushy, curly hair tickled my neck and cheek. I breathed in her aromas—the perfume she got from that one store in the mall and clove cigarettes. She smelled like the best flavors I ever tasted. Her lips were waxy from layered black-over-red lipstick but her breath was sweet smoke and tart wine and her tongue was a moment of ecstatic bliss every time I felt it slip into my mouth. She was thin yet soft and pressed up against me like she wanted to pass through my body like the Club ghosts could. I thought that sounded romantically poetic. The way angsty kids without hard experience think of things like ghosts—tragic but without consequences. It was only tragedy as *we* imagined it, with ourselves empowered by the history of their sacrifice and beyond grief.

Grief comes on its terms when it does, at no one else's pace or preference. I hadn't learned that yet. All we knew then was that this place was ours and no one else's because of the ghosts we imagined circling and protecting us from a town that didn't know how to live with us in it. We called the bluff, "The Ghost Club," and imagined ourselves drinking fancy cocktails with the victims of the speakeasy fire and dancing in a ballroom filled with defiant, secret revelry. Really though, we were just five kids waiting to be broken by Ripton. Like everyone else is, eventually.

Dustin pointed across the valley. "See that?" he said.

"See what?" Maia asked, taking a deep drag of a menthol. Her cigs tasted gross, but she bitched that cloves were too expensive and made her cough like her gran.

"That," Dustin repeated, stabbing his finger in the same direction.

"What? Ripton?" I said, spreading my arms like Lucifer tempting Christ with dominion in the desert. "You're gonna have to be more specific."

He frowned. "Those lights on the hillside over there. The ones by where the hospital is."

"Yeah, I guess so," Julian said. He was nursing the last of a stolen pint of gin. We'd all been drinking out of it, but it was stronger than the bottle of Boone's Farm Maia brought and I was already feeling a little too dizzy to risk more since I still had to make it down the stairs alive later.

"What are they?"

I shrugged. "Who fuckin' cares? It's all the way over there."

"Yeah but—"

"Yeah buts run in the woods," Maia said.

Dustin's face scrunched up. "What the fuck does that even mean?"

She smiled and blew out a plume of minty-fresh smoke. "The hell if I know. My grandaddy says it."

"*Grandaddy*," Dustin laughed. "What? Are you from the fuckin' country now? Gonna yee some haws for us next?"

"Eat me, loser."

"Spread 'em," he said. Maia reared back to hit him, and he skittered back, laughing. "Don't make promises your body can't keep."

"I'll fucking keep this one right here, Dusty." She held up her fist.

"I told you not to call me that," he said, serious now. Maia raised a finger from her fist.

"Come on, guys," Dany said. We all knew later on Maia and Dustin would be at each other like a pair of piranhas trying to eat the other's faces. They traded barbs as foreplay. Maia idly threatening, Dustin teasing until they were both so worked up the only choices were fight or fuck. Their thing wasn't as much fun for us as it was for them.

"Yeah, what *are* those lights?" Julian said before polishing off the pint.

"*Now* you see 'em?"

"I saw them before, dipshit. But you guys don't listen to me."

Dany nuzzled closer, making me plant a palm on the ground to stay upright. "It's that new place. The Anderson Clinic or something."

"Andrews Institute," Dany said softly.

"What's that?"

Dany didn't answer. Instead, she snatched the bottle of strawberry wine from between my legs and took a healthy drink.

Dustin said, "I heard about it. People send their kids there if they think they worship Satan or whatever."

We'd all heard horror stories of friends disappearing—thrown away by their parents for being queer or druggies or whatever. The Balfour Alternate School on the south side was for actual delinquents: kids who sold drugs at school and threatened teachers. Even then, those kids got to have lives after school and on weekends. The other kids, the ones who just vanished … the whisper-stream carried their stories through the halls of the school like hints of wildfire smoke on the breeze.

Betty Tichner got busted fingering Susan Pak behind the track bleachers. Don Langley's folks caught him taking acid. Paula Washburn tried to hang herself. Marina Yasnick took Maddie Medina to get an abortion.

All of them ended the same.

No one's seen them since. I heard they got sent to The Andrews Institute.

Julian shivered and tried taking another drink out of his empty bottle before stuffing it in his bag. He never said, but we all knew he was gay. It wasn't a well-kept secret and he'd taken bad enough beatings because of it to have a permanent limp at seventeen. As long as he was with us, people left him alone. Not because we were tough. We most definitely weren't, but we *were* witnesses. If one of us said someone called him a fag and threw a beer bottle at his head, nothing. If all four of us said Donny Cabot, Jimmy O'Neill, and Mark Taylor ganged up on him and kicked him until he was coughing up blood, well then, they *might* go talk to Donny and Jimmy and Mark's parents. That happened exactly once and we heard later on from someone else that Donny Cabot was out for Julian's blood because his old man had threatened not to pay for college if he fucked up his run for mayor. Not, if he fucked up another kid. His campaign. Cabot wasn't even in the same universe as someone smart enough to go to college, but he thought he was and he wasn't gonna risk his free ride since neither his grades nor his football skills were good enough to pay his way.

"They can't do that," Maia said, unconvincingly. What couldn't adults do to a kid if they wanted to? They didn't even need to keep it secret if they were "respectable" enough.

"Let's talk about something else," Dany said. She slid her hand into mine and my focus telescoped down into the feeling of her smooth palm in mine and her breath on my neck as her soft lips grazed my skin with transient affection.

"Dead Can Dance is putting out a new album," Dustin declared as if Lisa Gerrard and Brendan Perry had called him directly to tell him so. Still, it was a better subject than the one before. So we talked about music and drank the rest of the strawberry wine and wished we had some weed—all of us except Dustin, because his mom "has a snoot like a bloodhound," he'd explained. "She said she'd narc me out to my dad if she catches me smelling like pot one more time. He won't even wait until his weekend to fuckin' kill."

I cued the chorus. "Just tell him ... "

"I learned it from watching you, Dad!" we all crowed in unison to uproarious laughter from everyone except Dustin who did his best disapproving sneer. He ended up looking like he smelled something bad. Like his mom smelling him, I thought, and stifled more laughter.

"What time is it?" Maia asked.

"Ten-ish," Dustin answered. As the only one of us with a watch, he was our official timekeeper, though only the girls had hard curfews.

Maia stood, slapping the dirt off of her ass. "Shit! I have to be home in like a half an hour. I gotta go or else my mom's gonna have a fuckin' cow."

We brushed ourselves off, stashing bottles and blankets back in our packs. If we wanted our place to remain *our* place, we had to make sure nobody got wind kids were up here doing illicit shit. That meant no empties of any kind left behind, bottles, condom wrappers, or baggies with seeds and stems. Leave no trace, like my weirdo Vietnam tunnel rat uncle always said.,

"Already?" If it was hard to slur a single word with no sibilants, Julian did his very best.

"Come on, Jules." Maia and Dustin gently took hold of him, one on each arm, and led him carefully down the stairs so he wouldn't fall and die. Dany held me back as they disappeared below. "Just a little bit longer." She wrapped her arms around me and we stared out over the city, pretending the new lights on the distant hill were something else and we'd never ever heard of The Andrews Institute.

I walked Dany home from my place a little before her midnight curfew. Her flavor lingered in my mouth and the electric feeling of her touch persisted, even after we dressed and snuck out of my room. Sneaking wasn't exactly necessary. On a Saturday night, my mom wouldn't be home for at least another couple of hours, if she didn't end up at someone else's place entirely.

The night was cool and quiet. We lived far enough on the outskirts, noise from downtown didn't reach except faint sirens and really loud motorcycle pipes. Roots had broken up the concrete and made the sidewalk as even as a mountain range, so we walked in the middle of the street, looking out for headlights. Dressed all in black, it only made sense to not be standing in the road if someone came tearing around a corner on their way home from the bar. Not even a good bet even if the driver *did* see us. A friend of ours got run over in broad daylight. They finally found the kid who did it and he told the cops he was scared because she reminded him of "one of those people in Temple of Doom who rip your heart out." He got community service and she ended up with long metal rods fused to her spine that gave her perfect posture and constant pain.

Dany lived just over a mile from me. I clocked it once in my mom's car. Unlike us, her parents owned their house. It wasn't huge, but it was nice enough to feel the difference in how we lived. We stopped at the end of her block and made out for a while. I'd have walked her up to the door, but her folks were most likely waiting up for her. They'd know I was with her because their yippie little dog that didn't like me and started barking if it saw me from its perch in the window. On top of that, they had an agreement with the old, nosy neighbor next door to call them if she ever saw me "creeping around their house." This time of night she was probably asleep, but that fucking mutt was ever-vigilant.

Dany reluctantly pulled away from me, and I watched her walk the rest of the way home. She climbed the steps and looked back at me standing in the dark before letting herself inside. In the porchlight she glowed like a warm halo of fire lit her sepia skin. She disappeared inside and the night closed around me.

MONDAY

Homeroom, as well as first and second periods, came and went without any sign of Dany. After third period I ran down Maia in the hall and asked her if she saw Dany in gym. She shook her head, said "Nope," and ran off. It was morning break and she had ten minutes to get to the alley at the other end of the school to smoke *and* then piss. Nicotine before bladder relief. If she ran out of time, she could always get a hall pass to use the bathroom.

I shoved my binder and math book in my locker and leaned back into the gap, scanning the hallways, searching for her. Dany never skipped school. She was never even late. Her parents were wicked strict and would come down on her like a federal case if the front office called them. Wicked religious as well, they made her go to mass with them every Sunday. After that, she was free to go hang with her friends at the mall. That's what she told them. But I hadn't seen her the day before, either. I stayed home the whole day waiting for her to call, but the phone never rang. I tried calling once and got the machine. Now, she wasn't at school.

The hum above my locker made me grit my teeth. I'd learned to recognize the buzz of the electrical current in the second before the clapper started to bang the class bell. Despite knowing, the fucking thing made me jump every time. The custodian had removed the rag I'd jammed inside of it out again. I'd have to fix that later.

I grabbed my French stuff out of the locker and slammed the door hard enough to latch. If I didn't, someone could brute force it and my shit'd be all over the floor before next break. Jimmy O'Neill passed by, shouldering me into the metal door. I fumbled my books and he kicked my binder down the hall. The rings snapped open, spilling my papers everywhere. Kids snickered at the spectacle. It was a masterful play by a stunning intellect, perfectly punctuated with a pithy, "Watch it, pussy."

I kept my mouth shut and got down to rescue my pages from my classmates' feet. Dany would've called him a dickbag or something.

She wasn't afraid of him or his wrestling buddies. And as a result, she was the only person outside their own clique they didn't fuck with. Dany told me she flashed a knife at him once and said she'd cut his dick off if he fucked with her. I believed her. She kept one of those flip-around karate knives they sold at the shop over on First Street that we were supposed to be too young to shop at, but sold us rolling papers and packs of cloves anyway. She practiced with it all the time. I imagined her whipping that thing around, saying she'd wear his balls as earrings if he wanted to fuck around. O'Neill didn't know if she'd ever actually *use* it, but he seemed smart enough at least to not want to find out. He and his goons left me alone, as long as she was around. Since she wasn't there, he got to make up for missed opportunities.

I finished the day hiding in bathrooms between classes before rushing home. Any time she or I missed school, the other would call and we'd talk until her parents got home. They made her hang up "in case somebody else needed to get through." A bullshit excuse with call-waiting—but she couldn't argue. Like the day before, I got their answering machine again. Her dad's extra-serious voice outgoing message said, "You've reached the DeJourdan household: Daniel, Deborah, and Danielle. No one can answer, so leave your name, number, and the reason for your call at the tone and one of us will get back to you." After the tone beeped in my ear, I waited a couple of seconds in case Dany was screening calls and might pick up. She knew if the line was silent, it was me. As far as secret codes went, it wasn't sophisticated, but it worked most of the time. I hung up without leaving a message—her dad would erase it anyway. He liked me less than the dog did.

I tried to distract myself by reading, drawing, reorganizing my tapes, but I couldn't concentrate for more than a few minutes.

Nothing felt right, and I was too restless to stay still. I couldn't sit, stand, or lie down without needing to immediately change it up, do something else. I thought about going upstairs and sneaking a joint out of the stash-bag my mom hid in the back of her underwear drawer—kind of, but not really secret. It being Monday meant if there was anything left in it after the weekend, she'd notice it missing. Our unspoken agreement was the last was always hers. Fair enough; she paid for it and it was a long way to payday at the end of the week. Instead of seeking solace with a smoke, I grabbed my Walkman and a beaten-up paperback and slipped out the back door.

Outside, I felt the insistent pull of Dany's house. I ran there, slipping from the uneven sidewalk to the street and back when I needed to dodge a dog walker or car. I reached her place out of breath and feeling an increasing panic in my stomach that I tried to settle by telling myself it can't be that bad. She was probably just grounded for coming home late the other night after the Ghost Club and that's why she wouldn't answer. That didn't explain why she was absent. Responsible parents like hers don't ground their kids from school.

The driveway was empty. I peeked through the garage windows to make sure both of her parents' cars were gone. Coast clear, I crept around the side of the house to the back yard. Pausing at the chain link fence, I rattled the gate, in case the dog was outside. When I heard it bark inside, I pushed through.

Dany's room was on the second story with a clear view down to the back yard. No nearby tree or convenient movie flower bush lattice to climb up or down. It was too high to get any kind of look inside from below, though. I walked up to the back door and banged on it a couple times. The dog activated like a car alarm and rushed for the door, its claws clacking against the hardwood floors. They didn't have a doggie door, so I was safe from the little monster, and it would let her know I was in the yard better than throwing pebbles at her window. I backed up into the middle of the yard and looked up, hoping to see her come to the window to see what got the dog going.

She didn't.

Her dark curtains stayed drawn and still. If she was home and couldn't hear all that racket, she was …

dead

I tried to banish the word from my mind as fast as it appeared there, but once thought, ideas linger—especially if they're unwelcome. I couldn't get the image of her lying in that room, lifeless and alone in her room while I stood outside powerless to do anything except let worry twist my guts in knots.

The dog barked and jumped against the door. The sound of its fury dulled and grew distant as everything around me blurred and faded. It felt like that twilight between being asleep and awake. Everything was where it had been, but I wasn't. Something Dany asked me once up at the Ghost Club came to mind like I was reliving it.

Do you believe in astral projection?

What?

Out-of-body experiences. Do you think you could send your consciousness somewhere else while your body stayed where it was?

No. I don't think so.

I think it'd be cool, you know. Like a super-power.

I'd want to be able to fly.

Don't be stupid. astral projection is way better. Like flying with your mind.

My mind comes with my body.

Not if I knock you out.

The screeching whine of the fence gate ripped me from the memory. I pressed my palms to my temples as the color and brightness of everything slammed back into me hard enough I felt out of breath at the sudden intensity of it.

"What are you doing back here?" a man asked me. I looked down from the window which a second earlier I could've sworn seemed closer than it was. "I said, what are you doing?" he repeated. I looked at the man in the black uniform standing by the corner of the house. His silver badge glinted in the sun. Fucking neighbor called the *police* instead of her parents.

"I'm not ... I just—"

"Put your hands behind your head and lace your fingers." He had his hand on the handle of his gun but hadn't drawn it. I tried to make sense of what he was saying, but it still made no sense to me until he repeated himself, louder this time, with swearing. "Put your hands behind your fucking head and lace your fingers!" I looked around for a way out. He commanded me to turn around and "get on your fucking knees!" Athletic as I was not, even if I got over the fence, there was no way I was outrunning this guy. I did what he said and moved my hands from my temples behind my head. I knelt down and winced as he gripped one of my wrists with one hand and slapped the metal cuff on the other.

From the back of the police car, I watched the blue and red lights bounce off the neighbors' houses. People driving home from work slowed as they passed, craning their necks to see if they recognized the delinquent in their neighborhood. The officer who cuffed me sat in the front seat, head down, writing something while the radio crackled with a litany of unintelligible messages. His partner stood on the walk across the street talking to Dany's dad. Her mom glared at me like I was cancer.

No Dany.

Eventually, my mom pulled up in her red Thunderbird shitbox behind us. The cop got out of the car and led her by the elbow a few feet away to talk. Eventually, he pulled me out of the car and undid the handcuffs. He handed me over by my bicep like I was a pet. Mom took custody of me, as he put it, and told me to "wait in the fucking car."

As I trudged toward the Thunderbird, Daniel DeJourdan shouted, "Stay away from my goddamn house!" Deborah added, "Danielle doesn't want to see you ever again! She's done with you." The cop near them stepped in between us and said something low, intended for them only.

Done with me pierced my head like a spike. What did that even mean? I wanted to shout back, "She wasn't done with me the other night," but it was a childish retort that proved their point. Instead, I yelled, "Get Dany out here and have *her* say it. Go get her right now!"

"Get in the fucking car," my mom hissed from between clenched teeth. I didn't listen and walked around the other side.

I felt emboldened watching their stunned faces. I knew they couldn't say anything out loud about it. I tried playing the hand I thought I held. "You sent her there, didn't you? That's why she can't come out because you sent her to the fucking Andrews Institute to fuck her head up and make her a robot." Deborah's expression at hearing it out loud confirmed what I feared. They'd thrown her into that place and she'd either come out a pastel-wearing zombie, or maybe she'd just vanish like Marina Yasnick and Maddie Medina. Memories at best.

My mother grabbed my arm like I was a toddler; I shook it off, not thinking. "Let go of me."

The cop who'd been sitting with me in the car stepped in between us and put his hand on my chest. "That's enough, son."

I am not your fucking son!

"Get in the car like your mother says or I'll take you into custody."

"For what?" I turned on him with a sudden fury that made him flinch for his belt.

He scowled. "Disorderly conduct. Trespassing. Anything else I can think of. Listen to your mom and get going while you can. *Now.*"

My mother grabbed me again and shoved me toward the passenger door. "What the hell's gotten into you? You better believe we're going to have a talk about this when we get home, god damn it." She yanked open the door and I slithered in, staying as close on the bench seat to the door as I could without it hitting me as she slammed it shut. I looked over at Daniel DeJourdan. He returned my stare with perfect contempt. *I'd* done this. Forced him to drop his only daughter into the void. Because *I* was a bad influence, making her dress in black and take drugs and have sex.

Fuck him.

Mom dropped into the driver's seat and fumed as she drove us home. Once there, she shut the engine off and turned toward me. "If I ever have to ask my boss to leave work early so I can pick up my kid from jail, I'll fucking send you to live with your father. Understand?"

"It wasn't jail."

"Enough!" This was always the talk she promised. Never a dialogue. Always only her making threats and acting like a victim because she had to parent me. She'd threatened me with exile to my father's land in upstate New York more often than I could remember, though it never materialized, except for one summer. I went, and he couldn't send me back fast enough. Her words were as hollow as her I love yous after a couple of bennies and a Chardonnay chaser.

"Understand?"

I nodded.

"Fuckin' *say* it. 'Yes Mom, I understand.'"

"I understand," I muttered, waiting for the hit she always swung when she wanted to land her knockout blow. She saved it up until the end because I couldn't hide that it actually felt as bad as she made it sound.

"You're just like your father."

There it was. My eyes welled up, but I refused to cry in front of her. I gritted my teeth and waited there. She got out of the car and slammed the door. I closed my eyes and tried to imagine Dany next to me in the car, holding me and telling me it'd be okay the way she always did after Mom dropped that bomb.

WEDNESDAY

Julian leaned against his car and shook his head. "Fuck no. No way, man. Huh-uh."

"Come *on*, Jules. They way her parents reacted, I know it." If I didn't actually *know*, I felt a kind of soul-certainty. A bodied knowledge.

He slid an unfiltered Camel out of a pack and flicked his Zippo against his palm to open and light it in a single motion. What started as a joke to make fun of some guy he'd seen do the same thing had become as natural a part of him as smoking. He took a deep drag and French exhaled before blowing it out again off to his left. "You got hooked up by the pigs once already this week. Why try again?"

"It's not going to happen that way, I swear. I'm just going to go in and talk to the receptionist all calm and shit, while you wait in the car. If you even see a cop, just go; I don't care if you ditch." I knew it was a soft push to say he'd be "ditching" if he left me, but I meant what I said. All I wanted was a ride. Whatever happened after was on me.

"You can't be serious."

"Nobody's seen her in almost a week, and the teachers aren't saying anything about it. You know how they get when one of us fucks up." It was always the same. If one of our tribe stepped even a little bit wrong, they brought *all* of us to the office. Julian took another drag before pinching off the ember of the cigarette and returning the unsmoked half to the pack.

"Get in." He folded his lanky body into the tiny MG B Roadster. I don't know how he got in that thing without having to take the top down first, but he managed. I squeezed into the passenger seat with difficulty, despite being a foot shorter and not having a steering wheel in my way. He fired the ignition and the car roared to life like a throaty lawn mower. "You sure about this?" he asked.

I nodded. He put the car in gear, popped the clutch, and we lurched ahead, on our way.

The car drove like it sounded, rough and with more than a little feeling there wasn't much space or car between us and the road. Speeding toward the place, I felt the same pull I had running to Dany's house. This was the way I *needed* to go. Every inch ahead felt more right.

We pulled into the parking lot, passing a sign that read, "Andrews Institute: Residential Youth Treatment" beside an odd logo I couldn't tell what it was supposed to be. A sunrise over a mountain or something. The lot was smallish and half full. A beige and brick building stood behind a landscaped row of trees and a small lawn on either side of sidewalk. The logo was stenciled in white on the glass doors at the front of the place. No mistaking it. While it looked like any other medical building, aside from the lobby there were no windows anywhere. It was an institutional brick of a building that resembled a warehouse or a jail more than a treatment center.

Julian backed into a spot near the exit and parked. He gave me a "what now" look. "You're sure this is the place?"

I shrugged. "This is where Amye Blankenbaker said her parents threatened to send her if she didn't stop cutting herself."

"She's a cutter?"

"I watched her carve Bradley Hinson's name in her arm with an X-acto."

"The hell? The whole thing?"

"She only got as far as 'Brad' before the teacher took the knife away."

Julian shifted in his seat, slapped his Zippo against his palm and relit his unfinished cigarette. "What if they don't let you leave?"

I laughed nervously. He was trying to lighten the mood. I doubted that was possible, but played along. "If I'm not out in two days, send Search and Rescue." I got out and walked toward the building. Every footstep felt a little heavier until I reached the glass doors. Standing at the threshold of this place we'd whispered and wondered about felt like trying to psych myself up for willingly stepping onto the gallows platform. When would the floor fall out? Right inside the door? When I said her name? I swallowed hard and took a step inside. The lobby was small—a few upholstered chairs against the wall next to a couple of tables with copies of *Parenting* and *People* magazines left out. It didn't feel like a place where people disappeared their children. A woman behind a counter-style desk looked at me with some confusion. "Can I help you?"

"Uh, yeah, I think so. Probably." I moved closer trying to appear confident, knowing what I really looked like: nobody important. Another non-person. "I'm here to see Dany ... *Danielle* DeJourdan, Please. Thank you."

She titled her head and pursed her lips. "We don't have visiting hours."

"Can you at least tell me if she's here?"

"I'm not at liberty to disclose whether any individual is admitted here. Is there something else?" The way she said it, I couldn't tell if she was asking if I wanted to check myself in. I might've considered it, if it meant finding Dany. But of course, no; there wasn't anything else. How stupid of me to think I could walk in and ask to see Dany like that was a thing a person like me could just do. I felt my face fill with heat, my ears practically red-hot. "I was hoping ... "

The room swam like the world had in Dany's backyard. I tried to hold on, feeling in a fog of semi-existence. I heard the woman say something, but her words were too faint to make any sense to me. Something pulled at me like a current under the surface, trying to pull my feet out from under, draw me away where it wanted me to go. The door beside the reception desk seemed to gently vibrate before a man in a white coat emerged. He held it open for me, inviting me to come see for myself. I took a hesitant step before the current swept me through. I felt like stepping into an empty elevator shaft. I collapsed at the end of a blinding white hallway. Doors on either side ran the length of it. I staggered to my feet and rushed to the first one to peer through the wire-reinforced window. Amye Blankenbaker stared back at me, dragging her wrist across her mouth, smearing blood across her lips and cheek. I ran to the next and the next and the next one again, searching for Dany and finding instead Betty Tichner and Don Langley and Paula Washburn and Marina Yasnick and everyone else we'd ever talked about in whispers. Each one of them looked at me redly with slashed writes, slit throats. Alive and dead.

The man in the white coat waited at the end of the hall, holding open the final door, gesturing, like before, inviting me to inside.

"Is she in there? Dany?"

He laughed, his face contorting into a cruel mask of contempt. "No. This is for you."

I looked back the way I'd come, the doors behind me all gone, leaving only bare walls reaching away forever into a deep black shadow. I turned and tried to run toward the darkness. The man in the white coat grasped my arm, yanking me back. "It's not like you imagine; it's so much worse." He threw me into the cell. I bounced off the far wall, trying to get back to the door before he could slam it shut, but both he and it were gone, leaving me in the doorless, windowless room. The walls shimmered and pictures of her gradually appeared on them like things floating to the surface of water. Dozens of them, everywhere—all of her. The Danys all looked at me from them, smiling, laughing, winking, inviting me to come closer, be with her inside of them. I reached for one, but every inch closer always seemed another inch away. I fumbled toward another and another, never touching a single one. The images changed as I fought to possess them, her face growing sadder, frowning, crying, wincing with pain and open-mouthed terror. I squinted my eyes tight, shoving my fists against them until I couldn't see anything but stars blossoming behind my lids. The pictures still haunted me through fist and eyelid. Her face, grew ashen and slack, turning purple and swollen with rot, until her skin loosened and fell away leaving sinew and wet bone exposed that too fell to ruin. I screamed, mad with exactly what the man in white had promised: it was so much worse than I could've ever imagined.

"Are you on drugs?" the woman behind the desk shouted at me.

I blinked and the lobby returned, solid and clinical. No man in white, no hall or room or pictures of her. I stammered, trying to find words, but the vision left me mute, trembling and pale.

The woman stood, pen in hand and demanded I tell her my name. I held up my hands to ward her off as I backed away. She stared as if she was memorizing my face, cataloguing it for the next time. I turned and ran, the grasping, pulling current still there, but weaker, feeling like something slipping away.

I shoved through the glass doors and tumbled outside, throwing up on the walk beside the bushes. I heard the desk clerk say, "Send security to the lobby on the double. There's a boy—" The door on its hydraulic arm clicked shut, cutting her off.

I abandoned my regurgitated mess and stagger-ran to Julian, leaning against a low cinderblock wall next to the MG. "The fuck, dude?" he said, smoke carrying his words to me. The smell of it made me feel slightly less sick, promising something other than the vomit fouling my mouth and nose. His eyes widened as he looked up from me at the glass doors banging open.

"We gotta go."

"No shit!"

We jammed into the car and peeled out, leaving the blue-uniformed guards behind. Turning a corner too hard, I bumped against the door. Julian reminded me to watch out because sometimes it popped open. I pushed myself upright in the seat.

"Did you find out? Is she there?" he asked.

She was. I fucking *knew* it.

FRIDAY

I sleepwalked through the rest of the week, went to school, kept my head down, avoided everyone, and counted the minutes and seconds until it was time to go home. Every day, I walked an extra block out of my way to stand at the end of the driveway of the house behind hers and look up at her window. I could just see it from there through a gap in the trees, but the narc-neighbor next door couldn't see me. I hoped every time something would change, and she'd be home, sitting by the window. She didn't have to see me, as long as I knew everything was fine. But the view never changed: her window was always empty.

She wasn't coming home. Not this week or next. Like the other kids sent to disappear inside the Andrews Institute, it might be months before she got out ... if ever. Another unwanted thought I tried to unthink. I wanted to believe Dany wouldn't give up. But that was the whole point of the fucking place; it was a breaking wheel.

Home, I lurched into my room, threw my backpack on the floor and collapsed onto my bed. Mom was still at work, and the house was as dead as I felt inside. Any other Friday, I'd try rounding up the rest of the Ghost Club, but we'd spent the week tiptoeing around what none of us had the guts to say aloud, pretending the felt absence in our circle was something else. We quietly all pretended Dany had a cold, or her parents took her to see her Gran in Florida, anything but what really happened to her. What we knew could happen to any of us.

I lit one of Mom's joints and smoked half. Depending on how things went for her at the bar after work, I might have the place to myself until Sunday morning. I lay there trying to lose myself in a nothing of stilled sound and feeling until I was nowhere, floating in a haze of void-seeking disassociation.

The clanging telephone ripped me from my meditation, my heart beating furiously at the sudden offense to my quietly stoned peace. It rang again, and I scrambled to my feet lurching into the hall. As I reached for the handset fear surged in my gut. I could already hear his voice on the other end—the man in the white coat promising it hadn't gotten as bad as it was going to. Not yet.

I tried to reason with myself. *The weed's making me paranoid. It's just someone trying to sell us a portrait package at Olan Mills.* My rationalizations didn't help and the feeling persisted as it half-rang again. I answered. "H-hello?"

"Hey, Chance." The whispered voice at the other end sounded a million miles away but was unmistakable.

"Dany? Is it you, really?"

"Really."

"When did—"

"I want to see you."

My mind raced with fantasies of her sneaking out of that place, bursting through a door into daylight and running and hiding while Andrews men in blue uniforms and white coats searched. She broke my trance. "You still there?"

"Come over right now. I'm alone, no one will—"

"Can you meet me at the Speakeasy Stairs?"

"Sure, but my mom's not home. It's safe here. You can chill out in my room while we try to figure something out."

"Huh uh. My parents will tell them I'd go there. But they don't know about the stairs. Meet me there *after* it gets dark, okay?"

I tried to figure out why not now, but I supposed it made a kind of sense. The only light at the top of the hill was whatever we brought ourselves. Cigarette lighters and whatnot. If they were looking for her, we could hide there in the dark for a little bit anyway. She had to have a plan already. Something she'd spring on me later. I took a breath, my heart racing now with a different urgency. She'd escaped and we'd figure it out together. "Okay okay. I'm there."

"After dark."

"After dark. I love you.

The way she said it back, felt the words came from deep inside of me instead of across a phone line.

"I love you too."

⛧

Void-high ruined, I passed the hours until sunset scouring the house for things I thought she might need. I packed a sandwich and a bag of chips and a Coke, in case she hadn't eaten, along with some other stuff that seemed helpful in the moment. A lighter, a knife—I figured they took away hers. I went up to my mom's room and opened the bottom drawer in her makeup vanity. I dug around until I found the scented candle jar she stuffed deep in there. Unlike the weed stash in her underwear drawer, she thought the "mad-money" inside the fake candle was an actual secret. I counted out the roll. Almost five hundred dollars. It wasn't a fortune, but it seemed like one in my desperation. I stuffed the wad of bills in my pocket, unsure whether I'd give it to Dany or use it to buy us bus tickets or something. I put everything back the way it had been and looked out the window. The sun was going down. Not nearly fast enough.

I resisted the urge to go early, surprise her by waiting there. If they were watching, I might lead them there.

She wants to meet after dark for a reason.

⛧

"After dark" was difficult to pin down. When the streetlights came on still felt too early, but how long after that? Each second waiting for it to feel Goldilocks right was an elongation of the longing to fucking be there already. Finally, I decided I'd waited long enough. People by now were staring at TV sets instead of sitting at their dinner tables, looking out the window at the weird kid in black running up the street. I hefted my backpack over a shoulder and crept out the back. Our yard was small and there was nowhere to hide there or at the neighbors'. Still, I scanned for men in the shadows.

I hopped fences into the Potters' yard and then the Millers'. They were both cat people and their pets wouldn't give me away passing through. I skirted around the side of the Miller's house, emerging onto the sidewalk on the next street over from mine. It was a quiet night, and I didn't see anyone out. I made my way around to the bottom of the hill. I clambered through the roadside brush until I could step up onto the crumbling concrete steps a few feet up. They went up a few yards before they turned at a right angle and disappeared behind shrubs and bushes. I paused, listening for the sounds of men following. Behind the bend, I had a good shot at shoving the first one down the steps. Anyone he caught along the way was icing. I heard nothing. I continued.

Halfway to the top, a section of steps had crumbled and fallen away in a gap made by spring snow runoff. We used that space to hide things there for later. Bottles of wine and weed and, though we made fun of him for it, Julian's porn. If his dad caught him with "that gay shit" he was done for, so we helped him stash a few fuck mags in a gallon freezer bag and never said anything to him about it. I stopped and peeked under. It was too dark to see anything. Of all the things I'd thought to pack in my bag, a flashlight wasn't among them.

"You made it."

Startled by the sudden sound of her voice over my shoulder, I almost fell in the sink pit. "Shit," I hissed. "You scared the shit out of —" Dany wrapped her arms around my neck and kissed me to shut me up. It was the best kiss of my life. After what felt like both forever and no time at all, we pulled apart and I took her all in. Her hair was undone and wild and she wore no makeup, but it was *her*! The same full face and brown eyes I loved to see looking at me. Her long, slender neck leading down to prominent collarbones and sharp shoulders. Instead of a black blouse, she wore a tan t-shirt with the Andrews logo on the front, with matching sweats. AIYIR was stenciled in block letters up one leg. Shower sandals finished the unlikely outfit. I suddenly understood why she'd insisted on waiting until after dark. She looked like an escaped prisoner on the run. She *was* exactly that. I added a change of clothes to my mental tally of the many things I'd forgotten to pack. We were roughly the same height and weight and she often "borrowed" my shirts. I could go back and get her something that didn't look like a jailhouse uniform later.

"I missed you," she said.

"Me too. How'd you get away?"

"Come on." Ignoring my question, she grabbed my hand and led me the rest of the way up the stairs. She'd tell me how when she felt like it. I realized I didn't really care about the details as long as she was there with me. As we climbed, I saw the back of her shirt read, RUNAWAY / CALL 800-488-7211. I let go of her hand and unzipped my sweater, pulling it off. "Don't let go," She said, as if I might fall without her support.

"It's okay." I handed her the black sweater. She looked at it like it was something alien before slipping into it.

"Thanks." She held out her hand again, insistently. I wanted to ask if she had a plan. Instead, I quietly climbed the rest of the way up, holding tight to her like I was afraid I'd get lost without my hand in hers. We crested the top of the hill, and I lost my breath. I blinked trying to make sense of what I saw as my stomach turned, not ready for another nightmare episode like I'd had in the Andrews lobby.

What is wrong with me?

"It's okay," she said, as if hearing my thoughts. She smiled and I felt a quantum of calm, despite the view. Ahead of us loomed a two-story cottage house like the one she always drew in her notebooks when she was supposed to be paying attention in class. It had twin chimneys and the same embellishments she'd grin and name for me every time I forgot what something was called. *That's a finial. The siding is board and batten, and that's called an oriel window.* I'd nod and smile and try to remember the terms because this meant something to her. This house that she drew over and over, inside and out. She knew exactly what she wanted from life and seemed to have a plan to accomplish it, while the best I could muster was what I definitely did not want to do.

"I don't ... What is it?"

"It's a house."

I rubbed at my eyes. It rose high above us and I wondered how I hadn't seen it on the way up. "I can see that, I mean, how did it—"

"It's ours." She pulled me toward the porch, eyes alit with excitement. The front door hung open like a hungry mouth waiting to swallow us. I froze at the bottom of the stairs, waiting for it to grow huge nightmare teeth and roar as it bit into me. It didn't do any of that. It simply stood there waiting for us to enter, a welcoming inviting warmth escaping through the open door. "Let's go inside." Her eyes had that bright madness they got when something really excited her. An idea, a pretty thing that fell into her hands ... a house where there hadn't been on before. I followed her in, closing the door behind us.

She led me from the foyer, down a dim hallway. Framed pictures hung on the walls. I couldn't make them out as we hurried by. A staircase rose to our left, and I wondered if we might keep climbing stairs all night until we reached the roof or the moon. She tugged my arm and guided me past them. "Not that way."

"What's up there?"

She shook her head. I followed her through lovely rooms appointed with lush furniture and dim lamps draped with veils and a fireplace, dark and empty, yet still warm. She turned and took my other hand, backing into a bedroom with a wide poster bed draped in a red and black duvet and matching pillows. I opened my mouth to ask more questions without answers and she pressed her lips to mine, exploring with her tongue. Her breath tasted like cinnamon and clove and a sweetness from deep inside her body. She pulled at my clothes with urgent hands and I took a step back. "Wait a minute. Just wait. I don't understand what's happening."

"Please." She stepped toward me, the look in her eyes begging me to shut up and listen. "Let this happen the way I want it to."

"But … "

Her mouth turned down in a pout. Not the playful, fake disappointment she turned on me when she wanted her way. Her expression said if I didn't accept *all* of this, it was going to cost her—*us*—everything.

"This is our only chance to have this. Please. I need this one thing to be perfect."

I stripped off my shirt and stepped into her arms. We kissed and she worked my belt and button and zipper, freeing me. I finished undressing, waiting naked while she stripped out of the terrible tan clothes they'd made her wear. She pressed her body against me and caressed and kissed and breathed her hot breath against my neck, my chest, my stomach. She took me in her warm mouth and reached up with greedy hands, feeling my chest rising and falling with excited breath.

"Not yet," she said, pushing me back onto the mattress. She crept on hands and knees over me. "Stay with me."

"I'm not going anywhere."

"Promise! Promise you'll stay with me, no matter what."

"I promise. I'll stay with you forever."

She shook her head at the word, sadness returning to her mouth. "Forever's just tonight." She lay on me and kissed me again, tenderly, saying my name in my ear again and again as if it was an enchantment against… I didn't know what. I didn't understand the house or the furniture or anything at all, but I did as she asked, and put it all out of my mind, choosing to be there with her in that single moment as it elongated and we loved each other unconcerned with anything or anyone else in the world. Only we mattered as we felt each other's hearts beating against our chests and shared a continuous breath as we lost sense of whose heart whose mouth whose limbs were whose. An oceanic whole, unaware of ourselves as separate beings. Nothing could pull us apart.

    Together

              in that

                                    fleeting

                    moment

                            Forever

We came and kissed more and held each other, her smooth skin up tight against me, our bodies too warm to slide underneath the covers. We lay there, unashamed and afraid to sleep and risk waking from the dream. She rested her head on my chest, curly hair tickling my chin. Warm tears wetted my skin. I didn't ask. She let out a long breath and sat up, looking at me with wet, weary eyes. "I have to go upstairs soon."

"What? Why? What's up there?"

"Nothing, okay?"

"And what do I do while you're up there."

She traced a nail from my chin down my throat to my breastbone. "You stay here and keep thinking of me like this. Right now, as I am."

"And then?"

I didn't want to know "what then." It just came out.

Another tear slid down her cheek, dropping onto my bare stomach. She wiped it away and dragged her palms across her eyes, drying her face. "And then you go home."

"No. Fuck no. I want to stay here." I felt like a child making petulant demands. *I won't. You can't make me.* She smiled and kissed me, soft lips telling me not to argue. She straightened and moved to get out of bed. I reached out for her wrist. "Don't go."

She pulled her hand away and stood.

"What's happening?"

"This is how I'm getting through it."

"Getting through what? What the fuck, Danielle?"

"Don't follow me, okay? Promise." She stared at me, waiting until I said it.

"I promise."

She lay back down beside me and said, "Just a little while longer." I held her close.

I jerked awake and sat up in the bed, panicked and alone in the house. I heard the creak of the stairs in the hall outside the bedroom. I jumped up and flung open the door, chasing the sound down the hall. I stopped at the stairs, hoping to see her, stop her, bring her back down and tell her to stay. It was wrong. Don't go up the stairs.

She'd already disappeared.

I called up after her. "Come on, Dany. Whatever this is, we'll deal with it together. Dany? Dany!" She didn't answer.

I followed, her voice in my head telling me not to. *Stay in bed. Wait until it's time. And then go home.*

I am *home. This is our home.*

I put a bare foot on the first step.

You promised.

I followed her up.

I stood at the end of a bright, blinding white hall lined with doors. Frozen in place, I shouted, "Where are you, Dany! Which door?" My words died in the empty depth of the endless hall. I crept forward to the first window and looked in.

An empty room.

Forcing my eyes to stay open against its blinding obscenity of the unforgiving light, I went from door to door, knowing not one of them was the right one. Not until the end.

It got brighter and whiter as I moved down the row, searching cell after cell, finding nothing in the light but stark loneliness.

"Dany!"

The hall grew hotter the further down I went until my skin felt like it might blister, and still I pushed ahead, reaching for her, for that feeling that pulled at me. Searching for that oceanic oneness no one could sever. I promised to give myself to the current, not caring where it took me.

There it is!

The current carried me deeper until I couldn't see anything at all in the luminous void. I choked as it wrapped around my neck and the air became thick and unbreathable. My skin burned and I lost touch with the floor beneath me, feeling nothing but that tightness at my throat and searing heat. I hung and I burned and I tried to call out to her, say her name and conjure her.

And there I found her.

Hanging above the mattress they made her sleep on, torn elastic from her sweatpants around her neck. Her eyes were vacant and she didn't see me as I dangled with her as the fire in the mattress grew higher and hotter until it caught her skin and climbed her body reaching up and up and up toward those eyes I loved so much.

I burned with her until there was nothing of either of us left.

⛧

Sunlight shone red through my eyelids, waking me. I rolled over, dew slicking my bare skin. I sat up, naked in the grass. My clothes were in a pile where I'd thrown them at the foot of the bed. Absent now along with the house and the hall and the stairs and

Dany

I struggled into my things, wet cloth catching on my damp skin, resisting my attempts to cover up. I gathered my things and stood, concentrating, trying to make it come back. The house—our house. Dany.

Gone.

Along with the pull. Our ocean dried and gone.

I went home like I promised, ignoring the thick trail of black smoke rising from the hill on the opposite end of town, coming out of that place next to the hospital. You know it. The one where all the kids we once knew went to disappear.

LYING IN THE SUN ON A FAIRY TALE DAY

Once upon a time, the sun, high in the afternoon sky, shone down on a mountainside waking from a long, cold slumber. The snow had melted and new grass, straining to grow long, reached up for the shafts of light shining through the evergreens above. Early wildflowers bloomed in a paint stroke of color that shivered in the crisp breeze, and ferns unfurled their fiddleheads like tiny fingers opening to catch the light that had traveled through space to give its nourishment just to them. Green had returned after a long season under frozen white, and the woods were stirring to a bright, renewed cycle of burgeoning life. It was an afternoon so striking, he could have described it as a fairy tale day. If he weren't lying broken in the runoff gap in the middle of a glacier rock.

The sun was not as kind to him as it was to the green things. Though it was warm, he shivered with shock under it. His skin was hot to the touch and red from a blistering sunburn. Those blisters burst and wept tears that congealed and stuck in the hair on his arms and cheeks. His teeth chattered as another breeze swept down the mountain, carrying the scents of pine and pasqueflower. If blue had a scent, he'd once thought, it was the aroma of pasqueflowers. Under that, was the coppery smell of the blood stiffening his sock.

The sight of his shinbone sticking out through his skin seemed unreal, not only because he couldn't feel his left leg below the knee, but also because it was such an alien view of himself. His forearm on the same side was unmistakably broken as well, but that bone remained unseen. Until that morning, what was within his own body had never confronted him openly. Those internal parts had a hidden life of invisibility and received only occasional conscious acknowledgement. He thought of his stomach when it growled, and his heart when it beat hard. But he never considered his pancreas or bile duct at all. And he only thought of his bones when they broke, which was a rare thing. Even then, he'd never seen one of them—not with an X-ray, *actually seen* one. They say there's a first time for everything, but really, you hope not. Everyone honestly hopes there's no first time for being pulled out to sea by the undertow, or waking up in a house on fire, or … taking a bad spill down a slick glacial rock slope while hiking up before breakfast to watch the sunrise. Everyone hopes that their lives will continue apace without those firsts, because they are sometimes also lasts.

He called out for help, coughing as he tried to raise his voice, but he'd come to the woods alone. There was no one to hear. It was chilly at night still, and his girlfriend didn't like cold weather camping. His oldest outdoors buddy moved to Vail the year before to be a rich people's bartender, and no one else he knew was willing to pack in as far off the trails as he was. But, spring was his favorite season and he loved to sleep outdoors when the night air was crisp and the days weren't buggy and hot. So, he packed his gear and set out for a long weekend by himself. He told Shonna that he was going, but not *where*, specifically. She didn't ask for details, not because she didn't care, but because everyone knew this was a thing he did, and they all trusted that he would be fine, including her. He went deep into the woods by himself from time to time to recover from what he called "city poisoning". He had wilderness experience and didn't take stupid chances, so everyone assumed they'd see him on Tuesday or Wednesday, because they always had before. But it was only Saturday, and he didn't know how he'd make it back to the car to get help. It was parked at the trailhead, miles away, over a rough country hike. And that goddamned bone sticking out of his leg was telling him that even if he dragged his ass out of the rut, he wasn't getting any farther than where he'd made camp at the bottom of the slope. Not without help. And the only way to summon help was to use the cellphone he'd powered down and stuck in the jockey box of the fucking car.

With his good hand, he unclipped his daypack and tried to pull it out from under the small of his back. He could use the 550 Paracord and pocketknife inside to make a tourniquet for his leg. His signal mirror, whistle, matches, solar blanket, and sunscreen were all in there too. Tugging at it was painful and he couldn't arch his back enough to slide it out. His head ached and vision swam, and he gave up trying for a moment. More important to stay awake.

The sun shone in his eyes, so he closed them.

Just for a minute. It's so bright.

When he awoke, the sun had tracked more than a little farther along in the sky. He realized that he'd probably hit his head in the fall and was concussed. He tried to say something aloud, break the silence and provide a comfort to himself where no other was coming, but his throat was dry and it hurt to speak. He longed for a drink of water, but didn't know where his bottle had gone. He figured it must've fallen out of the side pouch of the pack when he slipped and bounced off somewhere he couldn't see, even though it was fluorescent green plastic. It was lost. Like him.

He was sunburnt and growing ever more dehydrated. He knew he'd die of thirst faster than starvation would take him. The reality of it was, though, that neither starvation nor thirst were his most pressing concerns. Exposure would kill him before anything else could even get started. Anything else except blood loss. Or shock. Exposure, he decided, was most likely.

He could spend what was left of his life contemplating all the ways to die.

The breeze blew again, raising prickly gooseflesh on his body. He'd set out from camp wearing a thick flannel shirt, but ended up tying it around his waist halfway up the climb. It too was gone. Lost in the fall. He was left wearing a thin, sweat-wicking tee-shirt and shorts, because he *always* wore shorts. It was a joke among his friends. He could be stomping through snow in a parka and boots, but he'd still be wearing pants that stopped above the knee. "I just run hot," he'd tell them. Shonna would snuggle up into his shoulder and smile, nodding. "Better than an electric blanket," she'd agree. That was at home in bed. Not so much here. Here, he was freezing.

He tried to push himself up out of the cleft worn in the rock by tens of thousands of years of trickling water wearing it away, but the pain of moving his broken arm lanced up into his shoulder and he pulled the limb in close to his body to protect it, slumping back down in the crevice. He cried, because everything was suddenly so in focus.

No amount of white pebbles or breadcrumbs would get him home.

He was going to die.

Just like firsts, no one ever thinks about lasts. Unless they're already sick or have a plan to kill themselves, no one wakes up thinking today will be the end of their story.

Once, a friend had shown him a video of some guy walking along the edge of a high building. The guy's foot slipped and he dropped straight down onto the ledge. He expected the man to catch on and the people with him to pull him back up and have a laugh at close calls and luck, but the ledge was narrow and offered nothing to grab on to. The guy's backpack pulled him over into open space right away, where he disappeared into the distance below. His friend showed him that ten-second video loop on his cellphone and, laughing, said, "Natural selection." But it wasn't funny. That person got up in the morning and put on his clothes and ate breakfast and met his friends for their adventure at the top of wherever that was, and not once did he likely imagine that there were only hours left in his life, because of one miscalculated step he had yet to take. That was the furthest distance between any person on Earth and dying. One step. A single second in time. The interval that launched your car through the guardrail, your skis toward the tree line, your foot off the edge of the building, or down a steep rock slope on a lovely spring morning, the sound of your breaking bones startling the birds.

"Up there! What's that up there?"

He raised his head at the sound of footsteps scrambling up the hillside toward him. It was hard to focus through his tears and disorientation, but he recognized Shonna's voice as she cried, "It's him!" He tried to sit up, but couldn't find the leverage, so he held his good arm up in the air for as long as he could. Which wasn't long at all, though it was long enough. Shonna settled onto her knees beside him, leaning close. "Shit! What happened?"

He coughed and tried to tell her that he slipped, but couldn't manage to find his voice. The dreamy shape of someone else, backlit by the bright blue of the late day moved behind her, but he couldn't make them out. "I've been trying to call you," she said. "You have to come home. We have to get you home right now."

"I'm...st-stuck," he managed. The figure behind her stepped around to the other side of him and he felt a tug at his wounded leg. The pain was unbearable and the world swam and his vision blurred again.

"Stay with me," Shonna said. "Don't pass out."

"Stop ... pulling. It ... hurts."

Shonna snapped at the other person, but he couldn't make out what she said. His head was fuzzy. But the one clear thought that resolved in the fog of it was, he wasn't going to die after all. Shonna and ... whoever it was with her, were there to get him off the fucking mountain. He pictured himself hobbling between them, an arm over her shoulders, while the other one held him at the waist. He knew he couldn't make the whole hike like that, but they just had to get to camp, and then he could tell them how to make a travois out of long sticks and his tent fabric. He knew how to get wounded people out of the woods. He could talk them through it. But first, he needed water.

He tried to ask Shonna to find his bottle. She didn't move. He tried to say it again. "Water ... bottle."

She cocked her head and just looked at him. "Come on. Get up. We have to go, *now*," she whispered. He didn't know why she was whispering. And then she pulled at his broken arm.

He screamed. She let go and backed away. Daylight dimmed, but it felt like it was him that had moved behind a cloud, not the sun. He clutched his wounded arm and tried to keep from passing out. But willpower never kept anyone from losing too much blood. No amount of intention was sufficient to overcome shock. Shonna leaned forward hesitantly. He wanted her to come close. He wanted—no, needed—her help. But, she was hurting him. He felt like a cornered animal. It was clear what had to be done to save his life. The problem was letting her do that. He wasn't getting out of this fissure without some measure of discomfort. In fact, *considerable pain* was a guarantee. He couldn't put it off forever.

He tried to sit up again, but his arm wouldn't cooperate, and the effort made him see stars in the daylight. He tried to tell Shonna to push him up from behind. Help him get into a seated position, so he could use his good arm and leg to stand. But he choked again. She leaned in and sniffed at him. He felt her breath on his face. Hot and moist. It was disorienting and it made him afraid.

Then, the other figure pulled at his leg again and a fresh jolt of pain brought him back into his body. He craned his neck around to tell them to quit pulling at his leg. "Fu … cking stop … it," he choked.

Another tug. He kicked weakly at the person with his good leg, and they let go.

He looked down his body at Shonna's companion. Who'd she brought with her anyway? Who would make the two-hour drive and then another hour-long hike to come get him, all on a hunch that he'd be at this spot and not some other? Not Dave. He worked the Co-Op on weekends. It had to be Kory. *She* would. Kory was kind and friendly, though not at all outdoorsy. She teased them about going to pretend they were homeless in the woods. But her heart was in the right place and Shonna could convince her to come along if something was really wrong. She'd make the drive, but she definitely wouldn't know what to do with a wounded person. He could tell her, if they'd give him a drink.

He blinked the sun out of his eyes, trying to force himself to see straight. The person crouched at his feet came into focus. Not Kory. *Dad?*

He coughed again. "How'd ... how'd you find ... me?"

His father looked up with furrowed brow and the judgmental expression he wore more often than not when looking at his son. "Find you? You're not found, boy. What makes you say that?" His father licked at his lips.

"You're not ..."

His father opened his jacket, showing his red heart hanging in the black cavity the chainsaw had ripped open when it kicked back into his chest decades ago. The heart snarled at him with long, yellow teeth. He tried to kick at it. The woodsman with the hungry heart shimmered and faded and whatever it was that had taken its first tentative tugs at him backed away, along with the ghost of his father, into the shade of the trees.

He turned back in the direction where Shonna was kneeling and saw only the rocks beside him and the low sun setting over the horizon. She'd retreated back to the shadows to wait as well.

Reality dawned on him. No one was coming to his rescue, because no one missed him, and they wouldn't until he was long dead, and maybe they wouldn't even find him until next spring when he'd be a collection of bones and some tattered cloth. Less than a memory, like the fading light of the sun on the spring mountainside. He stared at the line of jagged mountains along the horizon, lit the length of it all in a fire burst of yellow turned to red and then purple until the sky turned black and the wide band of the Milky Way arm replaced the single star of day with cool, diamond light.

And the dark things breathing in the woods waited for him to sleep.

He wished Shonna, or whatever she really was, would come back. He didn't want to die. But if he had to, he didn't want to die *alone*. Even if his only company was a dream of a wild girl who couldn't help but bite at him. He could die with a wolf by his side. As long as it breathed its warm breath on him so he knew he didn't have to do this all by himself. He wanted the company just so he didn't feel so lonely.

When he'd woken up that morning he'd never thought that this was the end of his story. But it was. Like a fairy tale written in reverse.

Once upon a time, there was a boy who had everything he ever wanted, but he left it all to go into the woods alone one beautiful day. There, he met a girl who was a wolf. And he loved her. He loved her hot breath on his neck and her sharp kisses that made new stars shine in his eyes. And there he lived with her, ever after, until the end of his life.

ACKNOWLEDGMENTS

Thank you, first of all, to Doug Murano for first taking a chance on me in *Miscreations: Gods, Monstrosities & Other Horrors*, and again now! I am absolutely thrilled to be able to play this Bad Hand.

To all the people who've read these stories in one form or another before publication, Ellen Datlow, Mark Morris, KL Pereira, Errick Nunnally, Christopher Irvin, Scott Goudsward, Tony Tremblay, Jack Bantry, Richard Wood, John F.D. Taff, Matt Bechtel, and D. Alexander Ward, thank you for making them better. Christopher Golden, Paul Tremblay, Benjamin Percy, Adian Van Young, John McIlveen, Dana Cameron, Gerald Coleman, Brian Keene, Tony Tremblay, Izzy Lee, Tom Deady, Ron Oliver, Michael Rowe, Kasey and Joe Lansdale, Billy Martin, Todd Keisling, and David Baillie, thank you for your true friendship and constant support. I also must acknowledge new friends, Sofia Ajram, Katherine Silva, Clay McLeod Chapman, and Eric LaRocca, as well as Agustina Bazterrica and Mariana Enríquez (not friends—yet—I should be so lucky) for writing such wonderful prose. Every word of yours I read makes me want to do better.

Finally, for the rest of my life, my love goes to my amazing spouse, first and perfect reader, and best friend, Heather. And to our son, Lucien, who always far exceeds my expectations and hopes with his boundless compassion, intelligence, and talent, I love you kiddo! You two are the very best parts of my life.

Bracken MacLeod
Sudbury, Massachusetts
6 June, 2025

ABOUT THE AUTHOR

BRACKEN MACLEOD is the Bram Stoker, Splatterpunk, and Shirley Jackson Award nominated author of the novels, *Mountain Home, Come to Dust, Stranded,* and *Closing Costs.* The New York Times Book Review called his first collection of short fiction, *13 Views of the Suicide Woods,* "Superb," though he imagines the reviewer pronouncing that, "supOIB." His short stories have also been recognized in the summation and honorable mentions of several volumes of The Best Horror of the Year. Prior to becoming a full-time writer, he survived car crashes, a near drowning, being shot at, a parachute malfunction, and the bar exam. So far, the only incident that has resulted in persistent nightmares is the bar exam. So, please don't mention it. He lives outside of Boston with his delightful and loving family and a loud murder of crows who like to be fed much too early in the morning.

PUBLICATION HISTORY

"Epilogue (For a Story Yet Unwritten)" is original to this collection.

"Pigs Don't Squeal in Tigertown" was first published in 2018 in *New Fears 2*

"Weightless Before She Falls" was first published in 2021 in *Fright Train*

"Lost Boy" was first published in 2017 in *Wicked Haunted*

"The Loneliness of Not Being Haunted" was first published in 2019 in *Echoes: The Saga Anthology of Ghost Stories*

"Not Eradicated in You" was first published in 2020 in *Miscreations: Gods, Monstrosities & Other Horrors*

"A Short Madness" was first published in 2019 in *The Seven Deadliest*

"Memories of ~~Me~~ You" is original to this collection.

"The Girl in the Pool" was first published in 2021 in *Beyond the Veil* (The Flame Tree Book of Horror)

"Extinction Therapy" was first published in 2017 in *Splatterpunk: Fighting Back*

"No One Who Runs is Innocent" was first published in 2020 in *The Dystopian States of AMERICA: A Charity Anthology Benefiting the ACLU Foundation*

"Dreamers" was first published in 2023 in *The Never Dead*

"Pareidolia" was originally published as "Cambridge" in 2024 in *Winter in the City*

"Back Seat" was first published in 2018 in *Lost Highways: Dark Fictions from the Road*

'Everything We Lost in the Fire" is original to this collection.

"Lying in the Sun on a Fairy Tale Day" was first published in 2018 in *Suspended in Dusk II*

CONTENT WARNINGS

There is much debate about the ethics and utility of content warnings in fiction and horror fiction, specifically. Your well-being is important to me, so I've done my best to compile this list of potentially sensitive content throughout the collection:

- Violence/blood
- Child abuse/neglect/pedophilia
- Verbal and physical abuse
- Self-harm/suicide/suicidal ideation
- Alcohol/Drug use
- Sexually explicit content
- Stalking
- Body dysmorphia
- Death and dying

- Pregnancy/abortion
- Depression
- Homelessness
- Animal injury
- Sexism/misogyny/homophobia

National Sexual Assault Hotline: 800-656-4673

National Suicide Prevention Lifeline: 800-273-8255

Please be safe and take care of yourself.

Printed in the United States
by Baker & Taylor Publisher Services